DIAGNOSIS

DIAGNOSIS

Darryl Leslie Gopaul

iUniverse, Inc.
New York   Bloomington

iUniverse books may be ordered through booksellers or by contacting:

iUniverse
1663 Liberty Drive
Bloomington, IN 47403
www.iuniverse.com
1-800-Authors (1-800-288-4677)

Because of the dynamic nature of the Internet, any Web addresses or links contained in this book may have changed since publication and may no longer be valid. The views expressed in this work are solely those of the author and do not necessarily reflect the views of the publisher, and the publisher hereby disclaims any responsibility for them.

ISBN: 978-1-4401-8224-2 (sc)
ISBN: 978-1-4401-8223-5 (ebook)

Printed in the United States of America

iUniverse rev. date: 12/18/09

1

SHORT STORIES

Tales Of Myths & Fantasy

IMAGINARY TALES

Fantasy & Science fiction

DISCLAIMER

This is a work of nonfiction as far as the stories are concerned. The case histories used as examples belong to the writer but the stories are embellished by the author's imagination and his knowledge of the Medical Sciences. However, the characters portrayed in this novel are products of the author's imagination and are used fictitiously. The physical settings named are those places where the author has actually worked but many have since closed and no longer exist. The names of the university are where the characters work and include the author's alma mater in the city -university in Waterloo. Only the persons to which this novel is dedicated are the real characters and only their first names are used in the dedication. Those characters used within the book have given the author the approval to use their first names.

Contents

DEDICATION:

This work is dedicated to the wonderful medical technologists (now referred to as Medical Laboratory Scientists) of the 1970s with whom I have had the privilege of working as a 'team member'. This was long before present administrators of hospitals discovered the word 'team' and brought it into the jargon of contemporary management. Most of all, it is especially dedicated to the wonderful Sisters of St. Joseph, who were the administrators at that time. Without their knowing, a new Medical Laboratory Technical Chief was allowed to grow and prosper in a profession free from the many difficulties that normally plague a professional in his lifetime. I would like to mention a few of my colleagues by their first names MaryAnn, Ginny, Brenda, Bhushan, Mary, Caroline, Pam, Pauline, Emily and especially my colleagues and friends Sandra Causyn-Brown and Paul Hostetler. There are many others but I was unable to trace their whereabouts and ask their permission, so the omission of their names is for that consideration. If you are out there, please accept this novel as a *letter of thanks* for the many hours that we have worked together.

Finally, I would like to dedicate this book to the memory of the late Dr Leslie Hatch, who was my Medical Director and mentor. I apologize for being the bane of his life when he was willing to settle for a quieter and safe retirement. Instead, he had to put up with my newly acquired scientific innovative ideas, youthful enthusiasm and my need for change. This meant that my persistence for improvements continuously bombarded him, which he inadvertently fuelled by passing the latest journals (all 15of them), to me every two months. Most of all, he will always be a rather undervalued clever gentleman but this was by his design. He played the part of an obtuse English gentleman and acted the buffoon deliberately at meetings. His wink to me on these occasions meant he was needling members of the administration, his colleagues, medical residents, students, technologists, nurses and interns. It was our secret for as long as we worked together.

Our professional collaborations pushed me to achieve more than I ever thought was possible. He may not have known this until his end but in spite of all the changes that took place in healthcare, I finally completed my PhD and went on to do an MBA. His part in my academic ambition was profound for he was and will always be remembered by me as a gentlemen.

dg

Foreword

Case Report

Peritonitis in a C.A.P.D. Patient due to Micrococcus mucilaginsus

Microbiology Department, London, Ontario, Canada.

The above headline was taken from one of the published articles by the group of scientists in the medical laboratory where Leslie Paul worked. He was the head of the Microbiology laboratory in a teaching hospital in London Ontario Canada. Peritonitis is an infection or inflammation of the normally sterile fluid that fills the wall between the abdomen and the intestine. CAPD is the process used to assist patients with damaged or irreparable kidneys to clean out the waste products accumulated from the process of the body's metabolism. This task is normally done by healthy kidneys. This process entails puncturing the abdominal wall and attaching a dialysis machine to remove the body's wastes which can become toxic to such patients.

While there is great care to ensure that all the attachments made in this CAPD process are sterile, occasionally an organism, a saprophytic one (usually a non disease causing bacterium) slips in and causes a low grade infection. The healthy human body is covered with numerous bacteria, fungi and parasites which do not cause any disease. However, when one of these normally non-pathogenic organisms finds its way into a normally sterile body fluid in CAPD patients, then a medical problem arises. The bacterium *Micrococcus mucilaginous* is normal on skin tissue in different external parts of the body such as the human mouth where it causes no harm. When it enters peritoneal fluid in this group of patient's, pus is formed indicating infection. This becomes dangerous to the health of these already compromised patients and can become a threat to life. Antibiotics are used to cure such infections. This is what occurred in this case history but the unusual thing was that this bacterium was also found in the patient's mouth. Punctures are made through the abdominal wall through which, built up toxic products, are removed by the CAPD process. The placement of a plastic stent allows more frequent CAPDs to be done removing multiple puncture wounds into the abdominal peritoneal space. This opening is clamped shut when not in use but it allows the patient to have dialysis on a regular basis. The presence of this plastic must itch continually. It is normal for the patient to give this wound an itch especially, when the skin area is red and dry. Occasionally, some spit may help to moisten the dry area but in doing so an organism enters the punctured area.

The role of the laboratory is to find the infectious bacterium and to report it quickly to the attending physician so antibiotics may be instituted. In other severe infections, when a major pathogen is isolated, then isolation techniques may be enforced to prevent cross infection between patients and the staff. I have read many case histories from my friend and colleague, the author, over the years. He may have been the reason for me entering this worthwhile profession. I only worked in the profession for a short period of time during which the author and I met only a couple of times in over 30 years. I left this profession and went on to be part of an organization that assisted in the establishing of our Olympic speed skating organization in Alberta. However, I have always found diagnostic laboratory work very interesting, the workers dedicated but in truth my friend's enthusiasm bordered on an 'infectious obsession' for he truly enjoyed his work. It was a pleasure to read his manuscript. I strongly recommend this story and novel for anyone who wants to know more about the Laboratory Diagnosis of infectious diseases, the silent profession that assists in keeping us well for these workers are the right and left hands of all physicians in practice. This novel will make a great gift to the mothers of young children, older folks and high school kids may get a chance to see a fun profession worth considering.

Lynda Murch.

Administrator Calgary Alta.

Preface

Working in human health services is generally no different in principle to working in any manufacturing, high technology, industrial companies or other industries in North America. The essential difference is that our product deals only with 'ill human beings.' The main role is to make them better, health-wise so that they can continue to work, be physically comfortable and continue to contribute to their community. Since healthcare is funded by the tax dollars, then healthy people are able to pay their taxes and be a part of the working society. Every human being becomes ill sooner or later and so they should have an idea of all those workers who assist in their recovery. This includes the primary physician, the nurses, the phlebotomists (those who take our blood sample into tubes), the technicians and technologists in radiology, nuclear medicine and medical laboratory scientists. The public needs to have some idea of all those workers that play a part in their treatment using their tax dollars in this modified socialized medicine as practiced in Canada.

There is an empiric intrigue in the medical laboratory diagnostic work itself but especially for those staff that 'touch' the patient. This is not the case with other staff such as the Medical Lab Scientists, who use their scientific training and skills to assist in the diagnostic process. This staff member is an integral part of the healthcare team employing applied scientific knowledge and powerful technological tools to analyze samples taken from the patient. Apart from a blood sample taken through a stab wound, syringe and needle or vacutainer tube, there are urine, stools, sputa, semen, vomit, pus and a host of other samples that are processed in the laboratory of hospitals, private medical laboratories and physician labs in the North American continent. In many instances patients may or may not know that their 'specimen' of excrement or stool, urine, vomit, pus, fluids from around the heart, joints, lungs and gut have been collected. The information gathered from testing but really examination of patient specimens' allows lab workers to inform the attending physician of the normal or abnormal findings. The lab scientist gains a better understanding of the normal and abnormal aspects of human anatomy, physiology, biochemistry, hematology, microbiology/ virology and immunology. Standards of normal values when matched with those of an ill patient assist in the diagnosis, verification of illnesses, monitoring the progress of treatment or the effects of treatment on the internal organs and their normal biochemistry. The author is a retired medical microbiologist with over 40 years practice in three different countries. His book *Bacteria, The good, The Bad The Ugly* was designed for the public at large and was made up of his lecture notes to the lay public.

Medical laboratory practice allows for the monitoring of a patient's ongoing cure in defined illnesses and of the clinical progress in such diagnoses as in cancer patients while on therapy. It is important to document the case history of a patient with an initial clinical diagnosis but the diagnostic laboratory supportive evidence assists in proving or disproving the original clinical diagnosis. Scientific information is vital to the continuing education of the medical practitioners in healthcare. This type of laboratory Medicine never remains the same because the immune system, the physiology and the nutritional status of every human being are individually different and they all vary. The author's intrigue in this part of scientific medicine began as a young man working with the World Health Organization and the UNICEF in the malaria eradication program in Trinidad, West Indies back in the late 1950s and early 1960s.

Introduction

First assignment – for Les Paul:

"Young Les Paul, have you not just passed your practical examination in Malaria and Filaria by examining over 250 blood smears, recently?"

"Yes Sir," Les gladly and proudly replied to the Chief of the Malaria Division Laboratory. I was seventeen going on eighteen years old and had just had a scholarship to be trained as a scientific assistant by a joint program sponsored by the WHO/UNICEF programs.

"Good! then you can do the diagnostics for today, there is a plane in transit from Africa to the USA and there is a 'sick student' on board. He has had sweats, feels cold but is running a high temperature. The presumptive diagnosis is malaria for he comes from an environment that is highly infectious with all the different kinds of malaria." He continued," you know, malignant tertian and benign tertian and maybe the rare Plasmodium ovale", he winked and smiled. I thought for an instance he had wickedly averted his face and winked to his next in command, Calvin, better known as the 'Doc'. I was too keen, too naïve and just wanted to please my new first time bosses.

"Right away Sir," I proudly responded jumping up smartly from my seat, casting my white lab coat on a rack in the closet room, picking up my blood collection tray and heading outside the lab to catch the jeep which was driving out to the airport in Arima, a busy little town that had this major industry. Such was the power of youthful enthusiasm. I now wonder where and when did I lose it or where did the energy go. It was a sunny tropical morning on the then beautiful island back in 1960, with its surrounding high green mountains in the northeastern area where we lived and where I was lucky enough to work.

On arriving at the airport, after a very chatty short brown skinned Negro driver took me into the VIP area, I put on my new, clean, white lab coat used just for outside clinics. I was shown to a room where I found a very black African man who had tribal marks scarred on his cheeks which looked like the healed wounds from sharp knife cuts. He was laid out on a cot and he was wet with perspiration as was his shirt. There was no air conditioning. A sharp command from the attending physician directed at me echoed across the small crowded room. "Move quickly young man and take a smear. Let me know what we are dealing with here before I have to make the decision to hospitalize him. If it is Malaria I will just begin a regimen of treatment and send him on his way to the USA where they can monitor his treatment." This was 1960 when the combined organizations of WHO & UNESCO began a malaria eradication program on the island of Trinidad and its sister island of Tobago.

I cleaned the patient's finger with an alcohol swab after using a drop of iodine first over the skin area that I would stab to get a drop of blood. His finger was soft, obviously not used to hard physical work or any outside sport. I 'pranged' his finger with my sharp Hagedorn needle. He did not flinch but slowly opened his eyes then shut them again amid his perspiring face. His white shirt collar was soaked. I saw a large drop of blood at the opening of the stab, which I placed onto two spots of two clean glass slides. One drop was allowed to spread out into a thick smear, the other I spread out thinly using the edge of another glass slide to push the drop across the empty slide. I placed the slides in front of a small electric fan and allowed them to dry. I fixed them with a drop of alcohol then stained one of the slides over a sink using Field's stain.

While the stain was reacting I lit the lamp of the new Swiss Microscope. The light passed to the outside through a hole in a black painted cylindrical metal can that housed a light bulb. From that hole or opening, the light was interrupted by a glass bulb-shaped flask with a blue copper sulphate solution. This dye acted as a filter for the light before hitting the convex mirror at the base of the microscope, which directed the rays of light through the condenser of the microscope. This filtered white light passed through the internal optical lenses to the eye pieces. I placed a control smear on the stage and adjusted the microscope using the fine adjustment. I recognized the control smear blood cells clearly stained as a dark purple (white cells), with red cytoplasm and the known malaria parasite. The red cells were a pale pink to red in appearance.

I removed the control smear in time for the patient smear to be washed off with tap water then blown dry. Carefully placing a drop of oil onto the smear of the patient, I focused down through the oil objective to the plane of patient's cells. To my quiet delight, almost immediately, I recognized the 'banana-shaped gametocyte' of Plasmodium falciparum or malignant tertian. Not wishing to jump the gun in my enthusiasm, I continued to search for the confirmatory 'signet ring' and found two in the next two fields. With further searching I was confounded to see the dark brown Schuffner's dots in a trophozoite followed by ring trophozoite showing 'spreading cytoplasm' or pseudopodia. I was witnessing a double infection and began to sweat. This was a rare finding on the island of Trinidad where we were working on a program sponsored by WHO/UNICEF to eradicate malaria and its spread throughout the other islands of the Caribbean.

I began to sweat as the temperature of the room appeared to have risen to even hotter levels as the sun came overhead and the day wore on. After wiping my wet brow with my clean white handkerchief, which my mother had given to me that morning to tuck into my side pocket of my new grey flannels, I went back to the microscope. I began to search the smear under the microscope to find a perfect banana-shaped gametocyte of P. falciparum, the type of malaria in the early part of the twentieth century that recurred in supposedly treated patients after 20 or 30 years. I went back to examine the brown dots, the ring trophozoite with pseudopodia, for there were so many parasites. A loud baritone voice shouted impatiently across the room that was filled with other patients, an ambulance driver, attendants, a nurse and other personnel. "Well young man, what is the diagnosis? What the hell is keeping you?"

Les moved his head from the microscope stood by the chair and quietly replied, "It is malaria, Sir."

Then the physician, who was an older white man, came over in an intimidating manner and his voice boomed loudly, "Yes, yes I know that. But what type is it?"

Sweating because it was a hot, humid, over-crowded room and my nerves were shot, I stammered, "It is a double infection Sir, of malignant and benign tertian."

"What nonsense!" exploded the voice as the physician came over and said, "Move over and let me have a look." He sat down, widened the eye- pieces, and adjusted the light to brightness too much for my own youthful eyes and he began to move the stage rapidly from field to field.

He stood up suddenly, turned and looked at me. "God, you are right!" He stuck out his hand and I automatically shot mine out. He squeezed my hand and turned to the nurse shouting loudly, "Get the ambulance to take him to the Port Of Spain General Hospital immediately. Get the Malariologist on the telephone for me quickly." He disappeared into his office. The patient was whipped away as I quietly began to pack up my kit, picked up the patient's smears both stained and unstained. I had in fact made two smears but only stained one for my use. The other was left in the alcohol fixative then dried for the main lab to stain by a better method later on. It was placed in a shallow cardboard box two inches square. The purpose was to keep the flies from eating the blood smear off the glass slide.

As I approached the door, the driver of the jeep in which I came, was standing there and he looked at me with a big smile. He was smiling awkwardly as he took the tray carefully from my hands and quietly said, "Sir, we are almost ready to collect the last of the insects from the plane. Boss. I have a 'boy' who sprayed as soon as the passengers left so he is

*going around looking for dead mosquitoes and other insects."
I looked at the kindly older grey-haired man who was looking
up at me. I was an 18 year old Indian boy, recently graduated
with a second diploma from Fatima College. I had six months
of practical training in the diagnosis of malaria and filarial
worms in blood smears of untreated and treated patients. This
was my first trip out of the lab to do diagnostic work on my first
live patient. This driver field worker called me 'Sir' and my
embarrassment was probably unseen for the highly nervous
state that I was in. My ears were hot, flushed red and burning.
My back felt as though small ants were crawling across it. My
discomfort was acute. I had my first patient and had to make a
diagnosis in the field.*

*I looked at him, smiled and said, "Let us go to the jeep,
Oliver." He again smiled looking at me questioningly again
but pushed ahead of the other people unseen by me at the
time. He guided me like an important person, letting me follow
him quietly and briskly. My sweating brow was automatically
being mopped with the now damp white handkerchief that was
part of a white collar vestment back in the 1950s. My mother
ensured that I was properly dressed for the new work world as
did the older Negro woman who did all the washing. She used
a washboard and the sun to dry the 'washing', and then she
starched and ironed the white shirts for me. This task had been
done for my father and my sisters who wore school uniforms
for many years.*

*As we entered the reserved parking lot, the other young
Negro man Cyril, (called 'boy' by the driver) came running
over carrying a varnished wooden box with a closed brass
handle containing the insects that he had collected. His dark
brown face was wet and his perspiration had dampened his
clean khaki shirt leaving wet stripes. He said anxiously, "Sir,
look at what I found," looking directly at me. He placed the
box into the open hatch at the back of the jeep. He cautiously
opened the lid which revealed two rows of small round cream*

coloured pill boxes lined and labeled with a lead pencil. On them were the local names of the insects. I looked as he cautiously opened a small round pill box, as if to show me a precious diamond or jewel of unknown wealth. Nestled on the white cotton wool was a mosquito and I could see the blood in its proboscis when I used my jewel's loop which I carried in my pocket. I then looked at the small collection of house flies, fruit flies and a small spider all in their individual little cotton wool lined coffin boxes. They were lying peacefully on their snow white beds of cotton wool coils in their brand new round pill box coffins.

Then both Oliver and Cyril brought the forms that they had filled out with lots of columns denoting the time, date, type of spray used in the plane and the demographics of the patient along with the Doctor's name and many more details. I was shown another list of the passengers' names and addresses and those who could be contacted by telephone, a rarity in those days. In the silence of the heat, bright sunshine the surrounding green mountains that overlooked the Piarco airport and my sweating comrades, I automatically signed and initialed the spots as they pointed them out to me. We were all sweating, mopping and smiling when Oliver said to me, "Sir, that was great work that you did in front of that 'bad doctor', you know!"

I looked up still quite stunned, a bit confused and asked, "Bad doctor?" I nodded my head and looked back at the building where I had just spent the better part of two hours.

"Yes Man! He is a terror and none of the boys in de lab like to work with him, Man. He gives dem hell for taking too long, even Mr. Ram, de boss get his shit as well."

He continued in his sing song accent that was encouraging and to some extent comforting. "Yeah Man, but when ah saw you look at him and say there is a double infection, I thought he would shout you out of the airport. But he shake your hand, Man! Ho! Ho. Dat is the first time I see dat! He cannot be bad with the Malaria Lab this time Man. You did good Sir," he said as he extended his hand for me to shake.

I automatically shook his hand, smiled awkwardly and said, "Oliver and you too Cyril, never call me 'Sir' again. My name is Leslie Paul, so please call me Les or Leslie."

*They smiled and looked at me then Oliver said laughing loudly, "But we will call you Sir, in front of the Malariologist, you know the doctor from Sweden, Scandinavia. He said that is what we should do, but he let us call him by his Swedish name, Sven, when we are out in the field just like you said." For some unknown reason, we all laughed as we entered the hot jeep and Oliver started the engine. On my way home when we were not laughing, I thought quietly to myself, I now understood the reason for the boss's smirk that morning but I **was well and truly hooked on this type of work,** after my 'idiot savant' diagnosis.*

I knew then that I wanted to be a member of these unsung background professional workers in the diagnostic laboratory. The stimulus began as a child observing the sick and the approach by the Negro lady friend of our family. We all called her Nennen (a patois word for aunt), and she appeared to know how to treat many of the common illnesses during the war days of the early 1940s. It is the profession that I have had for over forty years of practice and it remains an' infectious topic' after being retired for over eight years.

We move forward fourteen years later, after being trained in the UK for five years and emigrating to Canada, working for awhile and then heading to university to get a Canadian degree. I began all over looking for a job.

Biography

&

History

His name was Leslie Paul and he was the first of eight children born to an Indian family on the island of Trinidad, West Indies. It was a time of rationing for the Second World War had just about come to a halt but more importantly a time when his parents were building a family. Being the first boy, he was told that he was too skinny and had gained weight poorly but seeing the size of his girth today, one would never believe that he would have made it to the tender age in his sixties and appearing quite healthy.

As a young lad, he saw his newborn baby sister in the arms of his beautiful fair- skinned, still pale mother, who had such a peaceful face as she gazed at the young brown-skinned, closed-eyed skinny baby. She opened her blouse and proceeded to withdraw her bloated right breast, under the close scrutiny of the Negro midwife who cooingly said, "Rita, it is important to place the first few drops of milk into the eyes of the baby." My mother did not argue but quietly squeezed her now dark brown nipple. A drop of white milk dropped into her baby's eye and she again repeated the task on the next eye. The little baby whimpered and cried out as her little tears mixed with the milk, welled up then rolled down her cheeks.

The midwife gently wiped the little face. She again quietly said to my mother, "OK Sweetie, you must do this again today while your milk is still new. After today it will not have the same effect in protecting her eyes."

Les was to witness this practice well into his teenage as the members of his family grew up, his family expanded and younger babies were added to the family brood. It is strange but he never heard his mother ask why this was necessary. She was invariably thankful to her midwife. Twenty plus years later, he saw the results of an infection in a newborn baby's eyes in the UK. The specimen received in the lab had large amounts of pus and the cultures grew an organism known as 'pneumococci. The mother had delivered her baby in a poor part of London's East End under probably not the most sanitary conditions. As a result, silver nitrate was not administered to the newborn baby's eyes, which was the clinical practice back in the early sixties. Coming through the birth canal is neither an easy passage nor a clean one for a baby and there is a high risk of the eyes becoming infected. Silver nitrate killed numerous bacteria in the tender eyes of a baby. It also had no side effects on babies as far as Les knew. Thirty years later he was part of a study group that made the change, in Canada, to use chloramphenicol drops, a broad spectrum antibiotic, instead of silver nitrate as there was the potential for the development of resistant bacteria which could establish themselves on the susceptible membranes of the young eye.

Back to the Island:

There was a group of women of an Afro-French background, who lived in the hills of St James. They made their living by selling herbs for food as well as, for herbal medicines (also called bush medicine). They dressed in bright highly-flowered floor length skirts and wore brightly coloured head scarves and bands. They spoke a broken French known in the islands as patois. They came to Les' home once a week to sell their herbs and spices from their wooden trays, which they carefully balanced on their heads leaving their arms free. In the hot tropical sunshine, these women walked in small groups and were called-out by their customers asking for their products. There was an exception made for their 'regulars' when they dropped in to deliver standard herbs every week. His mother bought chives, thyme, ginger and other herbs, which were used for making teas. Any kind of herbal tea was considered to be an elixir or medicine for various mild problems. A side product of these easy going brusque and saucy women visiting their home, was to 'catch up' on the local gossip.

He noticed that they were always paid in pennies. They would rest briefly in the shade of the great mango tree and judging from his mother's giggles and their straight-faced comments related tales and gossip of a very saucy nature. Carrying these heavy trays on their heads in the hot sun was a recipe for headaches and mild fainting spells. It happened a few times at their home and his mother would offer cold water. On one occasion, one of the ladies asked to see his chubby brother. She asked if he ate meat and Les' mother laughed out loudly answering affirmatively.

"Madam, I want the little boy (5years old) to pee on my head if I am to return back up the hills." His mother, still laughing, was aware of their strange cures and must have known much more about these unknown ladies' (known as 'Martinicans') traits, than Les could have imagined.

"Why do you not let the big boy, Les pee in your head cloth?" his mother still giggling asked. "No! I bet he does not eat meat and besides he is too skinny," was the retort. His chubby brother was called and he laughingly climbed up on a stool and gladly peed on her head band. She used a cloth to pat her head, breathed in deeply and said, "I feel better already." She closed her eyes briefly, breathed in again then smiled and handed my brother a half cent (known as a farthing). She was correct for Les did not eat much food; indeed he could hardly stomach any food and lived only on fruit juices as a young boy. He just could not bear the taste of meat in his mouth and often chewed it in front of his mother but spat it out for their dog to gobble up. He was jealous that his younger brother was so well liked and stalked out quietly for these women made a fuss over his fat brother. Later on, he worked out that the urine from his brother was high in ammonia as a result of his digesting meat. Fat people tend to have more ammonia in their urine hence their strong body odour and urine smell.

It is said that one's environment makes the individual but in this case it gave Les a profession for so many folks on this little British colony did not have many scientifically trained physicians in the 1940s and '50s. While he did not become a physician, he became a professional member of Laboratory

Medicine. He is the right hand of any tertiary trained physician who had a patient with an infection. He isolates the infecting organism, identifies it and recommends the antibiotic most appropriate to use against *bad bugs*. He also monitored all hospital and institutional infections and recommended procedures to reduce the risk of spread or cross-infection between patients. Les is a Medical Microbiologist, retired.

Les' story is about the world of diagnostic medicine from its earliest days to the era that he left in the early 2000. When the television or radio announcer says that the laboratory tests will confirm or that the inspector, coroner are awaiting the lab results, it is these professionals, who are not known to the public for they work in labs in the back ground where the lab work is done. This is a profession that is a combination of detective work and scientific curiosity, which makes every day exciting.

Of Reality

and

Diatribe

Reality:

Les Paul is the character who has a similar upbringing and career as the author and this is his story.

At the beginning of the 1970s, there existed a power play between the 'Human Gods' in medicine - the physicians - and the 'Human Devils', the 'holders of the finances' or the administrators - and in between were the 'Goddesses of Suffering' - the nurses. It was a time when power was the name of the game and autocratic behaviour the norm. It was the era of powerful egos, puritanical enthusiasts and naive workers trying to do everything to get even better results in diagnosing diseases. The beneficiary of all the struggles was invariably the patient and that was and is the whole purpose of working in a diagnostic medical laboratory. A secondary benefit is sharing the knowledge obtained from the practical and sharing it with colleagues across the country and globally through lectures and publications.

DIATRIBE

Of course, in the midst of these human resources stew was a sobriquet of the best and worst of human traits especially when the academic souls are thrown into the pot. However, if this brew is poisonous or close enough to toxicity to the normal worker, out of the brew emerges a most unusual very human trait, humour. This is the uncommon and unexplained thing about human beings. Even against all odds there is often a modicum of success. Why and how does not matter for in the midst of 'close shaves in battle' within the health service battle ground, is that unknown meeting with destiny. Often a human being may be the first to discover a difference in his scientific practice then unbelievers go out of their way to destroy the work with no thought to the worker. Often under the guise of professional purity and a noblesse attitude to uncover the truth, rash statements and deductions are made with supposedly good intentions, usually presumptively. This is more common than the lay public could ever imagine.

The policing of a professional by peers are noteworthy and are a sign of maturity in a profession. However, one should never be naive nor forget jealousy, the angry green-eyed monster of a few. A few of these reptilian humanoids are often there because of their 'politics' and desire to keep power or obtain power rather than for their input into knowledge and often show little leadership in promoting excellence. They may use the verbiage loaded with the humility of condescension reflecting noble thoughts but are often caught up in their own practical or academic stagnation of thought and scientific ignorance. The fact is, if an individual, especially a young researcher, has spent many hours on a subject project that has his interest, and then one can safely assume that person would know more about that subject than someone who had no interest in that field but rather a general appreciation of the subject. To reject the youth's work for a concrete misdemeanor in his experimental design or a flaw in his hypothesis is one thing but to cast aspersions on the integrity of the project is unworthy.

In the end, nothing really matters for time takes care of what the truth is with no glorification to an individual, group of individuals or professionals or even of our human existence. People come and go but the scientific truth, like the truth of everything in the cosmos, will eventually be uncovered. Fame and fortune are fleeting awards in life leaving little substance behind especially, for those with large egos. The really big discoveries and the smaller conquests by the rank and file workers, all combine to educate in the long run. This book outline Leslie Paul's trials and tribulations of a single lab scientist, who worked through his daily tasks, day in, day out, for many years. It outlines the discoveries made by his fellow lab mates and is expressed through the patient case histories which were published in medical and technical journals within the profession and are noted throughout this book.

However, the journey of this single lab scientist is not unusual as described in this novel. It is when the gallant lab scientist attempts to go further than he was thought capable of doing, that problems arise. It was like the humanity outlined in Huxley's *"Brave New World"*. Stay as an alpha or a delta, and know your place in society. If one dares to follow up a curiosity for details based on unusual findings, one is often thwarted and even belittled by the then departmental hierarchy at least that was how it was in the 1970s and '80s in Canada. This gauntlet of scrutiny includes the academic folks, the publishers of the technical journals and their advisors. At the end, through all of one's trials and tribulations, one has and enjoys a wonderful career and as John Lennon said, *"Life is what happens while you are busy making a living"* (paraphrased). The missing parameter is that Man as a species does not like puzzles for that piques his curiosity, which is a very human thing. The lab scientists are often 'too busy' to follow up the puzzle and are often encouraged not to do so for the priority is get the results to the patient bedside so treatment may be initiated. This is quite the noble demand but what a waste of scientific and clinical information. What a loss of knowledge for daily our patients bring vital new knowledge to us with little twists and turns that often fog the accepted norm. How more efficient diagnosis would be if that knowledge was uncovered and added to the pool of clinical information? Alas! The administrators now run the labs and every scientific thing done has to be cost accounted for and when the lack of knowledge is basic as with these new folks then much is lost to ignorance. The breaks in the system are showing and maybe common sense will once again return before many more lives are put at risk to such routine misunderstanding as multi- resistant bacteria as the erstwhile multi-resistant staphylococci or MRSA...

Success and an Appointment

"Really Dr Gutch, if I knew that I would have had a dissertation instead of an interview with you today, I would have boned up a bit," Les said laughingly to the big Englishman known as Dr Arthur Gutch. He had the same first name as his prospective Lab Technical Director of the large teaching health centre. He had heard that the then chief lab scientist of the department of Microbiology was quitting and returning back to his native Scotland, having recently obtained his science degree from the local university.

"Well to be honest, old boy! I do not want an over-educated person to be Chief of Bacteriology who is incapable of doing applied work in the Bacteriology department. To be truthful, my interests lie with the Virology Department and I do work at the bench level but as Head of the joint departments I have to trust the Chief in doing a good job in Bacteriology. I only wish to do my Virology lab work and to teach at the University Medical School," replied the giant of a six-foot-seven inches tall red-bearded pathologist Virologist, who smiled while stroking his beard. His large blue eyes cast askance with his head slightly turned so that he could better hear Les. His meaty earlobes appeared to have closed out the outer ear canal making it difficult to hear. 'Over-educated' lab technologist in charge, again smacked a little of Huxley's '*Brave New World*' in wanting only the gamma citizens (or was it the deltas?) brain dead in this man's world. They made good technologists but he smiled to himself thinking at the time, this is good information to be used later in life.

"You know, I did train in the UK for five years using day release intern and night classes so I can fully run the routine operation. As well, you should know Sir, that I have worked with the WHO & UNICEF in the Caribbean. I initiated a basic micro-diagnostic lab at the community hospital in Ajax Ontario which had to open in time for Expo '67," Les replied with a smile.

Dr Gutch got up from his chair, pulled open a filing cabinet and seemed to be studying a file. Ignoring Les' yammering, he asked abruptly without raising his head, "Yes, sure. Who did you say you trained with in the UK?"

"Dr Ken Saunders of the Woolwich Group of Hospitals in London back in 1961 – 1967," Les replied. This was 1972 and all this talk was history for he had immigrated to Canada back in 1967. Dr Gutch was from the 'old boys' club of ex-pats that gave appointments to those preferably trained in the old country, the UK. It was a standard but unwritten practice by men of that era. The premise being that, if one was British-trained then there was an unwritten fortitude that could be used to maintain the empire.

Essentially, Les had no problem with this unwritten philosophy since he had brought over a chap from Cornwall, unseen, to take over his old job as head at the Ajax Hospital Laboratories. He never thought of this until now for he had thoughtlessly promulgated this same concept that he was now experiencing. He smiled quietly, reminding himself that what goes around comes around, and he had behaved like all the ex-pats from the UK for they were indeed better trained in those dark days of the middle 60s. There was also a great shortage of home-trained medical technologists to work in the medical labs. There just were not enough training centers and the compensation as a beginner was less than encouraging. Les had been told by a student about to leave high school in a month's time and that he will get a job at GM in Oshawa as a floor sweeper. He would have a car in a month. He would be making Les' salary in a week more than what Les could ever dream of in those days.

The Interview Continues:

There was a loud clang as Dr Gutch slammed shut the filing cabinet with a hard a shove. This was a sound that Les would grow accustomed to in the future. He would become used to this physically powerful man slamming the filing cabinet drawers and skating around on his wheeled armchair on the terrazzo floor. In his office this man moved about loudly and forcibly. His voice was a deep baritone that was further made incomprehensible by the 'strangled burble at the back of his throat'. "I see your wife is a cockney like me," he beamed at Les.

"Yes" he replied. "Her grandparents had a butcher shop on the old Kent road. But both her parents are deceased now."

Les bent his head thoughtfully, and then continued in his mild British accent. "I met her while we were in training in south east London at the Brook General Hospital. She did the London classes and I did the Bromley Tech night classes. Dr Saunders did however, send me on training courses at the Brompton Chest Hospital, you know." He looked up suddenly. Les continued, "Yes I have had lots of experience with old tuberculosis patients and those with Mycotic infections." Then, Les paused and looked at his inquisitioner and smiled broadly as if they were speaking in a code that no one else would be party to, for unknowingly he was now participating in the same 'old boy' club.

"Oh! Good, were there other places that you interned?" Dr Gutch asked in his throaty 'upper class' growl.

"Of course," Les smartly responded. "There was the company at Sandwich, you know, the experimental facilities where Pfizer did some work on Thalidomide using pregnant beagle dogs," he thoughtfully replied looking down on the floor for a moment. He quickly raised up his head and looking at the far away pensive face of Dr Gutch, he instinctively knew that he would get the job as head of the Department of Bacteriology.

"Just as a matter of interest, Leslie, how would you identify an isolated colony that looked like Salmonella?" Dr Gutch asked as he again went back to looking at simple details that any bright undergraduate student would know.

"Well," Les thoughtfully responded. "When you say it 'looked like Salmonella' one would assume that it was either a sample of stool, blood cultures, food or vomit that was processed on a suspect sample of the questionable Salmonella-infected food. Then it would also be necessary to again assume, that the specimen had been cultured onto an appropriate range of culture media that would be inhibitory and selective. Then the lactose positive coliforms part of the normal flora would appear red when grown from either stool or vomit that had some stool contamination. Then again assuming the media commonly used on such specimens would let the suspect colony of Salmonella to grow as a pale non-lactose fermenter, with a characteristic appearance of a pale to translucent colony with, maybe depending on the age of the culture, a small black centre which would be indicative of hydrogen sulphide production. If there was such a colony, together with a case history of the patient having some gastro-enteritis, the usual fever after five days, then blood cultures should have been taken earlier as well. This would capture the organism in the bacteremic stage. Other clinical indications would include vomiting and diarrhea. Such a pale yellow bacterial colony isolated (not pink or red) would be suspect of a Salmonella species."

"Such a colony should be sub-cultured onto a blood agar plate in pure form. If there is enough of an inoculum, sugars from a peptone broth suspension of the colony should be inoculated and incubated at 36 degrees C for 18 - 24 hours. The next day such a pure culture would show a biochemical pattern of lactose and sucrose negative but positive for mannitol and dulcitol. Using polyvalent antisera, slide agglutination testing for the O & H antigens from the blood agar plate would be appropriate. The slide agglutination tests would be performed and depending on the degree of positivity one would proceed to complete the serological testing that would confirm the identity of the infecting organism. However, it would be better to use a nutrient agar plate without the blood for the agglutination testing," Leslie paused for he could go on to do further testing but in his mind surely this is too simple and wondered what this man really wanted from him.

He looked at the ever thoughtful man in front of him who was now looking at the file that he had taken out of the filing cabinet earlier. Dr Gutch raised his head, looked directly at Leslie and said, "OK, I guess that you know your job. I am willing to hire you at an annual salary of $9,000 per annum with an increase after three months probation. I should tell you we have a crack technical staff and they may know a bit more than you do but mainly in the Canadian training, which leaves much to be improved. They have had some internal social problems but that has all been settled by Mr. Ryan; a few people had to be dismissed. Things have settled down now and I would like you to look into the quality control of the media used, along with the lab procedures. However, do not make any changes until you have discussed them with me. Miss Jill is in charge of Virology and she is to be your technical supervisor. I suggest that you listen to her guidance."

Just then there was a knock on the door as Mr. Ryan, the head of personnel, accompanied by Leslie's wife, entered the room. Dr Gutch stood up from his chair quite suddenly for a man so large, moved over to shake my wife's hand and to welcome Mr. Ryan. "Well! Dr Gutch, I took this young man's wife to Hematology for she is also well trained in that department. She met the head technologist."

"How did you two get along?" Mr. Ryan asked in his old croaked voice, peering through his half glasses at both Dr Gutch and Leslie.

Dr Gutch said, "I have made an offer to Leslie for him to consider and have written the details of this offer in my notes. Maybe, I can have a brief chat with both these London folks, you know from the old country, before they come down and see you on their way out. I have asked for a reply by the end of the week."

Les stood up and again shook the old Personnel Officer's hand. Mr. Ryan said, "That is wonderful Dr Gutch! This young man has great qualifications." Mr. Ryan winked and left them.

This was Wednesday so Les and his wife had two days to decide whether to take the job. Before Mr. Ryan left he said to him, "Come down and see me before leaving anyway."

Leslie politely responded to this gentle kind-looking grandfather of a man, "I will Sir."

Dr Gutch then sat down with the candidate, Leslie, and his wife Alice, and began on a nostalgic journey of the old days and places in London. He asked where she had gone to school for night classes and where they had taken their exams. When they replied that they had to go to Russell Square and some were done at St Mary's in Queen Square, he was thrilled. He continued saying that he too was a cockney although his accent betrayed that of an upper class inflection.

This accent thing is purely a British trait and Bernard Shaw's *Elisa Doolittle* was well based on this British affliction of matching accent to class. However, this turns out to be an asset to Les throughout most of his career. The little group of ex-pats in Dr Gutch's office began to jest with a few words in the cockney slang such as the common one, 'apples and pairs'. Leslie saw his wife and the big Englishman disintegrate into a friendly laugh and discussion as folks with a similar cultural, ethnic background tend to do. After a while, Leslie and his wife rose to shake hands and then left the office with Dr Gutch, who gave a loud over-exaggerated bellow of a laugh. They both felt welcomed not knowing that a long phase of intellectual sparring was to take place in the future. Leslie told his wife what his salary offer was going to be to begin with and that there was to be an increase after three months probation.

His wife felt that they could just make things work with that income since they had worked with a lot less in the past. This was prominent in their minds as Leslie had just left the University of Waterloo where he had graduated but not under the most pleasant of circumstances.

Finances:

Alice worked full time at the hospital labs in Kitchener-Waterloo Hospital while Leslie moonlighted on weekends and nights doing 'on call' work. The staff in the Micro lab preferred the time off. He also had income from his teaching fellowship at the university and a few dollars, in cash, from work he did for a Professor, who was a consultant in food Microbiology to a few of the local firms. They had no debts and by the standards of the day one would say that they had a healthy bank balance. This did not come easy for they deprived themselves of little things like movies and eating out. Instead, they went walking and hiking with other couples and grad students with whom they had befriended over the 27 months that Leslie was at the university.

Background of the job:

The couple went down to Mr. Ryan's office and again shook hands. This old grandfather of a man, with his Pickwick glasses sitting on the middle of his nose, politely said that he would like to meet Leslie separately. He led Leslie into the enclosed adjoining private office. Alice remained sitting in the outside office. Just then Mrs. White came into the office bringing a file for Mr. Ryan to deal with saying, "You had asked for this information."

Mr. Ryan introduced Leslie to his assistant Mrs. White, who said, "Well I hope that you will join us soon." For the first time in a long while, Leslie felt as though he was wanted and there was a feeling that he was coming home to a comfortable environment. Leslie was shown to an interview chair and after the assistant left he was sitting opposite Mr. Ryan.

Mr. Ryan then stood up waving a hand to Les to remain sitting as he began to pace the carpet behind his desk. "I will be frank with you Mr. Paul; it has not been very easy with that lab up there. We have had to fire a few trouble makers. I do not know what Dr Gutch has told you but you must be aware of what has gone on up there. I put the whole blame on Dr

Gutch's shoulders for he is in charge but he did not appear to know what was going on in his own department." Mr. Ryan paused before continuing.

"He needs a lot of help but he will now try to control everything. He needs someone who is strong and willing to make the hard decisions. I believe that you can do it for you have had the training in a small hospital as a Chief. You will be able to take on the few staff, now under threat of suspension but still working up there. Should they step out of line you must know with whom you are dealing? I just feel that you should know the facts of that department. I would really like you to take the job. Just call me and I will inform Dr Gutch for he would like to know when you would like to begin work."

Les stood up as the interview was abruptly over. "Thank you, Mr. Ryan, for your openness and frank discussion. I appreciate your 'heads up' and we will get back to you by tomorrow. We have a lot to do to meet the employment deadline, such as giving up our apartment, finding a new one and then moving into town." The old man came around and said sotto voce, "He is a tough old bugger to deal with but he is a very kind man and I believe that you can work with him." With all the warnings Leslie and his wife had decided to take the job.

FROM ONE UNIVERSITY TOWN TO ANOTHER

Details and a Move:

The young couple left the hospital and set out to find a local newspaper as a precursor to finding somewhere to live. The aim was to search for an apartment that cost more or less what they were currently paying. It would be nice to have the same as their comfortable 3-bedroom home which they had in Waterloo. After about three hours of driving around to check the location of the apartments and their relative distance to the hospital, they drove into the parking lot of a local grocery market. The sat quietly and again perused the section of the local newspaper dealing with apartments for rent. They found a 3-bedroom one with 2 bathrooms about fifteen minutes away on the northeast part of the city. There were two high-rise tower apartment buildings, which were painted white and they backed onto a wilderness area. They found the superintendant and were shown to the 3-bedroom apartment. There was an ensuite to the master bedroom, a full walk-in closet and the L-shaped dining/sitting room was large enough to hold an upright piano comfortably. They signed a lease for one year and promised to move in by the weekend. The landowner said that he would throw in a parking spot in the indoor parking garage, located under the building. The caretaker went on about the wildlife area conservatory through which a small tributary of the Thames River flowed.

This was perfect for this young couple as they had made up their minds to settle down into a permanent job and to raise a family. They got into their bright red 411 Volkswagen and sped back to Waterloo stopping in Stratford so that Leslie could meet with his contact Mr. Hughes. Mr. Hughes was happy that Les had decided to take the job and he reminded Leslie that the position had been open for quite awhile. He was very encouraging even when Leslie asked what the difficulties were. He said openly, "Look Les, he is an Englishman who is very strong-willed. He is a bit tough, even arrogant, but you can handle him. He likes you because he knows that you are well trained and with your new degrees from Waterloo, a teaching hospital is where you should be located." Mr. Hughes continued, "I would work with him and, in time, you will control him completely."

"Go for it Laddie!" smiled the ever canny but prudent W.W. Hughes.

Mr. Hughes was an old codger and many of the staff tended to stay away from him for his presence demanded an automatic response. He too had a pleasant accent that was very British and he had no intention, even after 30 years plus in the country, of changing or adapting to a more Canadian way of life. Leslie knew that this irritated many on his staff but he said to himself that he had no intention of becoming the same as this Chief of the Stratford Hospital. He would however, keep his refined British accent.

Leslie knew that his wife was in the early stages of the first trimester of pregnancy. He had to take the job to earn an income capable of supporting them both. As soon as they returned home to their apartment in Waterloo at around 4 pm, they telephoned the hospital in London and Les spoke directly to Mr. Ryan. He in turn said that he was pleased and will be sending a letter after he spoke to Dr Gutch the next day. Les and Alice then called up their friends Gary and Carol as well as, Courtney and his girlfriend Susan to come over for supper that evening.

One More Last Supper:
Their close friends were very happy at the news and accepted the invitation for that evening, bringing bottles of wine. They were also intent on assisting Les and his wife with the move from their apartment on the weekend. Such were the friendships that this couple had made and such is the generosity of the Canadian people they had encountered. The question was why one would choose not to change and adapt to such a pleasant environment? A question that Leslie and his wife Alice would ponder over the many years. The metamorphosis to adapt completely would also be schizoid for one never truly leaves one's cultural past. It was a feast for the three couples for they knew that it was the last supper in Waterloo. It was an unspoken pact that they will meet regularly to celebrate many more suppers in London Ontario.

Prehistory:
Yes, it was a great meal for no one in Leslie's mind, could put together a traditional meal such as roast beef with roasted

potatoes, veggies and with appetizers to begin with, like his wife. Their friends brought the apple pie and Alice made the custard. Several bottles of wine were consumed. On the Friday of that unforgettable week, three ladies and three men together began to pack the furniture, beds and dishes. Leslie went out the evening before to book the rental truck for early Saturday morning. He then went to the local liquor shop to pick up many empty cardboard boxes, all of which were free. To be ready for an early morning start, the two couples decided to bring over their sleeping bags and stay overnight until Saturday morning. Leslie and Alice brought a stock of eggs, bread and bacon.

Leslie and their friends again celebrated with a meal on the Friday evening after having packed away many boxes of clothing, food, dishes and all that a home is made of. This again meant another celebration and so there was more food which Carol had prepared and brought over. After the packing all she and Alice had to do was to heat up her dishes. Les brought out the wine and Scotch and everyone had a lot to drink that night. They were ready for the big move on the Saturday.

Essentially, Les and Alice were moving from one small city to a larger one that was a drive of over one and a half hours away. The two males began moving boxes of books, mainly from Les' university days but also several boxes from his small library. The large wooden desk which was bought from a second hand store in Toronto was the pinnacle of Les' university education. It had kept Leslie company for the past three years, night and day through endless papers, typing agony and ecstasy. His two friends dismantled the desk for it would have been a nightmare to carry it through the apartment door at the new digs. Early next morning Leslie went to pick up the rental truck before the others were up. When he returned a half hour later, the three men began loading the heavy furniture, as the ladies began to bring down an interminable number of boxes that held clothing, dishes, trinkets, linens and the end of the groceries. Within two hours after a hearty breakfast of eggs, bacon, toast and marmalade, they were on their way to London, Ontario, a normal hour and a half away. However, it took more time for there were only single lanes in the back highways in those days. The couples followed in their respective cars as in a procession of a dearly departed one. Leslie decided to use the gravel road that led down into the east end of London and brought them very close to their new apartment in the city.

Two hours after arriving, they were completely unloaded and Leslie took the truck back to the secondary office in town. All afternoon, they were all involved in putting up the bed, furniture with mirrors, assembling the book shelves and putting the dining room table together. The three ladies went out to get fresh groceries but also had the task of bringing home a barrel of Kentucky Fried Chicken. They also brought in a case of the local beer that had a well-known blue label.

The old black and white television had a blow to its insides for there was a cable attachment in this new apartment. It had never been exposed to such technology for Les and his wife did not watch much television in those days. Their singular recreation, if and when they had time was reading voluminously. The telephone man also came that afternoon and they had a telephone attached in minutes on a Saturday. Leslie and Alice were always surprised at the speed and efficiency at which this North American society moved. Their bank balance had been transferred to a branch very close to their home. Their friends left early Sunday morning as one couple headed back to Waterloo, while the other couple headed north to their family farm just close to Kinkardin.

Settling In:

Les and Alice settled down immediately into their new home. Leslie left their newly collected red Volkswagen 411 car for Alice to use just for first few days while he caught a lift to work with a member of staff in his lab. Leslie went in to the hospital for orientation in the first week. This allowed him time to go around and meet his peers as well as many other staff members. He met with a group of men; all expats from the UK that comprised a background of Scots, Welsh and English, and all were in charge of different laboratory departments. He was invited to have coffee breaks with them. He had the benefit of the old chief who was still on staff for his first week before leaving for Scotland. In the early days, he met with the boss every day and slowly he was being placed into the pecking order.

New Lab, New Job, New Beginnings, New Battles

The Laboratory Space:

In a nutshell, Leslie's major task from his perspective was to initiate a quality control system that would ensure accurate and reproducible work in this small laboratory. In fact this was put to him many times by his new medical director when they had discussions over what quality control really meant and how it should be measured. The main work area comprised essentially of one large main laboratory room, a walk-in 'freezer room', an annex "broom closet" that he used as his office and a large culture media production room with an attached office for a resident or medical student. The top part of the walls of the main laboratory area where the patient specimens were planted and examined microscopically was painted green. Matching small blue tiles lined the walls from the bottom near the floor to the height of six feet. Whoever, designed this laboratory, which were tiled like a toilet, thought that the cleaners would wash them with a mild disinfect daily to remove the aerosols charged with bacteria, which might have settled on the wall. There was a central wide bench made of heavy maple wood. During work time there were 6 technologists surrounding this workbench area. As the activity built up during the day the bench would be loaded with many Petri dishes or plates and small vials of sugars used in the identification of the isolated bacteria as well as vials of antiserum.

Along the walls surrounding the whole room was a bench that traced the periphery of the room. Placed on it were tabletop centrifuges used in spinning down patients' spinal fluids and other specimens. There were two microscopes used only for the wet preparations of urine deposits. However, this area was also used every morning to spread out the work done on stool specimen. Our interning students also used parts of this bench to study real patient specimens as well as to do their practical projects. The Bunsen burners numbered around seven and when they were all being used the room became very hot and smelly and at times quite unbearable. This was especially disturbing when the many stool specimens had to be planted or wet mounts made to detect pus cells or parasites. In a word, the room was a very 'shitty one'. The stool culturing procedure was followed at the end of the day by the massive numbers of urine deposits that had to be read microscopically.

Smell – a Microbiologist's Asset:

The odour of that room changed from one toilet smell to another depending what type of specimen was been planted onto the media in the Petri dishes. However, these smells were nullified by the odour of Lysol, pots of formaldehyde solutions and other disinfectants. Leslie initiated a policy that all benches had to be swabbed down at the end of the day with a weak solution of Lysol. This was followed by wiping down with a 70% alcohol solution. Les had done an orientation with all the staff members before taking over as the head of the department. Invariably when he was called to give a comment on what he thought the organism was on a Petri dish, he would smell the culture first before looking at the plate. His comments were "Mm ... smells like *Haemophilus* or someone is working with *Pseudomonas*." Then the other staff would laugh for almost everyone had a different way of detecting a micro-organism or type of organisms by smell.

Of course there would be differences in interpreting what a smell was but it was the cause of much frivolity. Yes, these technologists could detect many of the common bacteria by their smell. This keen sense of smell had the odd bad side effect for one could smell the breath of a person with a chest infection and guess what the causative organism was most likely to be. A number of the staff was single females who were either dating or living with a male counterpart and their revelations to each other, whether Les was in the room or not, while disquieting was revealing from a microbial perspective.

While the scent of the room improved for Leslie had found the maintenance staff and went down to chat with Peter, the head of the department. He was a tall, blond slim man with a pleasant accent which he was pleased to tell Les was Dutch. He was a quiet man with an almost shy smile whenever he was approached. It took quite a bit of time before Peter befriended anyone and Les was lucky for it did not take long for this to happen. If there was a shelf to erect or one to be taken down Peter would come up to the lab at the end of the work day, have an inspection then in a few days time the alteration would be done. Invariably, Les would send down a card or a note thanking Peter and his staff for their assistance and promptness in responding to his department's need.

Over the years Les had a great deal to thank the maintenance hospital workers for because they kept his labs changing and adapting as well as being kept tidy and presentable. The next task was to get an extractor fan put into the window which had an air conditioner. When Dr Gutch saw too many quiet improvements taking place, he became very annoyed and aggressive at Les for his not being informed first. Les found that when he asked if little adjustments could be made invariably the answer was "it was not needed." That usually put an end to ever having anything done to improve the work conditions. Les learnt to circumvent this obstruction over the years by having the maintenance staff on his side. They would just turn up and say they were told by their manager that such and such a task had to be done. Dr Gutch would just smile walk in a manner showing that he was in control and state loudly, "Les, the maintenance department is coming to clean up the air conditioner and do some adjustment, would you assist them, old boy? Thank you."

The Virology Laboratory was located next to Les' Bacteriology operation and it was constructed essentially the same way. The Bacteriology staff stayed away from the Virology work but the staff by and large was civil to each other. There was a storeroom which housed a fume cabinet with an extractor fan and an ultraviolet lamp that was used to sterilize the extractor hood after it was used. Both laboratories shared a walk-in incubator.

With meticulous precision, Les set about to begin the slow transformation of this, until now, poorly equipped laboratory, into one of the finest in Ontario and Canada. He built the reputation of being one of the best diagnostic units and this reputation was promoted through the many publications that he and his team of microbiology scientists amassed in the provincial, national and international professional journals. Accompanying the publications were the many lectures that he and his technical staff gave freely to their provincial and national colleagues. These lectures were followed by an annual symposium which was organized by the team of other lab professionals. This symposium was sold to the members of the profession as well as to the commercial exhibitors and the market was southwestern Ontario. Invitations were sent out to the technical and nursing staff of every health centre in that region. It took twelve years to accomplish this feat against severe odds. There were obstacles put up by administrators and pathologists who battled for budgets to build up their individual fiefdoms. The continual battle for limited resources necessary for equipment, staff and supplies was an endless one. Even Les' peers were part of this unwritten hostile bid for resources and they wooed the chiefs of medicine on many occasions to the disadvantage of each other.

At times, Les had to verbally fence, nay verbally fight, his own medical director, who used a disproportionate amount of funds for Virology rather than Bacteriology. However, Les learnt to circumvent these obstacles by developing a close rapport with the young ambitious new specialists in the department of medicine. Once he began to meet them in the medical student lounge venue on Friday evenings after work hours, it was the happiest of happy hour. The student's residents and chiefs of medicine, surgery, obstetrics and others, all chatted easily after a beer or two having an opportunity to express their needs and frustrations. Les' greatest task was to talk enthusiastically about the loyalty within a smaller hospital institution and the friendly atmosphere that was special because of the Sisters of St Joseph. The 'royal our St Joseph's Hospital' was bandied about with great happiness and enthusiasm. It was a time and a place where he could informally express what was needed in the laboratory. However it was all conditional on Dr Gutch placing these items on the budget. He would have these young powerful doctors support his items and slowly he began to receive the new pieces of technology he so desperately needed.

This modicum of success did not go unnoticed for then both the competitive and petty jealousies between the other lab chiefs came into play. The improving department was under continual criticism by the other lab section workers often expressing that his lab was being pampered and were unworthy of new equipment and the first computers. But smiling to all staff members and not answering or fighting back, along with many sleepless nights, allowed for progress against all adversity. Once the ball of success began to roll it took on a speed and timing of its own. After many staff changes, he ended up with a highly qualified scientific team, who were motivated by the continual challenges he designed and put before them. These included the continual comparison of new diagnostic reagents, new diagnostic kits used in identification of bacteria and rapid technology kits against the 'gold standard' of this old profession. Over ninety percent of his staff had developed their own sub-specialty of a technology such as the freeze-drying of stock cultures, fluorescent microscopy and specialist in mycology another in parasitology another in specialty stains and another still in immunology techniques.

On the other hand, some assisted in the sub-discipline such as fungal infections or mycology, or parasitological expertise. With the assistance of Dr Gutch the one point that they always agreed on was continuing education. Les bartered with the administrators for more funds for the education budget and here he had quite a bit of success for his staff traveled across Canada and the USA to gain the expertise needed for the Microbiology Laboratory. A huge network of professionals across the US & Canada began which in later years crossed over into Europe. He had his plan to make this Microbiology laboratory the centre of all that was practical and avant garde in his chosen profession.

The medical director refused to sign proficiency results for the provincial program explaining that the changes in technology allowed for little of his input, which meant that he was no longer up to date. This was a shame for this very clever medical director had focused on Virology to the exclusion of improving the Microbiology Laboratory. He made a policy decision that had far-reaching consequences as mentioned earlier in this book and there are many who owe their status as professionals to these early breakthroughs

As a result, through his professionalism and administrative skill, as well as powerful clinical input, the Virology laboratory had gained regional status and WHO recognition as a reference centre in Canada. However, there was little improvement in resources for this specialty-trained manpower. When he saw that the resources were taken over by the new administrators and his impact had waned, he felt professionally shunned. His legacy was that the top body in the world recognized his Virology work but he did not see that at the time.

This upset his feelings and pride as a leader but his mission was to develop a high quality service and in doing so, build his power base. By overly giving more of his attention to Virology his position was compromised. He did only what he wanted to do, which was to focus totally on Virology. The rebuilding of the laboratory remains a major achievement of 'both Leslies' (Dr Leslie Gutch and Leslie Paul). Dr Gutch put his career and job on the line by confronting the administration with an ultimatum of either providing him the funds needed to develop the Virology discipline or he would quit. The new leaders in administration were no longer the Sisters of St Josephs and they took him to task. Within six months he chose to take an early retirement at the age of sixty two.

The New Broom Syndrome:

In the 1970s Les's first year allowed for some very minor changes. The product known as culture media used in the laboratory to grow the bacteria from patient samples of ear, nose and throat swabs, as well as samples taken from all other orifices of the human body, had improved in quality and reproducibility. The culture medium is a 'jello-like' hot fluid which is poured into Petri glass or plastic dishes and solidifies when cooled. Other specimens of stools, urines, pus as well as spinal fluid needed special types of agar plates. To grow bacteria in 18 hours, it was necessary to provide a food source that encourages them to grow as colonies similar to the mold seen on old bread. The disease-causing bacteria needed to be in the warmth of 37 degrees C. At times, it was necessary to vary the food source, the temperature and the atmosphere in which 'God's little microscopic life forms' could multiply.

Once there was a good confluent growth of the infecting bacterium on the medium, then one could expose them to antibiotics to see if they were resistant or sensitive to them. It is straight forward if the bacteria are sensitive to the antibiotic then that antibiotic can be used to treat an infection in the patient. If the bacteria are resistant to the antibiotic then that specific antibiotic should not be used to treat the patient.

The light microscope is the most useful tool used by the bench technologist and microbiologist. For when a general practitioner sends a patient specimen sample to the laboratory as a swab (a Q tip-like sample), a small part of the swabbed material is put onto a glass slide. These glass slides are either stained or used as a wet preparation for viewing under the microscope. After staining, bacteria look like round black dots called coccoid forms (examples are streptococcus and staphylococcus). If they are rod-like in appearance they are called bacillary forms and in the case of syphilis they appear as spiral forms. To maintain these forms the bacteria have cell walls that maintain their physical integrity. Antibiotics in the early days were designed to destroy the cell wall allowing the insides of the bacterial forms to leak out and die.

This process is referred to as the bactericidal effect of an antibiotic. If the bacteria are only inhibited from growing then this process is called bacteriostatic. One problem that is an obstacle in trying to use the in vitro results to treat a patient is to determine the dosage to be administered to the patient. This depends on the role of the infectious diseases specialist today but who was not available back in the 1970s. Today this skill is left to the clinical pharmacist to educate the physicians on the dosages to be used, the combination of drugs and their effects as well as providing information on the newer types of drugs that come onto the market place. The major problem is that, in Canada, the greatest users of antibiotics are the general practitioners. Hospitals are able to limit usage and appropriateness by designing a formulary, which provides physicians with a list of drugs to use for different infections. This whole system which has evolved into modern pharmaceutical practice has been ruined by the major drug companies, who send non-medical sales people with a modicum of scientific and medical training, to explain the merits of drugs to these general MD practitioners. The process used may have a conflict but the information is usually from peer-supported publications and 'social means'. The commercial sales driving need is to get the MDs attention and explain the complexity of similar drugs and the merit of using their company's product over their competitors. The better ethical organizations use some of the professionals in the field as their faculty to present the latest information to the general practitioners under the continual education program.

General practitioners take one final examination to become a physician. Their options then are to advance into a medical specialty and work in a tertiary health care facility, with a teaching mandate or to become a family physician. The specialists must maintain a high degree of proficiency and keep up-to-date with the newer drugs that come onto the market place. If this carefully evolved system is not followed then the whole formulary system developed in tertiary care hospitals breaks down and the inherent cost effectiveness and hospital budget limitations of the hospital pharmacy *gang aft to glea.*

Other technology:

Leslie read in one of the many technical journals that there was a new electrode that had a flat head which could be placed onto the surface of a material, such as agar, and would give an accurate reading of the surface pH. This instrument piece was designed for the biochemistry and industrial laboratories. He called the representative of the company - a short smiling Swedish gentleman with a square jaw and piercing blue eyes. He was curious as to why a biological scientist would want an electrode to begin with. More importantly why would he want a high powered one like a flat head calomel electrode? Leslie began using his advanced biochemistry knowledge in microbiology as he explained that pH is a 'major part' in the successful growth of bacteria. Especially more so in his discipline of microbiology, since these microscopic living forms needed a strict narrow range of pH to grow optimally in vitro.

However, when making agar, again like 'Jell-O', needed for bacterial growth, there has to be thorough mixing of all the ingredients. Once the agar set firmly, the bacteria grew on the surface not on the inside or depth of the Petri dish. Leslie was curious as to whether the surface pH was the same as within the body of the medium usually measured in a liquid state when hot. If there is inadequate mixing of the hot brew, the pH may fluctuate depending on its state (solid or liquid) of the medium. He wanted to know if the pH was the same after the agar cooled into a solid state in the Petri dish. The old straight electrode was used in the liquid stage during the agar preparation and there was no way at that time of measuring the surface pH of cooled solid agar plates.

The Swedish gentleman was a biochemist but he knew enough science to understand what Leslie was describing to him so simply. He could also see a new market for his electrode and his company had the only one on the market at that time. After the publication of a letter outlining Leslie's success in measuring the surface pH of cooled solid culture media, there was a demand for calomel electrodes in the old discipline of Microbiology. There was a stimulus in sales for this Swedish salesman and this was Les' first lesson in applied work having a role to play in the commercial world.

The Experiment:

Leslie asked the two media production ladies, called Laboratory Assistants, into his office and explained what he wanted to do. They nodded in understanding for these individuals followed instructions with no variation for he had explained what he wanted and they understood the importance of the request. They began the process of testing the pH of the different media in both the liquid state and after cooling on the surface. Ph is known to change with temperature and the important pH criterium for bacteria is the temperature at which they will grow. Even though he had suspected that there was a marginal difference, the surprise still stunned him for there was a difference, especially in the highly specialized media. These types of specialized media were more expensive and are used for the difficult bacteria such as the more fastidious strains, like the gonococcus that causes gonorrhoeae and *Haemophilus* that can be the cause of deep chest infections as well as meningitis. Such fastidious bacteria required defined food products such as trace elements of iron and vitamins as examples. They also require specialized humidity between 10% - 70% and a specific temperature of 35 – 36 degree C temperature as well as an atmosphere of 5 – 10 % carbon dioxide or an atmosphere of no oxygen in which to grow.

Since bacteria grow at their optimum in a relatively narrow range of ph, Les decided to publish his findings in the Journal of Medical Technologists. This simple bit of technology usage revealed the small but significant differences in pH which allowed for the best growth of these difficult bacteria. The response from around the world to this insignificant little article was overwhelming. The technical staff was impressed and the Director of the Department, Dr Gutch, begrudgingly agreed that this was a marvelous way to improve the quality control program in this section of the microbiology department. The ice was broken. After the staff had left for the day, Dr Gutch came into the empty lab where Leslie was tidying up and checking out the reports that would be going out the next day. He looked at Leslie and said, "Hello old boy! Still tidying up?"

Leslie looked up and replied, "Yes Sir, just to ensure that the quality control sheets have been kept up-to-date and that any variation is within normal values, you know?"

Dr Gutch growled and leaned against one of the work benches, folded his arms and stated, *"Actually, I believe that quality control reveals that the leader is incapable of running a well-staffed laboratory, for he relies on the end results of science and not on what is going on at the bench level."*

The Battle:
Leslie could feel the hair rise on the back of his neck and replied, "Is that why you asked me to focus on the 'quality control' of the laboratory?"

Then the old director said, "There is no need to be oversensitive or rude old boy. If you stayed with the staff and read the plates with them then you would not need all this new fangled expensive equipment. Do not be upset by this observation."

Leslie stopped what he was doing and smiled broadly at his towering tormentor, "Did you not ask that I focus on the hither poor quality control part of the bacteria laboratory?"

The response was quick and biting. "I may have mentioned something but you are in charge and could have taken the proper 'hands on' way out. Instead you read about all this scientific 'claptrap' new gadgetry and spent scarce money rather than helping the staff to work better."

Les fumed retorting, "and ignore the quality control of the culture media as you do in Virology!"

"Excuse me Sir! Are you implying that we do not have as good as, if not better, quality control system in Virology?" boomed the voice of the old director.

Les became defensive and replied, "Yes Sir! We use the same media preparation room and the electrode that is currently been used is old. It does not give consistent readings and has not done so for many months now. However, no one has followed up to see what is going on with your tissue culture supplements. How many isolates of viral particles are you having these days?"

Again the booming voice enraged red face exploded, "Are you accusing me of poor proficiency? I will have you know that virus will not grow if there is the smallest deviation of either pH or any of the growth conditions. Our controls have all grown daily. I check them myself."

"Then maybe your culture stocks have become hardy to any changes in their environment," came the equally heated response from Les.

"You are rude and out of place Sir and I demand that you apologize immediately," responded Dr Gutch. With that there was a bang as the door of the bacteriology laboratory was slammed shut when he left.

The Positive Spin:

This scenario was played out between the two professionals many times over the next fourteen years. There were many weekends, when Les did not know whether he had a job to go to on the following Monday after these Friday sessions or discussions which invariably ended in a ranting. A stressful atmosphere could have built up in the laboratory but the staff of both sections appeared to be unaware of these professional disagreements. On the technical side, Leslie had worked with Dr Gutch on improving the educational short comings of many technologists back in the 1970s. They lectured together and when needed, Dr Gutch asked his fellow professors from the university or the city hospitals, to present topical subjects to the technical staff of the whole city.

They worked together on the first medical conference in all aspects of laboratory medicine sponsored by the Foundation of St. Joseph's Health Centre. Leslie felt that he had made a breakthrough with Dr Gutch and there was a working level where they could work together in a positive atmosphere. After this provincial symposium success, Les asked Dr Gutch if he would allow the publication of his lecture on urinary tract infection in acute patients in the provincial technical journal. This publication remains one of the finest lectures in terms of its practical application for bench technologists to follow but also for the third and fourth year medical students. Dr Gutch took many copies with him when he went to lecture at the university, as did Les on his touring lecture circuit for the national and provincial professional societies.

Although Dr Gutch had his name on several publications in Virology, many were written by other professors in Virology, whom he supported with practical work that he had done within his Virology laboratory. This was the first Bacteriology publication with only Dr Gutch's name on it for the Canadian society. Leslie was able to do this because he was the co-editor of the Technology Journal for the province of Ontario. He knew that Dr Gutch was very pleased or 'chuffed' especially, when he asked for extra copies to hand out to the medical students in their second, third and fourth years of training. He used this as a handout for many years after this publication. Leslie unashamedly gave away many more copies of this publication, as handouts, to medical technologists across the country for he was also in great demand as a lecturer to post-graduate laboratory scientists.

In the middle of the seventies an older female physician with a fellowship in pediatrics joined the staff to do a second fellowship in Microbiology and Infectious Diseases. She had been in Canada for over twenty-five years previously practicing as a pediatrician in the east coast provinces before moving to Ontario. She had a very posh English accent, a dry sense of humour. Les and his techs became friends very quickly as Les was appointed by Dr Gutch to be her laboratory mentor. She found Dr Gutch to be interesting but a bit over-exaggerated in his tutoring. In all fairness, Dr Gutch had said to Leslie on many occasions in quiet conversations that he had a great respect for her clinical knowledge. Her name was, to all who knew her, Dr Claire and she soon became known as a vital member of the new Clinical Microbiology Department that was developing at this small teaching Catholic Health Centre. She was a kind and willing older student who worked hard at her studies. None of the staff could understand why she wanted to change disciplines at this late stage of her medical career.

In the First Month:

In the first months of his employment, Les found the technical staff were quite efficient at what they were doing reading the routine cultures and identifying the routine organisms that were causing infections in the mix of patients. St Joseph's Health Centre was a 350-bed acute hospital which also housed 100 delivery beds, 20 ICU and over 150 surgical and medical beds bringing the total to 500 beds. The organization was run administratively by the Sisters of St Joseph's for over 100 years by 1988. They were also responsible for 150 long term beds and another 250 chronic care beds. These figures may be slightly out of balance for Les was trying to recall what had happened over 36 years ago when it was a thriving establishment.

Les found that there were a number of bright young specialists and the Grand Rounds revealed a dynamic group of knowledgeable physicians who were totally loyal to this, the smallest of the three hospitals in the city. As the new guy on the block, Les was invited to sit in at many rounds where I met the specialists in medicine, surgery, obstetrics, gynecology, neonatology and a host of other smaller departments. His first task was to serve as best as he could with the limited resources and ensure that the patients had results quickly so that decisions would be made in a timely manner. What was expected was a tolerance and support for a better quality of work. Over the many years, staff just adapted to the advances in technology as it applied to making the lab more efficient and streamlined while building up a knowledgeable team of mini experts.

Les' first task was to prepare a summary of the significant infections isolated from patients in the different clinical departments. Dr Gutch approved of this but wanted to sign off on it was his work and he approved of it. He also wanted have the copies sent to the respective medical chiefs. The following examples of our findings per month were:

Possible acute urinary tract infections
(based on presence of pus   = 35
cells, increased protein)
Ear, Nose & Throat infections   = 25
Wound infections   = 32 (surgical)
Eye infections (conjunctivitis)   = 10 (sympathetic or 2 eyes)
Possible septicemias   = 5

Venereal disease (gonorrhea)	= 3
Female genital infections	= 25
Diarrheic infections (adults)	= 3
Children	= 6
Peritoneal dialysis infections	= 2
Other samples with a pathogenic organism	= 15

This was based on an average of approximate 3,000 clinical specimens processed in a month. The names of the medical department and their chiefs were deliberately omitted. The infection control officer of the day found this list to be quite beneficial when she spoke with the medical and nursing staff. This list also placed the Chiefs of clinical services on alert that their quality of work was being monitored by the rate of infection, reported by the laboratory findings.

Case Report

Sub-Acute Bacterial Endocarditis due to Cardiobacterium hominis

Microbiology Department, London, Ontario, Canada.

Infection by bacteria of the heart valves or of any heart tissues is called endocarditis. Because of the nature of such a severity, Les improved the system of culturing for bacteria by adding a new plate of a nutritious medium to this type of specimen. This was a time, when a small number of bacteria were still being given names (the science of taxonomy) by an international microbiology body. After isolating this small red rod body from one of our new Petri plates, the staff did not have the technology to identify this organism so it was sent off to the CDC in Atlanta.

They were very kind to do this favour for us and so we clocked up another usually harmless bacterium found in the saliva of human beings. This normally harmless organism entered the blood stream of this patient. He wore dentures and his gums bled from time to time. It was speculated that was how this organism entered his circulatory system. Then it lodged itself into the damaged heart tissue causing an endocarditis. The unusual nature of this finding alerted more of our fellow workers across the country to look more closely at the association between their heart disease patients and the health of their mouths. This mainly applies in the wealthy northern countries and in the aged community.

Les' Postulate and

Predicament…

Les:

Over the years, Les thought that too little attention had been paid to the so-called *normal bacterial flora;* he had felt intuitively for some time that these organisms should be investigated as possible benign pathogens. The first time this registered with him was while he was an intern at the Brook General Hospital, London UK, where the first open-heart cryo-surgery was done to replace damaged heart valves with the first ones made of metal. Later on these prototypes were replaced by a plastic designed one followed by those made from pigs tissue. In these now perceived dark old days of heart replacement valves, which was a miracle of its day but by today's standards now appears rather crude but clever in its theory. Back in the early 19 60s, the whole process begins with cooling the body down to about 22 – 23 degrees C using a machine to keep the full 8 litres of blood circulating through the comatose human body. Les' fiancé was the one who was responsible for cross-matching the blood at the different temperatures, which were used to charge/fill the machine that replaced the function of the heart while the old heart valves were being replaced.

The major problem for the microbiologists was that the population of patients who had this surgery was much older. Many through poor oral hygiene had rotting teeth, porous gums, so it was easy for normal oral bacteria to enter their blood stream from their mouths, through their gum disease. Among the bacteria from the mouth is the largest population referred to as the alpha hemolytic streptococci. When these organisms get into the blood stream they tended to infect the heart valves causing an endocarditis. The presence of bacteria in the blood stream is called a bacteremia. These bacteria are easily killed off with penicillin in this older population but in the normal healthy body such organisms are dealt with by the normal defenses of the immune system. The normal flora of the human mouth is spread among individuals from the time of birth through direct contact such as kissing by parents, family and friends. Later on from the teens to adults the passage of these normal streptococci through this very pleasurable past time do not cause any problems. In this population of older patients, the case histories reveal that they had damaged heart valves many with low grade infections called an endocarditis. The labs isolated the causative infecting organism which was one of these alpha streptococci and reported that penicillin could be used.

In these old days of surgery, however, the mortality rate was well over 70% and the majority of these transplanted patients died from a septicemia, which is an overwhelming load of these mouth bacteria invading the blood stream. It was Les' task, given to him by the Chief Medical Microbiologist, to find out why these common organisms were causing such fatal septicemia in spite of being treated with penicillin. Les found out that these normal bacteria in the mouth had become resistant to the drug of choice in those days which was penicillin. This was shattering news back in the middle sixties for there were still current text books that stated that these organisms were 'always sensitive' to penicillins. In fact, every student was taught that there was no such thing as resistant alpha streptococci to penicillin. The moral of the story was that these little microbes that live in our mouths, while doing nothing other than occupying small nooks and crannies in the mouth, are considered normal flora. They also have the ability to survive and they do so by becoming resistant to any poison, such as penicillin, that is used to destroy them. Les thought of the irony when he looks at the public and their desire to have antibiotics to kill an infection but failing to recognize that it is a poison to a living life form. They fail to realize that there is little difference between us as a life form and that of a bacterium.

Of course a number of these strains of alpha streptococci die off when penicillin is administered but there is a small population that becomes resistant. When these increase in numbers then the patient hosts carry a population of resistant bacteria in their mouths. Bacteria learn to survive from the multitude of foods that make up our diet as well as the medicines that humans take in so they survive and exist in the folds of the mouth. This lesson was never lost to Les for he had to design new techniques to perform the needed susceptibility tests on these difficult to grow or fastidious bacteria, which required specialized food stuff. This meant that the standards used for susceptibility testing in the lab to many antibiotics would be compromised from the gold standard used for the fast growing bacteria. This then begs the question, is the test designed for these alpha streptococci without the gold standard details truthful? Could the results be trusted to treat the patients with different and higher doses of antibiotics? Were we really getting the real concentration of circulating antibiotics from our newly designed test, which did not conform to the 'gold standard'? The gold standard is one in which an antibiotic was given to a patient through their veins, orally or intra muscularly, then blood is with-drawn at set times and the concentration of the antibiotic estimated. It was found out after many such testing that 4 – 5 times the concentration of the antibiotic given will give the killing level of bacteria infecting tissues. This knowledge is used by the laboratory to develop tests that would consistently give close results related to the dosage given and to patients of different sizes and weight.

It was for that reason that he focused on publishing the many case histories throughout his career for many professionals in the business discovered what these organisms were but their devious biology had been ignored. Les' new philosophy was that he would put the lab scientist staff on guard to note and detect any combination of irregularity in infections that indicated either a significant increase in white cells or pus, unusual resistant patterns to the common antibiotics, or unusual bacteria in unusual specimens. If one bears in mind that all bacteria are opportunists, then should not all bacteria be screened for their reason d'être? All such unusual findings had to be followed up clinically, using the hematology and biochemistry results in specimens such as spinal fluids from patients diagnosed with meningitis.

The best example is that of using the biochemistry abnormal results of an elevated glucose and low protein content in a spinal tap fluid, the elevated white cell count to confirm bacterial meningitis from a viral or one caused by tuberculosis. The elevated white or pus cell count and the presence of bacteria when examined under the microscope indicate bacterial meningitis in microbiology. The reverse of abnormal biochemistry results for glucose and protein would indicate viral meningitis especially when backed with the hematology results which would report an increase of the white cell type called lymphocytes. If the cell type was polymorphs then it would indicate bacterial infection.

One of his first case histories, which was published together with the head of hematology, was on a patient who had a DIC (disseminated intra coagulopathy) or internal bleeding dysfunction which could not be controlled medically thus resulting in death. One of the common reasons for such a death is a low grade bacteremia and in this instance the only bacteria that was identified was a common organism found in all human mouths, called by its biological name *Neisseria mucosa*. In any other specimen, one would normally discard this organism as just a saliva contaminant from the normal human mouth flora. A literature search done back in the 1970s, showed this organism as being never pathogenic; rather it was called a saprophyte of the mouth and so was just part of the mouth's normal flora. However, with such an organism from a bacteremia, when combined with an ill patient with a hematological oncologic problem, immediate death becomes a possibility from massive internal bleeding. The moral of the story is that while our normal bacterial flora may assist in our health, when the body becomes unhealthy in any marginal way they could become our worst enemy speeding our demise. Of course at death, our bacterial flora in the gut, mouth and skin all combine to reduce our carcass back to its original elements of salts, water and a few chemicals, so there is another reason for having our microbes as continuous companions.

Over the years, Les has brought diverse consequences together in the relationship between humans and their microscopic companions by observing and bringing together their roles in exacerbating illnesses. He remembers his grandfather who died in the mid-1940s of gas gangrene in his big toe. Les was only a young boy at the time but he had quietly learnt to spell gas gangrene. When he asked his mother what his grandfather's illness was about, he was told that her father had damaged his big toe when he was riding his bicycle in the countryside where he had his Cocoa Estate. Although everyone thought his toe had healed, years later a deep painful throb developed in his toe. One night grandfather could take the pain no more so he hammered his toe with his walking stick. The skin was broken and it bled profusely. The ladies who worked in the home just bound the big toe up with sticking plaster for that was all they had in those days. However, his toe festered in spite of many dressings, became blue black against his pale skin and in weeks began to smell. His toe was amputated but his foot continued to become inflamed. He eventually died for the gas gangrene that had developed spread throughout his body and his old body succumbed to a massive infection. I feel that my grandfather was probably diabetic for many Asians tend to become diabetic as they age. He would not have known and even if he did know there was not the information or the insulation available to treat him

How to use this anecdote!

Again, during his internship at the Woolwich Hospital Group in London, England, he had leant what organism caused gas gangrene and what the clinical appearance of the patient presented itself. He learnt that this was an organism that grew in the absence of oxygen and hence, was called an anaerobe. Les knew the tests to identify this anaerobe, which was called *Clostridium perfringens* (the older name was *Clostridium welchii*). In those days back in the early 1960s, the organism was a suspect in infections from road accident patients. The story went that because horses defecated on the roads, the bacterial spores survived for long periods in the dust long after the stool had powdered away and to all intent, the streets were clean. When the spores of Clostridium got into the broken skin of wounds, the organism became vegetative, began to grow in the tissue and invade the blood stream causing severe septicemia and eventual death. However, Les had observed what many pathologists knew and other lab scientists took for granted but was never written up or discussed at technical rounds. This organism was especially dangerous in diabetic patients. In Les' family, type 2 diabetes is very much in the family genome for they were of East Indian race and together with their diet, poor physical state as a result of a sedentary lifestyle, this disease may have manifested itself without grandfather even knowing.

One day in the lab, after isolating the *Clostridium perfringens* which was common enough, one of the confirmatory tests showed the presence of a "stormy clot" when the organism was placed into 5.0 mls milk with a drop of litmus indicator. After 18 hours incubation anaerobically in a specialized jar, the huge clot developed (looks like soured cream when thrown into hot coffee). The litmus milk indicator changed colour from red to white and the clot expanded up the tube because of the gas produced from fermentation. It was a great test to observe for the reaction mimicked the text book completely. Les showed the results to the pathologist who had entered the room. This was a pathologist who had specialized in medical microbiology who calmly commented "You know Les, you are really enjoying your science, aren't you?"

Les thought for a moment before answering, "Well Sir, it is nice to have a confirmatory test to verify what I had known from just reading the colonial appearance of the organism. It is also a pleasure to identify these various organisms daily. When the key to their Genus is not broken it becomes a puzzle and that encourages me to look for other biochemical confirmatory tests to perform."

The microbiologist, Dr Sumner, replied with a grin on his face, "You must never forget that we must report the results immediately so that treatment may be changed or dosage altered accordingly."

Les responded, "Oh! I have sent off a preliminary report explaining what the possible organism was, along with the susceptible pattern to the antibiotics tested."

"Oh! Good, so this is just your full identification tests to confirm the identity of the organism?" replied Dr Sumner.

"Yes Sir. But there has been little information on the clinical history of this patient that I would really like to know," Les replied seriously.

"What would you like to know and why?" replied the now grinning microbiologist obviously enjoying the curiosity of his new intern. His incisor teeth were bent in front and were yellowed from his continual cigarette smoking and there was a light dusting of either cigarette ash or dandruff on his jacket. He bent his head down to the sitting Les with an almost animal leering laugh about to explode, large blue eyes focused on his student.

"Well Sir, I would like to know if this patient is a diabetic. Secondly, I have noticed that diabetic patients often have this organism as a secondary infectious organism to the other primary pathogenic aerobic bacteria, such as a staphylococcus or enteroccous etc. Even when the main pathogen would be the known causative reason for the infection, I would go back to the cooked meat stock and seek out this Clostridium and in majority of instances I have found it. I know that the antibiotics used will also kill this anaerobe but I just want to seek out its presence. I will only do this check when the patient is a known diabetic because I wanted to see the correlation."

Dr Sumner said nothing. Then he stood up and said, "Give me the name and location of this patient," and Les hopped up from the workbench and wrote down the details for his boss who left the room. About half an hour later, Dr Sumner returned and asked Les to have the typed report brought to him. Dr Sumner signed the report and wrote at the bottom to the attending physician:

> *"As we discussed earlier, the reason for wanting to have the clinical diagnosis is that we can keep you apprised of the progress of the causative infectious bacteria that we have isolated. The pathology diagnostic laboratories are involved in the practice of medicine and as colleagues we need the information to assist you, the front line physician, in treating the patients earlier and with the appropriate antibiotics. .... Dr K. Sumner, Pathologist Consultant Medical Microbiology"*

In his later years, Les often thought of his former tutor and mentor after that incident who had said seriously to him, "Son, never stop tying things together. Never take these bacterial isolates for granted, so try and relate them to the cause of disease. It was clever of you to note the relationship between *Clostridium perfringens* and diabetic wounds, which we have taken for granted in the labs. But we fail to inform our colleagues, who do not have our training in pathology, to make this link between pathogen and a symbiotic disease process. Thanks for reminding me." Dr Sumner left the room and a very happy but stunned student intern behind.

Case report
Bacteremia due to Leptotrichia buccalis in an Immunocompromised Host
Microbiology Department, London, Ontario, Canada.

This lesson that was learnt so many years ago continued throughout most of Les' professional life. The organism isolated in the article above, was part of the "so called" normal flora of the human mouth. While the organism is normal in the majority of human mouths, when that organism invades the blood stream of many healthy adults, the body copes by restricting its growth and destroying the bacterium using antibodies or other gamma globulins working with the body's complement. In the immune suppressed patient such as cancer patients, the organism can become a serious pathogen because the body cannot produce the antibody needed. However such infections can be treated with antibiotics. This is another fine example of bacteria not OK in normally sterile sites in the body of certain patients especially, when their immune system is compromised.

The main purpose of publishing these unusual findings from his immuno-compromised patients was to bring awareness that while some bacteria may be saprophytes, that is none disease causing, many can become pathogenic in the wrong type of patient. This also occurs when bacteria find their way into normally sterile sites within the human body.

The Dilemma

&

The Question

Darryl Leslie Gopaul

THE DILEMMA AND THE QUESTION

(Whooping cough is caused by the organism Bordetella pertussis and a milder form of the disease-form caused by Bordetella parapertussis - the story continues).

If the research did not isolate any carriers of the whooping cough organism which caused pertussis in school age kids, who were the most susceptible patients and where was the source of these infections that continued to rise? Well over 125 cases of pertussis were isolated by March the following year and none of the patients had developed the prodromal stage. Those kids with the organism showed symptoms in the catarrhal stage which were severe symptoms. When the organism grows or infects the throat or pernasal space at the back of the nose, a tremendous amount of mucus is produced. As described before, this mucus traps the small hair-like projections known as villi (villus *singular.*) that waft air through the respiratory tract. These villi become trapped in the mucus and cannot move or waft the air through the respiratory tract, hence the strain in trying to breathe and expel the thick viscid mucus. This is traumatic to the child and the parents who witness these episodes.

It is safe to deduce that when the organism is present in children then there is always disease. At just about this time there was a single case published which stated that the vaccine against the whooping cough organism was the cause of brain damage in a child in the UK. It was verified that this damage was directly associated with the pertussis vaccine. This was published as a letter in the world renowned *Lancet Journal*. It was a Scottish physician that began the furor and said just one case is sufficient evidence that the practice of massive population vaccination for pertussis in newborn and school age children should immediately cease. This caused great consternation among mothers concerned for their children. As usual the purveyors of dread and infamy around the world are the newspapers and the news anchormen of the international television stations. They all pounced onto this topic and bombarded millions of homes with half truths. It was implied at the time that the spread of cases should be a case for legal action. The newspapers sold many copies and made a sensation; everyone knows that nothing can panic a population like the newspaper and television news stories. The Scandinavian countries, in particular the Swedes were the first to ban the vaccination of children with the pertussis combination that had protected so many millions of children. This was followed by the UK for a few years. Needless to say, there were outbreaks of pertussis in these countries. The national vaccination schemes were reinstated but there was a demand for better vaccines to be produced. Canada was producing vaccines used by many countries around the world at that time. The research being done to get a better vaccine was ongoing and fascinating to all medical microbiologists.

Les was fortunate to attend a convention known then as the Canadian Public Health Association Meeting held in Toronto back in the 1970s. This organization has long since merged with another professional group which is really a shame for the focus on public health work has been demoted for those who work in hospitals and private diagnostic laboratories. There was a major lecture being presented by the Microbiologist Scientist who was in charge of making the pertussis vaccine. He was an elderly Scotsman, who still had a very thick accent so at times it was difficult to hear all he had to say. However, it transpired that he had recognized that the antigen from the pertussis organism, used to make the vaccine, was missing a part in the inoculum. This small protein (or it can be a carbohydrate) is usually attached to the main antigen or body of the bacterium and is known as a hapten. He had sero-grouped all the different types of pertussis based on their cell wall ability to stimulate and produce an antibody in a rabbit.

In his grouping of organisms, he dismissed a less pathogenic form of the organism, which was called a parapertussis. Workers with these bacteria had long recognized this form of the organism that caused a mild form of a neurological disease. Leslie had two separate fluorescent-tagged antibodies from the Scandinavian Company for both forms of the organism so his laboratory was able to identify both forms of the bacteria for his statistics.

When the Scotsman introduced this hapten into the vaccine, he was convinced that he had developed a complete vaccine that would cover all stages of the disease by stimulating the human immune system to protect itself. Over the years, this vaccine has undergone close scrutiny by the medical staff concerned for the protection of patients against the pertussis disease. Thirty years later there may have been modifications to the vaccine but it has remained one of the victories against the scourge that killed so many children before the war and in the dreaded 1800s.

Leslie returned from this meeting happy about the new vaccine and its production that would assist the next generation of patients. However, after discussion with his colleagues he could not find out the repository for this organism's existence in a protected population as found in Canada. The dilemma remained for this little team of Dr Gutch, Dr Claire and himself. He reported what went on at the meeting to his group of GPs and to the medical technologists in the laboratory. He distributed his collection of handouts from the many lectures as well as, the latest material on improving the growth of bacteria in vitro. Attending the major medical conventions in one's discipline is one of the best investments that any institution could do for the promotion of the best practices in healthcare.

A Summer of Cricket:

As the summer of 1974 wore on, a cricket match was organized by the London, England-born Hematologist. The great thing about Canada at that time was the number of professionals who practiced in the city but came from the outer reaches of the British Commonwealth. Needless to say, cricket was the sport that inspired great passion in many colonial countries, even though this was very much a gentleman's game. The house team was made up of Kiwis, Australian, Englishmen and a Scotsman against a team comprising, an East Indian, West Indians of Negro descent, East Indian players, Pakistanis, Trinidadians, Guyanese Indian, South African Caucasian and mixtures of the different race types. Their places of origin were as diverse as the racial types but the wonderful thing was we all spoke English.

Being a West Indian of East Indian race and not a very good cricketer, Leslie found himself on the team. This game takes the better part of a day to play and for busy physicians, scientists and porters working in a hospital to get that amount of time off was very difficult indeed. However, it says a lot when everyone rescheduled their weekend routines and made promises to the family that the outstanding tasks will be completed or attended to if only they could get this time to play. The sport was addictive enough but to spend a half day on a green field, dressed in whites and 'waving the willow' was not too difficult for us connoisseurs of this complicated game. It was wonderful to see the home grown Canadians and US visitors trying to come to grips with the similarities to baseball.

These made-up teams were invariably fully attended and the fellowship was palpable and unexplainable. The passion displayed by the knowledgeable spectators of family and friends from the colonies made for great exchanges with non-cricket professionals. In so many instances, home grown Canadians of two or more generations know of the game but have never seen a game and so never understood the rules. It was left to the knowledgeable spectators, usually family members to explain to these folks caught up at the sight of

11 players spread out on a field and two batsmen. The game was splendid for it was a sunny day and there was a break for tea time. There was a lunch of roti and curry chicken brought in by the Indian supporters and there was beer at the end of the day. It was also an opportunity for the female members of the family to dress up and come to see 'their males' play in this national game of the Commonwealth. When the teams disbanded at the end of the game, it was not necessary to know who won for there was great hilarity but most of all, there was the opportunity for professional folks to get together and 'chin-wag'.

After this particular game, instead of going home, it was decided that the two teams would meet at a West Indian restaurant know as the Calypso. It was owned and run by a Guyanese expatriot, who was a medical biochemist by profession. The main dishes were essentially East Indian cuisine done West Indian style. The beer flowed throughout the evening and the conversation rose and dropped. Invariably, it would return to medical discussions and the problems that we all shared for curing patients were not a defined task. It was then that Leslie, who was known by all for his scientific publications, told of his stymied research in looking for the repository of the pertussis organism. A number of GPs were also present and they took 'the Mickey out of him'. He laughingly said that they had ruined his research by treating empirically, without knowing what the causative organism in many infections was. The caustic and comedic remarks that make for the fun in British humour were unlimited. When the laughter died down it was a GP who said that he was convinced that many of his twenty year-old patients in his practice had similar symptoms as presented by Dr Gutch at his Grand Rounds of a few months ago.

The discussion continued well into the late evening, with everyone mellowed by the beer and comfort food. Then it was the bleary-eyed Hematologist, who suggested, "Maybe the

GPs could assist in this study by swabbing the pernasal space of these twenty-somethings, just a few to begin with, and see if Leslie and his team can isolate the pertussis organism." It was time to leave as the evening was well into night time and it did look strange for this group of men, of varying race types, accents and range of complexions all dressed in white shirts and trousers as they left the establishment. It was then that a few of the GPs said to Leslie, "Call me next week and let me have some supplies, as well as rekindle my knowledge so that I can assist you and hence assist ourselves with this pertussis puzzle."

Post Game Beer Sessions and Understanding Spouses, a Key to Profound Thought:

The roles of beer sessions and of sport as repositories for professional staff to meet, imbibe to mellowness, to ruminate on comfort food, have unknown possibilities. Of course, it is equally important to have a spouse who understands that the beer or wine and the desires that these beverages stimulate were purely for profound thought and scientific knowledge and for no other Bohemian reasons. If that is believed then there would be so many more breakthroughs and more success in scientific research. Leslie took these GPs up on their offer of assistance. There was a small group who did not participate including both physicians on his team and so he was up against their old knowledge. There was a contradiction in focus for they (the GPs) had the clinical experience and he was not a physician but a lab scientist. They never failed (alas!) to let him know 'the greatest stab of all' - they were the physicians and he was just a medical scientist. One wonders how this perverse twist in the professions, especially the medical sciences came about.

History has shown that the PhD was the first doctor recognized. All that these medical doctors did was pass a final exam once or twice in their lives. The first time was to become a GP then if they specialized in a discipline, it took four to five, possibly seven years, to get a fellowship examination. There were no other methods for showing their continued proficiency through regular external peer reviewed examinations or for publishing regularly. Whereas, the medical scientist has to show his continual proficiency annually by publishing his work which was reviewed by his peers. His written exams and publications had to be presented to medical peers at rounds before acceptance by the majority of practitioners. He had to apply for, and some time he would be rewarded with, grants that take so much of his energy away from their scientific work but he was guaranteed of maintaining his proficiency for that year.

Leslie however, stuck to his arguments that this organism which caused whooping cough or pertussis needed to be isolated to fulfill Koch's postulate. He would stand by the guidance of this basic principle on which all diseases had to stand up. He broke the rules by stating that whooping cough was not just a clinical diagnosis but a diagnosis based on the scientific isolation of the organism in the laboratory in all cases of disease. These discussions were heated ones which did not leave a pleasant atmosphere but he was as dogmatic as his opponents were cynical of the need to have the lab verify their intuitive diagnosis of whooping cough. The British team, he kept mumbling to himself, *'they have ganged up on me'*. The arguments by both groups were quite valid. The clinicians knew first hand that this was a disease of children and history as well as, from their varied practices, verified what they had done repeatedly.

On the other hand Leslie knew that the opportunistic nature of micro-organisms and their ability to survive for billions of years were genetic facts. Survivability was one of the most significant forces in nature especially for these microscopic life forms that were probably the first life on this planet. He also felt that humans evolved with a natural micro-organism flora that lived, thrived and even showed the best aspect of the perfect parasite which is to keep the host alive. Following up on this treatise, he expounded to everyone who would listen that because the human body has a micro-flora of microbes that was a definite sign they were there for a purpose. He explained that the purpose was to stimulate the human immune system thus keeping the human alive through scourges of infections. He also felt that bacteria created humans to be a site for them to congregate and mix their genes but he had caused enough problems with his hypotheses.

These were evolutionary factors that were not being considered by his two team mates. Microbes that are ubiquitous in nature and are actually intrinsic to the major life cycles in nature, such as the nitrogen and carbon cycles, had the planet by its 'genitals' for they were the reason for cycle of life on this planet. These arguments were not just philosophical but were in his mind, a proven reality and were proven by many scientists. The fact that micro-organisms were put to industrial use, such as in the manufacture of dyes and in the food industry, many of us could not possibly forget. Les was like the character in Jean Anouilh play *Poor Bitos* saying aloud, *'Where would we be without our* beloved *glass of vino or our cheeses, yogurt and so many more quality food products?'* He postulated to all present that it was the ability to survive and to be genetically manipulated by nature. These life forms are not to be trifled with for they will survive our attempts to remove, destroy, immune block, spray or dose with toxic drugs for they will eventually just mutate and a resistant population will emerge eventually.

Leslie had a science friend from Waterloo who was a biochemist by profession. They maintained their friendship for many years and of course they shared many meals, bottles of scotch and unknown numbers of bottles of wine over their twenty-five year association. Until his friend contracted cancer of the pancreas and died within a year, they fed each other with scientific possibilities. Their support for each other was phenomenal in their varied arguments over politics but most of all in science. In his colleague's last few years, they had managed to work together well and before his friend died, they had over 10 scientific posters and 5 international publications that remain in Acta medica. They had taken a research tool and made it into a routine diagnostic instrument that allowed them to measure Pico grams of drugs, enzymes and hormones by using the newest technology of Mass Spectrometry. He had his colleague and friend over for supper, a routine that was in practice for many years, especially on the weekends. The women had left to clean up the tables, look after the dishes and the children were put to bed. These two long time friends met in the quiet surroundings of the sun room with a bottle of cognac.

Les poured out healthy glasses for the two of them while his friend poured liqueurs for the ladies. They settled down for an evening of healthy discussion and there was no holding Leslie back as he drove right into the problem that was bothering him for weeks, nay months. "You know old pal, my associates are wrong for they will not look at the broader and bigger role of bacteria in the cosmos." His quiet friend allowed him to rant on and remained silent while slowly breathing in the fumes of his Napoleon brandy. He knew of Leslie's problem in getting this healthy carrier twist sorted out.

He then waited for Leslie to stop and sip his own brandy before he interrupted. "*You know Les, why do you not just go ahead and do the project without their consent? You have control of the lab staff and they will do what you ask of them. Ask your close technical leaders to keep this project confidential, which is placing your good staff into a conspiracy. Think about this as a solution for it is eating up your energy and you will never get this thing started.*"

After his friend and his wife left that Saturday night Leslie slept like a dead man for he was invariably worn out after a week at work. The need for friends over for supper is a real respite for such socializations relieved the passion and stress from his restless mind. The following Monday, he decided to bring up the subject of going after a new population of young adults, with a prolonged catarrhal problem, which the GPs thought may be a good hide-out for pertussis. He asked if he may continue but again the combined physicians remained adamant, indeed Dr Gutch loudly shouted, *"I absolutely forbid any more talk on this subject. Take it off the agenda immediately and do not bring this subject back until you have a more novel idea."*

Going Underground:

This was all that Leslie wanted to hear for he was not told that he should not do any more practical work, he was just informed not to bring up this topic anymore at their Monday meetings. He took the bit in his teeth and called his two close senior technologists to a closeted meeting. They had heard how the complete project had to stop. They showed great concern and had in fact said to him, *"Les, why do we not continue doing the work anyway?"* but he had just smiled.

It was his Charge Technologist, Sandy, who spoke up before he had completed telling them of his plans to continue the project, in quiet confidence. *"Leslie, we will do the work and no one but us will know what samples they are. We will take down the results in a personal binder. Just get the GPs to draw a blue line at the corner of the requisition and ask them not to discuss this project with the lab physicians. I will interrupt the specimens and we will do the fluorescent microscopy, Paul will record the result of the cultures for he will be the scheduled worker on the pertussis follow-up project."* Over his thirty years, these two loyal colleagues became the backbone of many of his successes which he nobly shared with them throughout their combined careers.

The project of searching for the healthy carrier began in earnest without any of the lab physicians being the wiser. After six months, there was a modification to the project. Leslie kept the confidence of a few GPs whose patients were pertussis positive. He chose one hundred positive children who had been cured and asked the GPs to find out if there were young adults that remained in contact with those families. If there were any young adults, would they volunteer to have pernasal swabs taken. If they agreed, then it was necessary to have a case history of any upper or catarrhal infection recorded.

If there was a reason asked in order to take part, then the GPs were to state it was to prevent re-infection of the child in the family. It was a stroke of genius and again it was Sandy who did the tabulations. This time her work was seen by Dr Gutch and he quietly asked what she was recording and she accurately told him that she was keeping a log of the pertussis isolates and the patient demographics as to sex, age, GP and whether vaccination was given completely or partially or none at all. She truthfully related that the technologists that come for orientation from other hospitals asked many questions on the details of the epidemiology of disease in the city of London.

He was impressed with the details and depth of the work being done but he never looked at the results immediately. After six months Leslie brought the project to termination. They had well over two 225 isolates. The two senior technologists had isolated pertussis from the 100 children, their family's isolates which included big brothers, sisters and mothers. In this population of pertussis positive children, there were over 80% recoveries of pertussis and parapertussis in their elder family members who showed no symptoms of whooping cough. In over 75% of the cases, some of these adults had complained that they had allergies. Sandra then took the logged results, at Leslie's suggestion, to Dr Gutch. He kept the book for weeks until one day he called Sandy in to his office and she was asked to explain the results to him. He remained quiet and said nothing to her or to Dr Claire or Leslie. Leslie met with Dr Claire later on when Dr Gutch was away and showed her the results and she was flabbergasted at what this little hospital had uncovered. She said to Sandy and Leslie, "I do not know what to say. I am astounded." She remained quiet for a few minutes again looking at the results and then rhetorically asked Leslie, "You went ahead and did the work anyway?" She looked at him and smiled. "You have shown these results to Dr Gutch?" she again asked Sandy. Seriously, Sandy said that she had shown them initially but Dr Gutch had said nothing.

Then this older physician, who was struggling with the body of microbiology work that she, had to study for her exams, said, "Leslie, this is far too important to be kept as a secret. We were wrong to have stopped the project. We are wrong clinically, if the details that you have given to me are correct. I must check the patient notes and speak to the GPs, the adults who carried the organism" she volunteered. "Then I will go and discuss this with Dr Gutch." Leslie thanked her for her support and went ahead to stress that this was all his idea and that neither Sandy nor Paul, who had kept the slides all labeled and filed away safely in the refrigerator, were to be reprimanded.

Dr Claire did the work which she had volunteered to do. She made copious notes from the patients' case files and she had confidential discussions with the hand-picked GPs. She redrew the diagnosis of the adult carriers for they were capable of walking about tending to their jobs or attending universities. Speaking with their allergists, they said that there was really no response to the standard antihistamine treatment although there was some limiting of catarrhal build up. They could not state that this was due to the effect of the antihistamine drug recommended. She concluded that there was a possible 'carrier state' in the older adults but she could not definitively say that they were healthy.

This paper was published in a provincial technical journal and was never published in either the Journal of Pediatrics or any Journal of Microbiology. Both Leslie and Dr Claire used the data in their lectures. While Dr Gutch never said a word about this project, he was very pleased with the work done. Leslie did hear from a secretary that she had heard him say to his opposite number, Dr Campsal, at the other hospital, "Yes he is quite a chap and the work done on whooping cough is absolutely splendid. But he will go against the establishment and he will be hurt. Bob, as you know it is never good to be the first in anything for one opens oneself to criticisms by everyone, including peers and the establishment."

Whither Wisdom in Professional Life or Work-A-Holic:

How true that advice has been for that was pretty well the pattern of Les' professional life, the significance of which he never fully understood. It was only after his retirement that he has had the privilege of time to think. Les felt that one is often born with a personal trait, a skill, an unusual understanding as a gift of evolution and genetics. If one has the environment that is nurturing and was allowed, then one would subconsciously blossom. Such personal traits are often masked by traditional societal training and education. Often these gifts of birth and genetic selection remain as dormant hobbies but they remain for life. The irony is that if one perseveres through failure in education or has been displaced from a job or some other personal change in circumstance that leaves one locked out of the traditional acceptable growth arena. However, more often than not, these traits will persist and the end result is often success. How does one define success? Invariably, one is happier and if ambition is mixed into the brew, then there is external growth and personal wealth often follows. There are a number of such personal stories throughout our new high technology age but so many remain untold.

Les has often thought of his profession, for he was the first and now probably the last in his family to have undertaken such a scientific pathway. His family history is riddled with members in the teaching profession on his father's side, as well as the commercial world of business, with strong artistic traits on his mother's side. The quirk of random choice in the next generation of humans, works just as described by Charles Darwin. Les believes now that his contribution is a 'pot pourri' of the traits on both sides of his family. This cocktail appears to have worked pretty well for he was very happy in his chosen profession.

Caution in the Year 2000:

Today, in the twenty-first century, such an undertaking would have a host of proponents for and against the exploitation of the children. The lawyers would be standing by while one was taking a swab. The ethics committee would stifle epidemiology for months before granting their consent, thus losing the environmental period of the year when this disease predisposes itself. The lab staff would not be so willing to participate for the unions would get involved in deciding whether a teaching hospital should be the place for such work and should the public health laboratory not do this type of work. Months if not years later the researcher would then need to find funds to go ahead on the endeavor. It would take a year before getting off the ground and two years to publish if the editors thought this were a significant finding. Before they did anything they would seek the counsel the College of Physicians and Surgeons that such work was empiric and was needed to add to the education of the general practitioners. This would cause a further delay and very little would be achieved for time will be lost as would enthusiasm.

The whole project was completed between September and November back in 1974, using the department's normal budget but knowing that if there was some financial shortfall the sister administrators would make it up. The results revealed at that time that there was a carriage rate for beta streptococcus, which was the primary cause of a bacterial sore throat, in Leslie's group of school-age students of 12 - 15 percent in every one of the schools. None of the children showed the overt clinical symptom of a sore throat according to Dr Claire. There was an almost ninety nine percent (99%) correlation between the symptomatic sore throat syndrome and the isolation of the causative streptococcus, not necessarily the Group A species but other groups of beta streptococci. The major deduction was that there was a carriage rate and a non-symptomatic rate in this cohort of patients of 12 – 15 percent. At that time in the 1970s, no text book had recorded such a finding. While our population was small it was focused in the primary school age population of susceptible children. Secondly, there was no difference between the sexes for there was an equal number of females and males in the cohort. Third there was a direct correlation between the kids who had the bacteria (Streptococcus pyogenes or Group A streptococcus) and their parents getting a sore throat after the kids became inoculated from their peers.

Les thought to himself "Ah! The hugging of the children after their first few weeks at school ensures that the family becomes sensitized after a short period of illness. These 'little carriers' Oh sorry children, did their work well by inoculating the mums first then of course dad

Diagnosis In Lab

Medicine Is ...

Diagnosis tells the stories of what happens when patient specimens are collected and sent to a medical laboratory where highly trained lab scientists process them to obtain results. These results are used by the attending physicians in the clinical diagnosis of illnesses and in the treatment and follow up on the healing of the patient. These lab workers also follow up on any unusual findings. By publishing their findings, they add daily to the collection of applied knowledge essential to the education of the many physicians, nurses and lab scientists indirectly helping the patients. The power of such publications is shared across the country and the world of healthcare on this planet.

The path taken in doing this work is not however, straightforward. There are some checks and balances which have improved over the years partly due to a provincial proficiency testing and teaching associations. There are also many international and US-based quality improvement organizations to which an individual laboratory may subscribe. These quality improvement organizations are then followed by the many inspections made by governmental bodies. The health care in Canada is extremely well monitored. In spite of all these precautions, problems still arise. Much of this good work however, has dissipated because of the amalgamation of the smaller more efficient labs into detached mega lab outfits. There are very few scientific leaders in this new world order of mega labs which pipe out results with no intuitive analysis or introspection. The administrators of the new world order do not believe in leaders who must look for scientific innovation and pursue curiosity and the purity of knowledge that are essential for the future improvement of practice. The bottom line and the cult of so-called business world conditions are all that matters. The knowledge obtained daily from the labs used to be shared through lectures within house and at provincial, national and international meetings but mainly through the dissemination of publications of one's findings. The leaders of today's labs are administrators who only look at the fiscal details not recognizing the health-knowledge benefits that have been invested in the human capital. The results speak for themselves for there is now a worldwide epidemic of resistant microbes, where 'policies and written procedures' are ineffective in its control. When there were medical microbiologists or bacteriologists, virologists, mycologists and parasitologists, then there was control in the use of the type and dosage of antibiotic selected for treatment. This was based on the understanding of the biochemistry of the drugs and on the biology of the microbes that have been on this planet before mankind crawled on the surface of earth. These professionals went on ward rounds daily, led by the medical microbiologists as well as by his technical head. There was the continual monitoring of the hospital environment under their daily critical survey and they were present to enforce the protocols that they developed based on their skills.

To cut back on the housekeeping staff and their cleaning products in order to keep more money for administrators and office workers is being 'penny-wise and pound foolish'. The scourge of multi-resistance will continue as ill-educated individuals, such as administrators and other non scientific individuals take on the role of warden in protecting the hospitals and their patients. This may seem arrogant but Les continually tried to explain that the breakdown was because these other staff fails to understand the biology of micro-organisms. The overuse of antibiotics has now produced an iatrogenic disease or a medical induced disease state caused by a normal gut inhabitant *Clostridium difficile*. This organism is one that is selected out when too many or insufficient or inappropriate antibiotics are administered to a patient over a long period of time. From the normal gut flora of microbes this organism is selected out by antibiotics that destroy the other normal bowel flora leaving it free to grow into larger numbers that is normally present. Its biology is to allow movement of the stool through the gut by releasing a by- product of its metabolism. Large doses of antibiotics kill off the normal flora but do not kill these anaerobes for they survive by going into a resistant spore state. They therefore remain in the gut and when the antibiotics have been removed they revert to the vegetative state, proliferate and produce a higher level of this normal waste product, now called a toxin. This toxin is produced in higher than usual quantities, relative to the size of the intestine. Too much of a 'good thing' such as too much toxin, allows the lining of the gut to be disconnected. In the presence of large amounts of the toxin the syndrome known as 'pseudo membranous colitis" occurs. The organism thrives in the absence of competitors such as the other bacteria in the gut that were killed off by antibiotics. The toxin in large enough quantities begins snuffing off the lining of the gut.

Similarly, the selecting out of the newspaper-worthy 'MRSA' is the classic example, for it has now gained a foothold and is well established in retirement and long term care facilities. Recent studies reveal in geriatric patients there is a larger number carrying the MRSA or multi-resistant staphylococcus. These older people or patients have been around for a long time and in their life time there have been several episodes of antibiotics been administered. As a result, the normal bacterial species have been cleared out and replaced by the multi-resistant strains of which the staphylococcus known, popularly as MRSA maybe one of several found in and on the ageing body. Moving such patients into acute care hospitals without first screening them for the presence of the MRSA allows for the spread of the bacteria in the acute hospital setting. Such carriers could be treated prophylactically to prevent the epidemic spread of multi resistance. Accordingly these patients will continue the spread of their resistant micro-companions and will cause massive fatalities in the future. The healthcare administrators need to have these patients screened for MRSA in all of these transfers before the long term care to the acute care facilities.

Case Report

Of Mites, Rashes and Allergy

Microbiology Department, London, Ontario, Canada.

So far Les has been telling the tales of his growth into the profession of being a medical microbiologist. He stresses where resources are needed to do a proper job of indentifying the location of bacteria in the patient and where they are in the hospital environment. He explains how resistant bacteria occur using one example. He also explains how new medically caused diseases occur because of the lack of knowledge in the biology of the infecting bacterium. Later on he will explain that just setting policies, which are tidied up by being placed into binders on the wards of hospitals, is not enough for there is a need for inspection of all wards and monitoring of the hand washing technique of all staff on a daily or weekly basis.

However, when one works in the laboratory a whole slew of requests come in from physicians with different specialties in medicine and surgery. There are the normal investigations as outlined in any pathology manual or text book then there those asking for a scientific or technical opinion. Such is the case history above, which was published by the group of workers in Les' laboratory after the Chief of Allergy asked for an opinion on a rash that kept returning to a young patient who went up on weekends to the family cottage. It was found that he had a number of water mites that had been brought from the lake, where he played and swam daily, into his bed. They had somehow thrived and loved his epithelium or his skin. While this was an unusual case it was found that the lad had a specific allergic reaction to these mites. Thanks to the professor of Entomology who was surprised when Les asked him to key out or identify the mites as a favour to his laboratory. He did and this was the second recorded case when Les and a brilliant allergist physician at the time published this article back in the 1970s. The allergy specialist was turned away by his teaching university for he was informed that he needed to bring in more income from his practice. The shock was too much and the world lost another wonderful professional for he died shortly afterwards by this rejection. He committed suicide.

A Personal Warning:

The world of diagnostic medicine has got to reclaim the initiative but understandably using a more cost-effective strategy. If it is not too late to convince many students to enter the field of Medical Microbiology and Infectious Diseases, then the next generation must be trained to close this Pandora's Box. However, that strategy must include scientific analysis, abstraction through the myriad of statistical analyses; many blind alleys of future investigations will then be avoided if statistics are available and this can only occur if the professionals are in place. Most important of all, this knowledge must be shared with all practitioners in this human health industry. For if the wealthy nations adopt this strategy and protect themselves it will only be a matter of time before the epidemics of other countries cross the borders and find new susceptible populations to continue their survival. Microbes do not recognize man made borders on this planet or in the cosmos.

Leslie Paul's story explains the joys and tribulations of being a professional in this otherwise delightful industry. He recommends that the newspapers should have predigested articles so that there will be continuing education to the public and this is a worthwhile role for the better papers. These articles should not be used to cause panic or for sensationalism but to educate but then this may be too noble a suggestion.

Question:

How does one find out about a profession and how does one enter it? Today in the twenty-first century, in the curriculum of many universities and colleges it is a nightmare for students to get good personal information. The more savvy students would look up the World Wide Web of any university curriculum. However, the old fashioned way of having a mentor or an advisor in the 'business/profession', so to speak, is by far a better way. It worked so well in the past when there were students lined up for these jobs working through a co-operative program, where both the industry and higher training institutions combined resources to develop a highly trained applied worker. Such industries along with government support could conceivably produce future workers for all industries. There will always be room for the pure academia so universities know that they are there not for just academia for the world cannot support the large numbers of graduates. They should bite the bullet, climb down from their academic high horse and acknowledge that the main reason for their existence is to produce good workers.

The co-operative system used by the University of Waterloo has worked very well. There is the added advantage of co-op students not being penalized by having huge debts after graduation. Contributing and furnishing funds for tuition or through a practical work experience with the support of industry's input could eliminate this penalizing system to our undergraduates but this is too big a leap in Governmental thinking and even worse for the old establishment of teachers at all levels in the current well paid and non-monitored system.. All teachers should have a government legislated professional college to ensure that the professionalism of teachers are maintained through continual development.

Improved Technology on an Old Disease:

Leslie and Dr Claire struck up a professional liaison that resulted in a breakthrough in an 'old disease' thought to be only diagnosed clinically as was written in all the text books. It is a childhood disease known by many mothers in the early part of the twentieth century, as whooping cough. Dr Claire said to Leslie, "In my practice I have had many cases of what I thought to be whooping cough. I had no way of proving it to be so." Again in the recent literature, Leslie read that a Scandinavian Immuno-biology company had produced an antiserum against the whooping cough bacteria and these scientists of the company had succeeded in tagging a fluorescent dye to the antiserum. The significance of this new product meant that one could now dye the organism and look at it under a fluorescent microscope where positive slides from patients with whooping cough, would be seen as green rods against a black back ground He contacted many of the bacteriology companies in Canada and the USA but could not find a similar product.

He discussed the lack of market initiative in this aspect of microbiology with representatives of the large diagnostic commercial companies. He was told repeatedly that there would be no market for such a product. He was also informed that if there was a market as a result of Les' initiative, it would be very small and limited to the teaching hospitals. It was not worth the commercial development even though the major companies had antibodies to these organisms for testing in vitro. All that was necessary was to link these antibodies to a fluorescent dye that would 'become excited under ultraviolet' light. Specimens with the coccal-bacillary organisms would show up under a fluorescent microscope as bright apple green against all the other contaminating bacteria normally found in these specimens.

The argument for not making a fluorescent-tagged antibody was based simply on cost of production and the inability of the company to make a quick profit to rapidly recover those production costs. Here is a wonderful example of how the professions in both the sides of the medical and industrial worlds could not do what is right for the ultimate customer, the patient. Government must in the future develop policies and regulations to prevent underhanded sales of poor quality products and there are enough regulations in place to do this; it should also pass legislation to allow the professional scientists to work collaboratively with industry in an open, less threatening manner than is currently being done. Furthermore, legislation should allow the private industries to make a fair profit for a number of years so they would continue to do the research that the government poorly funded laboratories cannot do. Because of more politics than commonsense, there is now less development of newer antibiotics by the large ethical companies for use as the parasites of this industry the generic companies can produce the already developed antibiotics and other drugs cheaper for they do not have to do the research or development of the marketplace. This is a very unfair use of political power using legislation to disallow the profitability to remain longer with the developers so that they can make a fair profit. This government action will cause greater shortages of new drugs in the future and this is already happening in the health industry.

Les knew that scorn will be passed on this last statement for "profit" in health matters. Profit has become a dirty word in the public but there is a way out for both the legislators and the pharmaceutical industry. There should be a combination of resources from government and industry allowing specialists in ethics to become involved in clinical trials and in the development of newer drugs. However, there must be the foresight to recognize when cost must be recovered and when fair profit is recouped. After this process then the generic companies should be allowed to copy and make cheaper versions of these drugs. Alternatively, a strategic alliance between the generic companies and the original pharmaceutical industries would allow for a similar outcome and bring about a solution. This would ensure that it would not take excessively long periods of time before giving their blessings to begin a research project. It is fair to acknowledge that not every little product that the laboratory worker wants or wishes to try should be made available commercially. Profit is the elixir that allows people to invest and to take chances in the research world. When there is profit then more funds will follow. There are charlatans in every walk of life but there are also a greater number of honourable people in the professions who would not take a chance on destroying their professions through unethical practice. However, from history the one charlatan found has painted a far greater risk over the whole group of hard working professionals and this holds true for all professions whether in the academic or commercial worlds.

Les while contemplating, how he could get some of the Scandinavian fluorescent antibody product, decided to focus on the old fluorescent microscope that was collecting dust in a store room. He pulled it out cleaned it up and found that it had the correct lens and the right filters on this very old microscope. He knew that his eyes would not be in direct contact with overt ultraviolet light, he had the old chief technical officer check out the lens. He needed a specialized condenser, which strained the direct light that entered the microscope. It took many months before the old chief technologist got one from a microscope supply company that was going out of business. Next, Leslie reviewed the literature involved in the growth of this organism in the laboratory.

He found out that the medium used to grow the whooping cough organism, known as *Bordetella pertussis,* was developed by French workers back in the late nineteenth century. This old culture medium was named after the workers of the then known Bordet-Gengou agar. These early researchers worked in the days when the disease was a killer of many children. They had lots of clinical material with which to work. They used not an animal-based meat extract but rather a potato extract with dextrose added along with defibrinated horse blood. Of course, Leslie had learned this information didactically at his UK classes back in the early 19 60s but wondered specifically how they came to choose the products to grow these very fastidious bacteria in vitro.

In order to inhibit the contaminating organisms that are normal in the mouth and throat but where the pertussis organism cause the disease, it was necessary to add a trace of penicillin to the lab's medium. In this way, only the resistant *Bordetella pertussis* bacterium would grow. Leslie called up his colleague at the Sick Kids Hospital in Toronto and then visited the chief of the laboratory at that time. It was an interesting observation; he noted that the text books described these bacterial colonies as growing on the original French medium and appearing as 'split pearls'. Leslie thought to himself that he really did not know how many laboratory technologists had seen a 'split pearl' or could even imagine what they may look like. He knew what a pearl looked like and imagined it to be split like the 'split pea' used to make peace pudding or dhal.

The chief technologist at Sick Kids was an expat Englishman well known in the profession and was always addressed as Mr. Keith. He had said to Leslie that their lab had been successful in growing the whooping cough bacterium for many years. His modification was to add charcoal, replacing the starch, to the Bordet-Gengou agar medium and this removed any toxins that were produced by these organisms when they grew in vitro. In fact, Keith said the organisms would self destruct in their own toxins or autolyze; hence there would be no growth. After a pleasant day, Les and Dr Claire went back to their London laboratory and tried to reproduce the Sick Kids formula for the culture medium.

They had a few viable cultures from Mr. Keith and so would know if the formula was working for then the organisms, which they had received from Mr. Keith would grow. The medium worked and the test organisms grew but only after five days as small pinpoint colonies. It was difficult to remove these organisms with a straight needle for they grew deep into the medium. It is necessary to pick off these colonies so that a lab scientist is able to work with them and make smears on glass slides. It was very difficult to emulsify these hard small colonies in saline so that could be stained. It was like trying to dissolve a grain of sand in a drop of water using a fine needle. The colonies, when picked off with a straight platinum wire, were hard and granular and would not make a smooth emulsion in saline or water on the glass slide.

The reason was that the bacteria grew tight into the medium, almost embedded. Leslie then came up with a combination of techniques that he had picked up from diverse sources. Just about then a new set of antibiotic products had come onto the market which worked like the old penicillin G. They belonged to the family of drugs known as chalosporins. The organism that produced this family of new antibiotics was found and isolated in the sewage off the coast of Italy. Just like the penicillins, they were produced by a fungus known as 'penicillium'. The race was on for many of the large commercial companies to find the next new antibiotic produced by any micro-organism in nature. This was an exciting time for Leslie and the many microbiologists of that era.

Leslie had heard that the American microbiologists were incubating their cultures from respiratory specimens, in plastic bags which allowed moisture in the cultures to be increased. This research showed that the bacterial colonies which grew, similarly to the green fungus on old cheese, were larger due to the increased moisture. He replaced the penicillin with a trace of cephalothin in the media formula used for growing the whooping cough bacteria. This inhibited the normal throat bacteria along and with the addition of charcoal, which removed toxic by-products of growth and metabolism that disallowed the pertussis bacteria from growing. He also incubated the specialized Petri plates filled with the new medium designed specifically for the whooping cough organism into plastic bags thus increasing the humidity. The combination was a great success for it allowed giant- sized colonies of *Bordetella pertussis* to grow in 24 to 48 hours instead of five days. Les also lowered the temperature by one degree from 37 degrees C to 36 degrees C. In doing so, he had corrected the basic intrinsic factors that allowed for optimum growth of this organism that, up until now, had been difficult to cultivate. There had been a great deal of difficulty in trying to grow these organisms and so they had been ignored by many hospital and private medical laboratories for many years for the physician felt that he could depend on his clinical experience to diagnose the disease. This was called a clinically diagnosed disease

What was written in the older text books, still being used, was that the diagnosis of this disease was strictly a clinical one not a scientific laboratory one. The problem of teaching this to young medical students of the 1970s, is that with the widespread use of vaccines, the traditional clinical symptoms described in the older text books no longer existed in a society such as Canada and the industrial countries of the northern hemisphere. The symptoms that physicians were taught no longer existed. Indeed, the details of a 'whoop of a cough' followed by a paroxysm was not part of the new disease syndrome. These symptoms belonged to the era before antibiotics, good hygiene and childhood vaccinations. The new clinical appearance of the disease was that of *'gagging and or throwing up, usually at supper time,'* a general *'malaise, a choking sensation and wanting to throw up,'* but unable to do so for there was a blockage of the upper respiratory tract. There was no deep lung involvement which was what happened before the era of a vaccine.

The biology of the organism is one where this little microbe produces large amounts of mucus. Mucus builds up on the upper respiratory tract and traps the little tissue hairs that line the respiratory tract, called villi. These hairs allow for humidifying and wafting the flow of air into the lungs. When they are unable to waft the air because of the mucus produced by the 'whooping cough bacterium' this causes the choking symptom. With the administration of vaccines in early child hood, much of the disease has disappeared, however, diseases are never obliterated. This organism re-appeared in those children who did not get the complete vaccine dosage or the vaccine did not stimulate the full immune response. Hence, there was a change in the clinical appearance of the disease. If one takes this analogy further, with the role of antibiotics in the population, one can deduct that the changing face of clinical diagnoses taught way back in the 1960s and up to the 1980s were poor indicators of disease in the modern era of antibiotics and widespread use of vaccines.

Unfortunately, many of the general practitioners do not have an in-depth knowledge of the changing face of infections and infectious diseases. Changes in the theory of the biology of micro organisms dated the text books and up until the 1970s, no one had revised many of the text books. If there was a newer version then it just carried over the old information just to get the updated publication refreshed. This was understandable for many new techniques were never published in peer reviewed journals.

The Follow up of this Theory:

Les's task now was to see if organisms from ill patients would also grow as well as the control strains from Sick Kids especially, since so many children had the vaccine against whooping cough as infants. Leslie noted that the colonies that grew on this modified medium had a range of colonial appearances none of which was as romantic as a 'split pearl.' Rather, he noted that these colonies had a mosaic of colonial appearances after eighteen hours incubation. Their shapes and texture of the colonies ranged from small and round with an entire edge, translucent or like a drop of water on charcoal, to a turbid soft or hard white to grey. Many grew quite large because of the increased water vapour in which the Petri plates were incubated. The laboratory did not have the sophisticated range of antisera to sero-type these different colonial appearances into their biotypes. Only a stained smear of the organism revealed its coccoid-bacillary red form with the Gram stain. The text books have never described these changed colonial appearances or the texture and the variety of colonial appearances. The text books were outdated by the changes in the practice of laboratory medicine in a population of wealthy, well-fed people practicing good hygiene.

The use of a tagged antiserum with a fluorescent dye gave a ready identification for only positive pertussis bacterium glowed in an apple green colour.

The Technical Problems:

At the same time, Les knew that it was improbable to make plates of specialized culture medium available and in stock just awaiting a suspected case of pertussis to be investigated. He would be throwing out lots of expensive media for this defined media did not last long after being reconstituted into a usable form. He acquired a new piece of kitchen equipment that had been introduced into the market place back in 1974. It was the microwave oven and he successfully used this oven to melt the agar base, which allowed his staff to pour one plate at a time. So the staff made aliquots of 30 mL of this specialized medium and stored them in fridge at around 8 degrees C. He could rapidly produce a plate that was fresh and pour it quickly in time for a patient's sample. It was only necessary to add the antibiotic and pour a fresh plate for the specimen that was also fresh. In less than 30 minutes, he had a rich medium for growing these hither to difficult organisms from the specimen which came into the lab as a 'stat'. He published his findings on the use of the microwave oven as a letter and had over 150 requests for details on its use one week after the letter was circulated.

The Clinical Problems:

Dr Claire came into her own right, for she published the use of the tiny small sampler known as a pernasal swab, used to sample the pernasal space above the pallet in the mouth. This was a small wire handle with a tip of rayon fiber that was wrapped tightly at its end. The platinum wire was flexible so that when it was inserted far enough into the nose the patient eyes blinked and watered. The technique was to roll the flexible wire pernasal swab then withdraw quickly. It was placed into a small transport bottle containing the charcoal medium. The swab was used to make a smear on a clean sterile glass slide, then cultured onto the new medium and incubated according to the new standardized procedure instituted by Les' team.

There was another large flexible wire swab designed to sample the area of the larynx or deep throat. This was done by passing this giant swab down the throat when the patient was lying flat on the back so that the head dropped off the edge of the stretcher. This allowed for a straight channel from the nose through to the pharynx. After insertion, it was lightly rotated and withdrawn. This was much too technical and difficult for many GPs of the day. The lab staff did not wish to learn this difficult technique and not many labs would have a Dr Claire on staff to take these samples using this particular device known as a laryngeal swab.

At about this time, Les received the first shipment of the fluorescent-tagged antibody from the company in Scandinavia. He used the stock culture from Sick Kids and made a discovery that these organisms were coccoid or round in form on fresh culture. This was not as the text books described *"as rods or bacillary"* in shape. Only the other less virulent strain, known as parapertussis was like a very tiny rod. Dr Claire took hundreds of swabs in that first year teaching both the technical staff as well as many GPs in the art of sample collection. However, she had to change the clinical approach by looking at a population of children with a cough which became worse during the day especially at early evenings just before supper. The coughing had to be hard and showed that the children coughed to the extent that they tried to vomit and their eyes became enlarged with the effort.

Next she discovered that in those patients, who had been vaccinated, the disease did not develop into the paroxysmal stage or whoop in the chest. The disease remained in the catarrhal stage of the upper respiratory tract. Sampling had to be done using the pernasal swab and not the 'cough plate' method found in the old text books. Her problem was what she observed, which was that many of the vaccinated patients could not cough out the built-up mucus. If they tried, they strained their whole torso with the effort. In the science of diagnostic medicine, there are several phases summarized as follows:

*A new way of interpreting clinical diagnosis is recommended, not the old fashioned method of paroxysm and catarrhal blockage.

* A pernasal swab is to be used always not the *cough plate* of the old text books.

* There should be a smear made directly onto a glass slide and dried by air blowing. The rest of the specimen was to be cultured onto the new specific medium.

* The smear must be stained with fluorescent-tagged antisera and directly examined under a fluorescent microscope.

* Culture of positive specimens could be reported in 24 hours not five to ten days.

Clinical Policy Change # 1:

The presence of these organisms was not accidental for if they were present, then there was disease. This was no longer a clinical diagnosis but a medical laboratory diagnostic procedure.

This was the first time that Dr Gutch went along with all the work quietly undertaken by Les and Dr Claire. Leslie believed that Dr Claire had quietly stood up to the chief of the division and had him convinced of this technical innovation. This would have been expected, as she had the clinical experience that he and many of his colleagues lacked because of the nature of their clinical practice. However, Leslie decided to share this revised protocol on the rapid detection and identification of *Bordetella pertussis,* the primary cause of whooping cough. This treatise was published in the Canadian Technical Journal of Medical Technology. Almost overnight, the health centre's Microbiology Laboratory was bombarded with requests for the 'in servicing' of staff from hospitals across the province and the country. Dr Claire and Leslie went across the country lecturing and putting on workshops which began a provincial process of diagnosing pertussis using the new lab methods. However, there was one area that had to be researched and updated in order to convince physicians to change their method of diagnosis. That was their out-dated knowledge from medical school days of looking for a "whoop" in the presentation of this upper respiratory form of the disease. Because of the vaccination of the children in this country the disease remains in the catarrhal stage and does not precede to the prodromal phase of the disease.

The Trouble with Text Books:

It was Leslie who decided that Dr Claire should look at the population of patients and decide whether the criteria used in their diagnosis was related to the number of laboratory isolates. The reasoning was to try and find a cause and effect in that if the organism was isolated by the laboratory did that mean that there was disease. The assistance of Dr Gutch was necessary in presenting this latest material to the chiefs of pediatrics and medicine at Medical Grand rounds. With the staggering number of cases that were being isolated by the laboratory from swabs taken by the lab staff, he had to inform the local public health chief. He inadvertently described the population of pediatric patients as *having the symptom as 'some blockage' of their upper respiratory tract. This discomfiture usually took place when these patients went into "coughing and choking spells" usually at supper time. In many instances, there was a resulting vomiting attack by the younger patients. The case history of many patients, revealed a number of similar facts, the most important of which was incomplete vaccination for whooping cough and in very few instances no vaccine at all but these numbers were very small indeed in the population of London.*

There was the nagging question of why in a healthy population of children in a fairly wealthy and affluent community, such as London Ontario with fairly knowledgeable parents, did so many cases of pertussis occur? When the general practitioners heard his presentation, there was a massive increase of samples from these general practitioners on their young patients. By this time, the other teaching health centres in the city had learned to make the medium for growth, to use the fluorescent technique to identify the organism and had instituted the method of specimen collection. These health centres also began isolating a number of cases but the clinical diagnosis and patient case histories on the request forms were poor. It took Dr Claire many months of tracing up the local GPs and reviewing many patient files before coming to the conclusion that the classic symptoms of invasion of the respiratory tract, by the micro-organism did not follow what was written and described in the published text books. There was not the classic catarrhal stage followed by the prodromal phases of the disease. Today in the early part of the twenty first century, by the time a text book is produced it is out dated. The answer is that while in science the basic rules may survive for a fairly long period of time the knowledge of new treatments, interventions and new medical problems need to circulated immediately. One of these high powered IT companies should be working on this vital tool that directly affects all types of patients.

Epidemiology of Whooping Cough:
First of all, the 'classic description', that has been taught to generations of medical students during and at the end of the Second World War, included a catarrhal stage when the patients suffered with some upper respiratory distress. The disease then spread into the chest and this was when the patients had severe difficulty in breathing and suffered from severe coughing spells. Indeed, according to the text books the coughing was so severe that many young patients developed an inguinal hernia due to the force of their inability to expel the accumulated mucus from their lungs. The force caused the tissue to tear the abdominal wall in some instances. This information is quite correct but the question asked was, "why was this disease occurring in patients that had been vaccinated under a free health care system that included the whole population?" What was also uncovered in this population of positive patients was that there were no instances of the diseases spreading in vivo and causing lung infiltration. In all the London cases, the organisms remained in the catarrhal or upper respiratory stage.

The immediate conclusion was that the vaccine had partially worked in preventing the dreaded prodromal stage or lung infiltration phase of the disease. The problem with this deduction is the need for a control group of patients. Where in Canada does one find a group of patients who had never had the vaccine and who had the disease so that one could clinically follow the course as described in the text books?

The second statement in the medical text books stated that there was *'no such thing as a healthy carrier'* of pertussis. The deduction therefore follows that everyone with pertussis was unhealthy or showed symptoms of the disease or had the disease. If that is the case, then there must be a sick repository in the population of the society that was carrying and spreading the disease to these young patients.

Dr Claire, Dr Gutch and Leslie pondered this question and sought out the assistance of pediatricians and the general practitioners who knew their population of patients. It was decided that the parents of these infected patients ought to be examined by the specialist pediatrician and medical microbiologist. A cohort of twenty families was examined and there were no common clinical symptoms indicative of the illness, not even mild respiratory infections in either the children or adults. The few runny noses or mild sore throats just followed the cyclical path of children beginning school, bringing home streptococcus sore throat organisms and sharing it with mum. Mum passed it on to dad and the rest of the family had a mild infection that disappeared after a few days.

None of the symptoms were indicative of even a mild case of pertussis and these adults were cured with penicillin in less than five days. Penicillin is not the drug of choice to cure pertussis. It was Dr Gutch who suggested taking on an epidemiological study in eight Catholic primary schools who would be encouraged to participate in this search for a pertussis carrier. The disease usually began in late September through to October, and then flattened out until after Christmas. Then a boost in infections took place in April and May. It was necessary to get the permission from the parents. This task was left to Leslie to explain why there was the need to take swabs from the noses and throats of the children in order to look for the cause of whooping cough.

Dr Claire, as a pediatrician, was to assist in convincing the parents of the children but in reality, back in 1974, there was no opposition for this first-of-a-kind applied epidemiologic research. Indeed, the true merit of working in a Catholic Hospital was that the network to the Catholic schools was complete. The only task left for the researchers was to share the results with the general practitioners and the parents as well as, head masters and the health nurses. Dr Gutch knew his world very well and he used his influence to garner the support of all the parties concerned.

Leslie brought up the suggestion to Dr Gutch that he, with the assistance of Dr Claire, would like to train a number of technical staff in the technique of taking the pernasal swabs from the in-patient and out-patient clinics. Secondly, he would like to broaden the microbial search to include the isolation of beta streptococci, which was the commonest cause of sore throats in school age primary school children, especially in the first few months of returning to school. This meant that a second swab would also have to be taken. This was a wonderful experience for Leslie and his band of medical technologists who went about speaking to the children in their schools demonstrating what bacteria looked like and showing what grew from their throats. This was great PR work in the schools and assisted many GPs and the parents in understanding the need for prompt attention to this group of children.

Indeed, thirty years later Leslie was convinced that a number of applicants to become Medical Laboratory Scientists came from the survey done on the kids of that era. The work was long and tiring but enjoyable in so many ways.

Teaching the Public through this Field Research:

The staff working in the labs was fantastic in their ethic and understanding in handling the volume of work. The tabulation of the voluminous results revealed a great deal but nothing to better understand the case for pertussis. All results, with either a positive beta streptococcus or other significant bacterial isolate, were reported to the child's GP and to the parents as were the massive negative results for the pertussis organism. Leslie began going back to the schools and talking to the students about bacteriology and what a 'streptococcus' was, how they could prevent it and when the kids felt ill, they must tell their parents immediately. The parents in turn knew that a swab should be taken before antibiotics were recommended and reminded their GPs to do so. Les took transparency slides and showed the shapes of the different bacteria after staining, what they looked like when grown and how the results given to their doctor helped in treating them when they were ill.

There was a lot of fun included in these presentations for when he wanted to demonstrate where in the throat the infection was, he would ask for a volunteer. Invariably, it was the bravest toughest boy who would volunteer. He would have fun when he asked them to "open their mouth wide" then Les will pull away, make a face of disgust. Then he would say, "I smelt bad breadth or smelt hot dogs from the day before," and this caused great hilarity with the other class mates. Humour is still the best teaching guide to all educators for when one laughs one usually remembers the occasion.

The letters from the children at the end of the testing period were absolutely fantastic for the kids invariably saw the humour involved and the funny things that they experienced during this project. They all would remark on the brave boy who volunteered and how they laughed at Leslie 'taking the Mickey' out of him. The boys felt special for he would be the first to see the bacteria and the first to be asked to smell the cultures. Complexity in an evolving society may be unavoidable but necessary for so much more gets lost in the evolution of doing simple things and sharing simple ideas.

Examples of Case Histories

in Medical Microbiology

The human body and its orifices are home to a natural and normal microbial flora. Bacteria are ubiquitous in nature found in all the varied earth's environments. Humans are part of the earth's fauna just as the animals on land and the life forms in the waters that cover the earth's surface. We are no different from the plants flora and fauna on this beautiful planet of ours. It has been thought and is now a working hypothesis for NASA and other space investigators to plan around the whole idea of planetary life based on the smallest living form - the microscopic unicellular bacteria. It is now thought that they were the first forms of life on this magic planet long before the waters of the earth had any discernable life forms.

For this reason all animal and plant life forms of the earth have their own bacterial flora that is a normal contingent of microbes or bacteria. Indeed, it is safe to assume that many play a major role in the health of the plant and animal as these simple forms can digest complicated foods that the larger life forms of plants and animals cannot. The nutrients of their breakdown or metabolized end products are usually vital to the health of the animal and plant. However, there are parts of this microbial flora that just live on bodies both inside and outside without participating in any favorable or unfavorable past time with their hosts. Indeed, in humans it was thought that their presence in the gut, throat/mouth/nose, vagina, rectum, and skin were to enhance our immune system by slowly allowing our body to build up antibodies against their presence. These antibodies are mainly gamma-globulins which are natural and circulate in the blood vessels and tissues within human bodies. They are useful in keeping invading infectious bacteria from becoming destructive and possibly taking over. This happens when the body's immune system cannot defend itself against bacteria that are often considered normal, but in the immuno-compromised individual such as those patients with certain cancers, normal bacteria can invade and become lethal in their effect or pathogenic in action. Antibiotics can arrest some infections but if the organisms invade the body by entering the blood stream causing systemic spread (bacteremia) and if toxins are produced, the symptom leads to the often fatal condition of septicemia, if untreated early enough.

So there is a normal bacterial load on the bodies of both healthy and ill patients.

However, there are bacteria that are entirely pathogenic and if they get onto or into the body, disease follows. We refer to these as pathogens or pathogenic bacteria that are disease-forming. Examples of these are tuberculosis, Salmonella typhi, Enteropathogenic E- coli, Staphylococcus in surgical and accidental wounds where they invade any break in the skin where pus is eventually formed. There is another twist to the presence of these organisms. This occurs when two of the species, usually different, combine their forces to cause a disease to the host and this is referred to as a symbiotic infectious syndrome. This can occur in their niche when there is a simple breakage or the integrity of the membrane or skin is compromised.

When the tissues of the human body is broken from an accident or surgical wound or just simply from flossing the teeth and blood shows, then our normal bacteria will enter our blood stream. In the healthy person these organisms will be taken away by a combination of our white blood cells called phagocytes and our protective antibodies (gamma globulins) and a circulating product known as complement. The human skin is a miracle in the way it expands to keep up with our body growth but it also has fat or lipids glands that remove superficial bacteria and lower the heavy burdens of the populations of microbes. As long as the skin is intact then our body is protected from the multitude of bacteria in the air, in aerosols caused by the flushing of toilets and from the many fungal spores that float from trees, grasses and other of nature's habitats.

It is said in the business that a true parasite or pathogen rarely kills off its host for then it will have to find a new one and that is not so easy. However, the human body with all of its protection still does succumb to an over whelming load of bacteria and the body could die from an infection caused by any one of the normal flora strains. The miracle is that so many humans remain healthy and free from bacterial infection in spite of our indifferent hygiene practice.

The hospitals in Canada and the USA are divided into two major types; at least that was the case back in the 1970s. There were the community hospitals found in many small towns in Ontario and there were the tertiary care facilities, which included all the teaching hospitals in that category. Leslie was first employed in a community hospital when he and his wife came to Canada in 1967 but after two years he went back to University to get a Canadian degree. Since he was stymied in his attempts to get the 'highest degree', he went back to the practice of diagnostic medicine but this time in a tertiary health centre. The real benefit of tertiary care was that all the specialists in medicine, surgery and the other medical specialties were employed there. As a result, patients that needed the care and attention of a specialist had to go to one of these teaching health centres. Leslie felt the power of continuing education as the many young specialists were happy, thoughtful professionals who began to teach the large number of interns, residents, nursing students, and medical technologists as part of their weekly practice.

In this new job, Les felt that there was an atmosphere that made everyone feel contemporary for the education was shared at departmental rounds, as well as the major Grand rounds and specialist rounds for the city practitioners. The atmosphere was vibrant, the journals were always the latest and the unwritten policy that everyone who was a graduate had to take part in teaching the undergraduate courses at the University of Western Ontario and the Community Colleges, was an excellent one. It was a casual sight to see a departmental Medical Chief followed by three or more residents and these youngsters appeared to listen to every word that was dropped by their superior tutor. There were specific morning Microbiology rounds where the head of Pharmacy, the head of Infectious Diseases and all the technical staff took part. Results of laboratory findings were taken directly to the bedside of a patient. The physician in charge may ask for an interpretation of a lab report so that he was able to use it as an example for teaching the nurses, interns or other students. This was an invaluable experience for the lab scientists as they also learnt a great deal about the patient apart from what the specimen revealed in the laboratory. Based on the new information, the physician in charge would either initiate treatment or he would alter treatment according to the results obtained from the laboratory. He may also consult with either the Microbiologist or the Infectious Diseases specialist.

Patient care was a primary consideration for all our patients but more so when a patient came from a community hospital. This was major reason for tertiary health services to be staffed with specialists. The patient had the full use of the primary care hospital resources and if the physician felt there was a need for more detailed medical input, he would refer the patient to the teaching or tertiary health centre's advanced resources of specialists and technological tools. All the stops were pulled out and every departmental chief could be consulted in the treatment of such a patient. All in all, this was an excellent system of checks and balances with the obvious professional peer checks and balances open to discussion and review. It is noteworthy that, all the professional staff wanted to do was to do their work on the patients. This automatically meant that there was a need for resources and in many instances, in that period of time, it was unavailable.

However, science had its way and that was through publishing the medical team's findings as seen in the following case history:

Darryl Leslie Gopaul

CASE HISTORY 1.

Isolation of Bacteroides sp., Peptococcus sp., and Wolinella sp. from a Submandibular Abscess:

Les Paul, Sandra Causyn – Department of Microbiology Health Centre

Introduction:

A review of the literature on periodontal disease syndromes, with emphasis on the associated bacterial pathogens, revealed that many oral anaerobes combine to form synergistic low grade infections.

Case History:

A 31-year-old white male was admitted to St Josephs Hospital for extra oral incision and drainage of a right Submandibular space infection. Previous hospitalizations were for surgical removal of dermoid cysts on the patient's left neck. Aspirates from the Submandibular abscess were sent for culture and susceptibility testing against antibiotics.

Discussion:

Both microbial sampling of the oral microbiota as well as serum antibody levels have revealed the presence of many anaerobic species as normal residents. Serum IgG levels against the normal flora were positive. In this case the normal causative organism Actinomyces sp was not isolated. The patient did have an infected abscess and he was treated with high doses of penicillin and discharged after the infection had terminated. The organisms isolated were Bacteroides melanogenicus, Peptococcus and Wolinella sp., which were all sensitive to penicillin and had combined synergistically to cause an abscess.

Published: *CJ MT 47: 1985*

In times of Limited Resources:

The obvious 'fall guy' when there was no budget for equipment or specialist staff was the administrative staff. Les heard repeatedly from his medical colleagues their distress: "Why were these people here who did not have 'hands on' for the patient? What are they doing here and what do they do for the nurses, doctors and patients for they certainly do not touch the patient?"

Physicians and the other professionals who dealt with patients felt their hands were tied for they were not allowed to do many things because the administrative bureaucracy limited the available resources. Yes, the Administration kept a tight hold on all the finances and at times it appeared that any newly hired physician specialist became the 'golden boy/girl' for he brought prestige to the health centre. Then resources would flow, at least for the first two years until the newcomer gets everything that he wants. The older services had to meet their budget and not run into the red. So the question asked: "From whence did the resources come for the new guy?" was the query from the established service chief. Suspicion grew and many thought that the administrative staff held on to the funds; dishing it out as largesse to the favourite son of the moment, which was the common deduction.

This placed great pressure on the medical and technical heads who found more and more of their time consumed by meetings. Leslie often wondered if this was the best bang for the dollar, using highly qualified medical and scientific staff to solve budgetary problems. Then there began a massive infestation of increasing numbers of administrators, who all wanted to have a say in all decisions even into measuring the clinical activity on which to base costs. Gradually, the patient-focused highly efficient and streamlined system began slowly to disintegrate. This is where the inefficiencies began to multiply delaying the slick operation of the clinical services. It was also felt by many of the bright staff that Les spoke to that it was becoming apparent that the least competent individuals were kept on, while the clever ones were pushed out or allowed to become frustrated so they left. In those days with the administration becoming emboldened, Les saw a number of very clever, bright medical individuals flee the health centre for places elsewhere.

Those bright ones who stayed because of family, kids and other commitments became disenchanted and lost interest in the establishment where they felt stymied and trapped. However, the administrators kept marching on increasing in numbers even taking on the position of limiting numbers of patients' tertiary services by disallowing beds to be used. It appeared as though the governments wanted more clerical people to be employed, so much so that over 30% (this is a conservative estimate) of the massive healthcare budget is never used on a patient. What is the purpose of a healthcare service if the primary customer, the patient, gets an inefficient service? Les became frustrated especially, when his own Chief, the implacable Dr Gutch was told there were no resources for his Virology Laboratory expansion. He became adamant and said that he was deliberately being suppressed from doing his work. The response was that perhaps he should look elsewhere for a better opportunity. Les was shocked by the way this very proud dedicated man was treated. This was a warning and a lesson for him which became very useful later on as the health centres developed into a merged operation.

With a massive tax-funded budget in one of the most affluent countries in the world, why did we not vigorously look after our patients by providing the best? In his later years, Leslie looked back ruefully at the waste and the loss of professionals in nurses, medical scientists, laboratory pathology specialists but most of all interns and residents. The educational atmosphere of the medical disciplines and the loss of services to the patients, continued to ebb away. A facetious joke stated at coffee breaks by a few of Les' colleagues was,

"Hospitals were great places to work if only there were no patients".

"Not snobbery" quotes he, "but reality sets love of a professions such a task..."

This brought to mind the power of decision-making regarding the prevention of iatrogenic damage to patients. Leslie was in the media preparation room where he tried to have input into the formulae used daily to grow micro-organisms. These employees were very hard workers. They were less well- academically educated individuals who came from the housekeeping department and many had a grade 11 or 12 education. They made a product which was essential for the medical laboratory scientists to use on a daily basis. It was the product on which bacteria grew after a patient's specimens were planted onto it. Without this high quality media being produced by these lab assistants, the whole operation would stop. He invariably had to deal with the temperature of sterilization fluctuations, the ion content of the water used for making the media, the stability of the pH meters and a host of little problems. Les rather enjoyed this aspect of his job and his time investment proved worthwhile.

How so, one would ask but that would take a text book to explain how he juggled these parameters. He invariably returned to the main laboratory intermittently but always entered around 3:30 pm as the day staff was closing down the bench operations. He assisted with difficulties in the identification of the organisms and other technical difficulties. He reviewed all significant reports on patients with the senior technical staff before they left for the day, with one individual remaining to take over for the evening and night shift as the "On Call" individual. His real worth was the list of external professionals that he could contact for advanced support in case of a problem or an urgent request.

CASE HISTORY 2.

HODGKIN'S LYMPHOMA AND MENINGITIS
How do I perceive thee? Art thou a swollen bacterium or other!!

Case History Exactly as it Happened:

There was a hushed silence from the activity on the work benches by the technical staff and the whine of the centrifuges for the Chief of Pediatrics, a Dr Ling entered the main laboratory room with three residents surrounding him. They all held their insignia of importance, a stethoscope around their neck, which appears to be the single one thing that every young medical graduate wanted to have. It was the Charge scientist Sandra, who came to Leslie's office as he was tidying up invoices for the finance department for the following day and said, "Les, Dr Ling has just walked in with a 'turbid spinal fluid' in his hand and wants us to work on it immediately. We did the cell count and it was loaded with neutrophil polymorphs." This meant that there were pus cells (white blood corpuscles) in the spinal fluid indicative of an infection. Infection of the spinal fluid demanded an urgent response. The lab findings were indicative of a fulminating infection and meningitis for it was spinal fluid from the backbone or vertebra of a child. Sandra continued, "We also made a smear and stained it by Gram's Method to examine it under the microscope. We saw giant-sized 'round forms' and Dr Gutch has taken the smear away to his office to look at it under his microscope."

Leslie went over to meet the very serious Dr Ling, shook hands with the other residents and introduced himself as the Chief of Microbiology. Just then Dr Gutch came into the lab and said, "Will the residents, Dr Ling and Leslie come into my room next door?" He kept the door wide open as we entered his small crowded office. Bookshelves from floor to ceiling were on the right hand side of the room. Immediately in front of the door, was his lab bench with a microscope and a high chair for he was a huge man and the bench was almost waist high for many of the average smaller mortals! On the left hand side of the room was a cluttered desk and two six shelf filing cabinets.

Dr Gutch sat down heavily on his chair and began to light up his pipe. With the first puff of smoke he passed the fingers of his right hand across his beard and then stroked it downwards. He then passed his large forefinger across his moustache. He coughed loudly and cleared his throat as his face took on a red almost blushing colour. "Gentlemen, I need to know the history of this patient from Dr Ling. What can you tell me?"

Dr Ling stood opposite the sitting Dr Gutch and said, "Well Dr Gutch, this is a seven year-old female with type 3 Hodgkin's Lymphoma. She went to see her GP five days ago. She came into emergency today with a stiff neck and is running and elevated temperature. I drew a spinal fluid, for clinically she has meningitis. Before I begin to treat her I need to know what microbe is the causes of the meningitis for these cases are different, you know immuno-compromised patients."

Dr Gutch beamed then said, "You have met my Chief Leslie Paul? Les, will you have a look down the microscope and give us your opinion of what you see?"

Leslie obediently climbed onto the high chair, pushed the eye pieces closer so that his narrower eye span could see the field on the microscope glass slide better. He looked down and he saw a number of small round (coccal) forms with some appearing giant-sized. He said, "I see Gram positive cocci and some giant round black forms."

Dr Gutch then asked, "Are they small yeast forms?"

Leslie knew that some yeast can also look like giant-sized cocci. But a yeast cell is about one billion times larger and they usually have a small nipple on the periphery or edge. Les thought that the large round one could be a fungus in the yeast family. These yeasts are similar in microscopic appearance to yeast used in making bread. These smaller coccal forms in a spinal fluid invariably indicate a pneumococcus primarily, then next, a possible streptococcus and thirdly (rarely) a staphylococcus. The main difference is that a coccal bacterium compared with yeast is like comparing the size of a marble to a tennis ball. The main feature of a small yeast form (he had never seen a yeast as small as the one under the microscope) is that there is usually a small bump or nipple on its edge, like the tube of a balloon and he could seen none.

He continued to look down the microscope when Dr Gutch said, "Describe again what you see, Leslie."

Leslie looked down and again repeated what he had seen. Then he got up and asked the residents one by one to look at the field that he had under the microscope. Of course, they would not know what they were looking at but then Dr Ling said, "Dr Gutch, if there is yeast under the microscope then I must initiate the use of amphotericin B."

Leslie let out an involuntary burst. "No, that will be too toxic. This is a pneumococcus or a streptococcus, I can swear to it. Amphotericin will shut down her kidneys and all her peripheral blood vessels" he blurted out.

Dr Gutch interrupted, "Look Leslie and Dr Ling, the commonest cause of infection in a Hodgkin's disease is yeast. This is a well known fact for all these lymphomas and this is well documented in all medical the text books.

Dr Ling then boldly said to Dr Gutch and to Leslie rather assertively, "Look you two gentlemen, we can debate what the appearance of the bug is under the microscope but I need to know definitively what it is, and now, so that I can begin therapy immediately. I have started her on a low dose of penicillin as is the medicine protocol. I need to know if amphotericin should be added."

A True Consultant Makes A Decision:

Here is an example of the power of a true consultant medical professional being asked by another medical Chief for clinical assistance. Dr Gutch stood up, went over to the microscope, looked down at it, and then asked his sidekick Les to look at it again. He blew the blue pipe smoke high above the heads of everyone and smiled saying, "There is no problem, Old Boy. You have these young bright young residents with you," and turned to look at them. They backed away from the towering smoke inferno in the room and smiled with discomfiture. He again turned to Leslie and said, "Give me a definitive answer of what you think."

Leslie turned and asked Dr Ling, "Has this patient had any penicillin in the last few days?"

Dr Ling replied looking at the residents who were all carrying the patient notes and files, "There is nothing in her notes to suggest that she had any. Why do you ask? And what is the significance of this question?"

Leslie said guardedly, "If she had any of the beta lactam antibiotics such as the penicillins, then one would see such giant forms in a pneumococcus or streptococcus. They are also the primary cause of meningitis in older children and old adults."

Dr Ling turned to Dr Gutch who was no longer smiling and said, "Well Dr Gutch, what do you recommend that I do?"

Dr Gutch replied, "Dr Ling, because the patient is a Hodgkin Lymphoma, I would have said empirically that she probably had a yeast infection. However, there are no obvious yeasts present even though this could be a member of the 'small race yeast' that is present. I therefore suggest because there are definitely bacterial coccal forms present and as my Chief, Leslie, said that he strongly believes that this is an aberrant form of the bacterial coccus, step up the dosage of penicillin and have one of your residents or all of them take turns monitoring the patient's temperature and medical appearance and clinical profile overnight. If there is a turn for the worse then have the switchboard call me and I will give the approval for amphotericin to be administered. If there is no change or improvement then just keep the penicillin up until the cultures are read in the morning."

With that there was a shaking of hands as Dr Gutch inhaled from his pipe and chased them out of his room with a puff of smoke. He turned to Leslie, gave one of his smiles, winked and said, "It is all in your hands, my lad."

Leslie went back to the lab with the smear and asked the technical staff present to take turns in writing down what they felt was the microscopic identification appearance. He then took some of the spinal fluid and placed it into a blood culture bottle of broth for this would dilute any other antimicrobial substances in the spinal fluid allowing the bacteria to grow.

24 Hours Later:

At the end of the work day, many staff in different corporations around the world want to hurry away to their homes. In the diagnostic laboratories, where Les has worked most of his life, these unsung professionals will invariably always stay back when such an interesting case appears. Invariably it is always at the end of the day. The amount of spinal fluid taken from a patient is very little. Just think for a moment about pushing the needle of a syringe into the spinal canal and withdrawing some of the spinal fluid; not a procedure to be undertaken lightly. So that whatever volume of specimen that was given to the laboratory was treated with great care. However, it was Leslie's 'brain fart' as he often said to others that he should send a sample to the professor at UWO who was in charge of the electron microscope and ask him to look at the morphology of these unusual-sized bacteria.

A University Resource is brought in:

Now, this is applied research and is frowned upon by the intelligentsia and administrators of the hospitals in the days of the '70s. Today it so different, Les thought to himself, for while he is retired, he keeps in touch. Thank goodness for the

Gates Fund that encourages the great achievement in applied research. This was not the case in the days of the '70s when there were no such wealthy bodies that he had access to. It was workers like him who invariably did their applied work covertly while using the resources of the diagnostic laboratory prudently. Any extra resources went to fund their work but only for supplies and when possible a new piece of equipment or a defunct part to repair an old piece of equipment. The key to this successful work was to convince the technical staff to enjoy the novel work and to let them see the benefit of their work in a peer reviewed publication, as one of the authors.

How many times this brilliant team of young medical technologists would mention the joy of showing their parents or spouse their name on a paper that was published. Their pride in presenting their work to their peers at technical meetings either locally or provincially was unbelievable when seen in their flushed faces and bright focused eyes. Their academic strength, pride and intellectual curiosity were enhanced and this was thankless as it opened the door to more work for them. In all the years that Les was in charge, he could only remember once when a pregnant employee said that she could not take on the research for a meeting because she was in a nervous state. The fact that he has had over 130 plus publications, many with his team members sharing the limelight, never ceased to impress and to give him immense satisfaction. This does not include another 120 scientific posters shown around the scientific world at various meetings.

A Case History Interlude:

To expand the statement that bacteria are ubiquitous, one has to look at all of man's associations. Yes, we continue to get a rich amount of bacteria in all our daily contacts. This includes raw foods such as salads that grow close to the earth (manure), meats and fruits. But we also exchange bacteria with our pets. Actually, Les often thinks of how sad it must be for the pets that live close to the ground and look up at their masters who fart, cough and belch at them and the owners just enjoy a wagging tail or a purr in return.

CASE HISTORY 3.

Case History: A Lethal Septicemia in a Splenectomised Patient (1989) Caused by DF2. Les Paul et al

Introduction:

At that time (1988) a review of the literature revealed that worldwide there were only 44 cases of infection caused by this still unclassified organism known internationally as DF2. This organism is found in the mouths of dogs where it is part of the normal flora along with Pasteurella multocida in cats, and other human pathogens that is also part of the normal flora of dogs' mouths and saliva.

A 62 year-old female patient was admitted to the emergency after a 24-hour period of nausea, vomiting, diarrhea, myalgia and fever. The patient was not on medication on admission, had no history of foreign travel and she denied alcohol abuse. Her medical history revealed that she had a transabdominal hiatus hernia repair with fundoplication in 1975 during which an incidental splenectomy was performed. Her only exposure was to her daughter's dog which she was playing with on the couch for she had just come in that evening (within 24 hours) from Newfoundland.

Since this paper was written a long time ago, the DF2 meant dysgonic fermenter. Bacteria that are little understood are initially classified by letters and numbers. A dysgonic fermenter means that it is a fermentative organism that grows poorly on the simple lab culture media. The number 2 meant that a related organism was classified as DF1 at an earlier date. By 1990, this organism was thought to be a Capnocytophaga sp., which meant that it grew better under reduced oxygen tension but it was negative for the two enzyme tests, oxidase and catalase.

Laboratory Results:

Leukocyte count (white blood cells)	6.3 x 10^9/L (Normal 3.5 x 10^9/L)

(Marked shift to the left – toxic vacuolation)

Hemoglobin	136 gm/L (Normal 110 – 140 gm/L)
Platelet count	23 x 10x9/L (Normal 150 - 400 x 10x9/L)

** Key Result:

Coagulation parameters compatible with DIC (disseminated intravascular coagulation)

Prothrombin time	19.9 seconds (Normal 10 – 12 secs).
PTT	> 110 seconds (Normal 25 – 40 secs)
Thrombin clotting time	14.6 secs (Normal 6.9 – 9.9 secs).
Serum fibrinogen	0.62 g/L (Normal 1.7 – 3.4 g/L)

Blood cultures showed lysis after 4 hours, which microscopically appeared as a Gram negative bacillus. The antibiotics suggested for empiric treatment were piperacillin and cefotaxime. The organism was referred to the CDC, Atlanta, which presumptively identified it as DF2 or as a dysgonic fermenter.

Discussion: *(brief)*

The passage of saliva from dog bites and scratches has been documented in every one of these cases to date. Patients that have been splenectomized and those that are immunologically-compromised are at significant risk of having a fulminating infection by this organism. The symptoms of these patients are febrile, presence of petechiae, ecchymoses, leading to septic shock and over DIC as well as tissue infection.

This was an elderly woman who had just flown in on a Friday afternoon from Newfoundland to visit her daughter. She was relaxing on the sofa playing with the small dog, the family pet. Within 6 - 8 hours she began to feel unwell. The symptoms increased hourly until she was taken late Friday evening to the emergency department of the hospital. By Saturday morning, this woman, who was healthy 24 hours earlier, was covered with petechiae and ecchymoses. The intensity, in spite of the close medications, showed a deteriorating physiology and by Sunday morning she was dead.

Conclusion:

It is obvious that dog owners or other household members are at an increased risk of DF2 infection if they are splenectomized or have underlying diseases. Most patients report owning a dog and give a history of a recent dog bite or exposure to dog saliva.

Microbiologist Comment:

Human microbiological flora is being increased by our lifestyle but most of all through our contacts with our environment. The bacterial flora of our pets plays a part in the transfer of bacteria from the four-footed to the bipedal human animal. Kissing dogs or allowing them to take food from your mouth is not only revolting to non-pet owners but can be dangerous, if the owner becomes immuno-compromised at a later date. Do not invite 'me' to your place where there is a dog and after supper place the plate on the floor and allow the dog to lick it clean. That will be last time you will see Leslie Paul at your domicile.

The Team Diagnostic Labs

& the Medical Lab Scientists

University Brain Trust & the Professional Clinical Microbiologist and the Clinical Pharmacist

Darryl Leslie Gopaul

The Prudent Use of Resources:

With the billions of dollars spent on the health service in Canada, it is a shame that the initiative of so many professionals is stymied for lack of funding. The patients and the healthcare of the province all lose in the end for applied research is profitable. As for a shortfall in budgeting, many of the brightest lab scientists were asked to resign and the unions went along with these dismissals. The shock of these Machiavellian-conspired terminations was even more galling and revolting after it was learnt that the senior administrators gave themselves large bonuses after the dismissal of these young bright professionals. When a professional has focused on one discipline and built up great experience and an obsessive love for his/her subject of choice, what else can he/she do for a living? What else does a well trained laboratory scientist do or a trained nurse do if they are laid off from their chosen profession? The bean counters have broken the career path of so many health professionals and the government wants shorter waiting lists and better patient care. How strange to want to drive in a direction after removing the driver and conductor!

Clinical Advice:

While Dr Gutch showed a remarkable cleverness in its simplicity by advising the pediatrician, Dr Ling and his entourage to take the conservative way of handling his Hodgkin's patient, the major work was far from complete. After twenty-four hours, several pieces of information came to Leslie's desk when he arrived the next morning. He focused on the details of this particular case. The overnight cultures revealed a growth akin to a drop of honey on a specialized medium made for spinal fluids and appropriately known as chocolate agar. The medium does look like a melted bar of Cadbury's dark chocolate. On the sheep blood agar plate, which is red in appearance, the honey-like colony had a greenish hue to it. The colonies were so large that the honey-like drop colonies appeared about to run across the Petri dish.

Leslie and his chosen few very clever lab scientists examined these plates, made microscopic preparations and stained a few slides with the standard lab routine stains, while another did specialty stain work. All the laboratory staff immediately knew what the colonies were indicative of and was happy that the 'lab call' was correct. While the text books informed all that such organisms had large capsules and grew as droplets of honey, it was Les' experience that this was also the appearance of an organism exposed to an antibiotic. He could never say this to anyone but his trusted few for it was not recorded in a text book..

The lay public is unaware that when a topic is written up in the text books, from the beginning to the time of publication the text book is almost five years out of date at the time of its release. The isolated organism causing the meningitis illness has killed many patients rapidly when not treated with appropriate antibiotics. It is described for lab personnel as a Gram positive coccus and not as yeast. The organism is called a pneumococcus. It is the common cause of primary lobar pneumonia and is biologically called *Streptococcus pneumoniae*. The organism also causes meningitis but usually in older patients. The penicillin treatment was the correct antibiotic to use but the dosage had to be increased.

It would be safe to say that the patient had recovered and went home after five days but laboratory medicine is not quite that straightforward and it is a shame to find out how many labs practice at this simple level only. Granted, if this case happened in a primary care community hospital there would not be the resources to do any further work. Some of the lab scientists in the community hospitals however, knew the need to do more and a few developed strategic liaisons with tertiary care facilities to fulfill that need. Knowledge in medicine increases with every case that is brought to the facility where the specialists can practice their advanced techniques and execute procedures that only they are skilled to do. Of course, Leslie knew that the primary emphasis was to treat the patient but he also felt the responsibility to maintain the knowledge for the future and to share it with others in the same practice through case history publications.

Within twenty-four hours, the identification of the organism was done, the appropriate antibiotics were tested and the report was placed onto the patient's chart and into the health records. However, one of the young residents had decided to follow-up and review the documentation of details with the child's GP to complete the information on the patient's chart. He felt that there were deficiencies and he decided to fill in the gaps in the patient's record. He came directly to see Dr Gutch who was away up at the university teaching medical students. The intern came to Leslie and related that there was some interruptive antibiotic treatment that the GP had undertaken. Essentially, he said, "Mr. Paul, I called the GP and he said that the female patient with the Hodgkin's lymphoma had come in to see him five days ago. He said that she had a mild increase in temperature so as a precaution he gave her 500 milligrams of penicillin and had her taken home. I thought you should know for you had asked if the patient had any antibiotics during our session yesterday"

Leslie listened and asked, "Did he order a full treatment course of penicillin for 5 to 10 days?" The resident looked at his notes and replied, "No, Sir. He just gave her the one shot of penicillin." Leslie remained quiet for he too had a problem. He was contemplating the mucoid colonial form or honey-like appearance of the pneumococcus grown directly from the spinal fluid. He felt that the organism just had a large capsule around it but now he knew that this was significant of something more important.

The few lab scientists who were working on the stains verified that there was a coccal form. The other stain used revealed a large capsule around the organism isolated from the Petri dish colony. One lab scientist went down to the hematology department and checked the blood work with the chief of that department and learnt that the white cell count of her peripheral blood count was abnormally high (>25,000/ml) indicative of infection. In the biochemistry lab, the sugar level was low but the protein content of the spinal fluid was high. These laboratory results verified that this was bacterial not viral meningitis. Leslie then asked for the organism to be challenged to dilutions of penicillin beginning with very low concentrations. This type of testing is very complicated and it is difficult to use the results to predict what dosage should be given to the patient.

The real value is if the patient does not respond to treatment in a timely manner, then it gives a guide as to the dosage that should be used. The extrapolation was a vague science back in the '70s. However, it was he and Dr Gutch who introduced and assisted in the development of the advanced technology which changed this type of qualitative work into a quantitative test a few years later.

He thanked the resident and explained to him the significance of this information. Leslie explained, "This is the theory at this stage of the investigation. Penicillin works on the cell wall of the organism, in particular, of this type of organism. It attacks the cell wall, punching holes in it so that the insides of the organism leak out and the organism dies. However, if the level of antibiotic in the spinal fluid is too low, as in this case, only part of the organism cell wall will be removed. As the antibiotic is removed from the body through normal excretory systems, the organism is not really killed. The partially removed cell wall leaves a membrane similar to the inner tube of a bicycle tire. The cell wall is the outside tire. If part of the tire is removed then the inner tube would be visible. It is the same with this bacterium, the pneumococcus. However, in the case of this organism, the gap that shows the inner tube is osmotic permeable in that it allows water to enter the bacterial cell and osmosis takes place between the organism and the fluid that surrounds it. This passage of water allows the organism to blow up like a balloon when there is no cell wall to maintain the integrity of the bacterial shape.

The concentration of fluid in the cytoplasm of the bacterial cell is concentrated and the gap 'inner tube' acts as a semi-permeable membrane allowing water from the spinal fluid to enter the cell. The process of water moving from a low concentration solution to a strong solution is known as osmosis. The resident looked intently at Leslie, smiled and said, "I remember that in my undergraduate notes of many years ago."

Leslie reciprocated the smile and continued, "Yes, you should. It is not very complicated to understand. The problem is when the organism swells up with the increased fluid; it takes on a distorted shape which can be confusing to the microscopist. In this case, it began to look like a yeast cell. It is very difficult to differentiate between the microscopic appearances of such a deformed bacterium and a small yeast cell. This is further complicated because of the clinical diagnosis of the patient as a known Hodgkin's case. This immediately leads one to assume correctly that the primary pathogen is most likely to be a yeast infection. The text books will all define this as a fact and again this is the conflict in taking text books as an absolute for science is always changing."

Both the resident and Leslie remained quiet as they thoughtfully digested this line of thinking. It was Leslie who broke the silence. "Have you read up on the side effects of amphotericin B?"

The resident was taken aback by the question and replied, "No, not yet, Sir. One of the other residents is meeting with the clinical pharmacist to look into its usage for we would have started to use it this morning, if there was any deterioration in her clinical appearance." Leslie reached up for the text book on the book shelf above his head. It had a yellow paper cover over the hard back and was entitled *'Antibiotics and Chemotherapeutic Agents'*, an old edition from his days back in the UK. Its pages were well worn with the crease marks from being bent back at their edges. There were still slips of paper marking spots that were used in his publications. It also had pages of his study notes that Les had used in preparation for a lecture. It was one of those comforting tools that were the extra brains that one needed even if one memorized many parts of it. He opened the page to the anti-yeast section and to the antifungal drug agent named amphotericin B.

He handed over the book to the resident who obediently sat down and began to read. He stood up after awhile and blew his breath out of his mouth. "Wow, this is terrible man. It shuts down the capillaries at the distal ends of the body. The kidneys can be damaged and the liver also..." (silence). He shut the book. He looked up at the patient Leslie, who felt for the first time like the old man for he had shown the damage that this drug could do in this vulnerable young patient. "Mr. Paul, if we had followed the course based on the diagnosis of yeast meningitis without the assistance of the laboratory then we should have surely killed the patient in hours faster than the meningitis," he stated quietly. This was the killing blow (not wanting to pun) that Leslie would have relished in his debate with both consultants. For pathology labs that are portrayed on television as heroic work being done by physicians and not by his breed of laboratory scientists grossly misleads the public. But this was not a matter to boast about; in fact it really put the scare into Les and his fellow lab scientists.

He said to the resident, "There is a great deal of knowledge and support in these laboratories. Get to know the workers wherever you go after graduation to set up practice and use all the resources available to you. Please remember that this current lab diagnosis is still in the theoretical stage and we are still awaiting the results of the electron microscopy from the university but this will take awhile."

The resident went into the lab accompanied by Leslie who introduced him to the staff. There were smiles and, strange as it seems, a few staff said to him, "Come back for your patient results at any time, we will give you the current status of where the work is and you can talk it over with Les or Dr Gutch."

This was said completely unsolicited by the older technical staff member and Leslie was proud to hear the young resident take the initiative. Les turned away and headed back to the office. He thought that he should get a preliminary report out of the lab for Dr Ling to have on the patient's chart. This was done and he signed off on it. Dr Gutch, who after his lectures, liked to have lunch at the faculty club usually returning around two or three in the afternoon. True to this routine he did come back at that time but made a bee line straight for Leslie's office. Before he could ask, Leslie smiled knowingly and had laid out the results for him. Dr Gutch looked up with confidence with his eyes askance at the ceiling, an unconscious affliction. He sniffed, passed his forefinger across his moustache, and then stroked his beard. He turned his head suddenly and looked at Leslie. "Come into my office, old boy," he quietly asked.

Leslie knew that when this happened, that was the end of the day. The door would close and a quiet soliloquy would begin in confidence. Before Les could say anything, Dr Gutch began, "You know old boy? That was pretty clever work that the staff has done. It was extremely well done, showing great efficiency. Please let them know that I am very pleased with their work and the speed of getting the results out."

Leslie was happy and smiled for he knew that Dr Gutch while not being a Bacteriologist, got more of his 'jollies' from the immediate-ness of this discipline compared with his own Virology lab that took weeks to get a report out. Leslie then said, "That was pretty clever guidance by the Consultant Microbiologist, if I may say so as well."

Dr Gutch shot a quick glance at Leslie and smiled. "You think so?"

"Yes I do," replied Leslie.

Then there was the involuntary clearing of throat from the post-nasal drip that all smokers have. "Well really you made the call, Les, so do not sell yourself short, old man," he replied back. Leslie should have left well alone but he had to be a bit of a smartass and said, "Thank goodness that it worked out. I wonder what would have happened if the lab specimens grew yeast this morning?"

"Then you would be responsible in part for the death of the child. Amphotericin would have had to be used quickly to raise her blood level to the therapeutic dosage. In doing so that would have caused all sorts of physiological problems, as you well know." He smiled and said, "Do you think that you were set up?"

Leslie again should have said nothing but instead blurted out with a laugh, "Like you would not believe. Ha! Ha! Ha!"

"Oh! Stop that. Surely you do not think that I would leave you in the lurch?" Dr Gutch replied in false coyness and pretended anger; we would all bear that responsibility. "Yes I certainly do. I also think that you would have lowered your esteem of my work, Squire, and not trust me much in the future," replied Leslie still laughing.

Dr Gutch would not bite and removed the barrier by saying, "What I think is not important. What is important is that you believe in yourself. You will make mistakes. I make fewer than you since I am older. I have, however, made my share of mistakes and so I have learned. It is the only way for you and everyone to learn, really. You are still too sensitive you know, Les! That will be the end of you if you do not harden yourself up."

His comments to Leslie were true and Les knew that his own prestige and pride in his work were supremely important for that was all he had to show the world. He took any suggestion that his work was not up to par as a direct criticism to his education and integrity. He took all criticism badly and he did allow little asides on his work to bother him. In the end, he made sure that there was always a good check on all work leaving the lab and in all his publications. After many years, he knew there will always be critics of everything that he ever attempted but that did not help. This is especially so, for now in his twilight years, he continually puts himself into the public by writing his 'silly novels' as he quietly says to his close friends.

He has never really learnt to take criticism in his stride and to allow it to roll off his back. Criticism however, is what has made him continue to strive for perfection. The perfection that he intuitively knows will never be found for he has an inherent distrust of his ability to achieve such a state in his work. However, he has invariably sought solace in his alma mater's motto, *'Nitendo Vinces'* translated from the Latin as, *'By striving you shall conquer'.* The Holy Ghost Fathers, who were his mentors as a teenager, also gave their young prodigies the answer that to attain success, the key was 99% perspiration and 1% brains. His personal battle will always be with himself. It was his cross to carry for the rest of his life.

Les after a quiet contemplation with his equally quiet Chief says "You know, boss, amphotericin B is called 'ampho-terrible' and it is really the last option open to physicians, in cases of fungal-like infections. The same situation occurs with complications in immuno-compromised patients (the example Hodgkin's disease) who are already incapable of protecting themselves. Administering such a toxic drug is really the last resort but what are the alternatives?" Leslie asked quietly.

Dr Gutch responded, "I know, I know Les, and that is why I asked that the patient be monitored all night long by the residents. It is also the reason that I placed myself between the pediatric consultant, Dr Ling, and the patient. I needed to be the person to call if there was deterioration in the patient's medical assessment." For an instance Les thought of his little problems but his boss had to sleep on his decision waiting for the unknown and he has to make the call. What a position to be in as the Consultant in charge!

Then Les mentioned quietly, "I hope that you do not mind but I used your name with that German professor who is the authority at UWO, and who is specialized in Electron Microscopy, asking if he would look at the bacterium in the spinal fluid."

"Why would you want him to do that?" asked Dr Gutch.

"Well, one of the residents decided on his own, to call the patient's GP to complete the notes in the patients file after our discussions yesterday with Dr Ling. He inquired of the GP asking for more details on what had happened when the patient was first brought to him five now six days ago," reported Leslie quite casually. "He learnt that after the assessment, the GP had given the patient one dose of penicillin 500 milligrams and sent the patient home," Leslie continued.

Dr Gutch enquired in the middle of Leslie's reporting, "Why would he do that? Did he start a full course of penicillin for the standard 5 days?"

"No!" replied Leslie. "He only gave one shot of pen G with a syringe for that was all he had in his office."

"Oh! Christ, these chaps do not know their asses from their bloody elbow," he shouted in his little office. "That is why we are in business Les, to make up for their bloody shortcomings," he continued. "My God! He was probably treating the mother rather than the child. You know these pesky mothers who want instantaneous miraculous treatment for their sick child," he added. "We were all caught up in this fiasco, Les!" Dr Gutch summarized. "I know that this is an ill child, Les so I am not blaming this parent in particular but the GP for not remembering his basic pharmacology"

Les Reports:

After a moment Leslie continued, "The colony of pneumococcus that grew was quite mucoid in appearance almost like a drop of honey." Dr Gutch remained quiet and Leslie let this information sink in before he continued.

At this delay he then heard the response from Dr Gutch. "Did you try to sero-type the pneumococcus?"

"Actually, no! We do not have such a broad range of antisera in stock in our refrigerator," he replied.

"Why not?" asked Dr Gutch surprised.

"Oh! Come on Doctor, you were the one watching the budget and you did not see the need for having such supplies in hand," retorted the distressed Leslie in a stern tone.

"I did not say not to purchase such important antisera. You are mistaken, old boy!" retorted Dr Gutch.

"Well, maybe I misinterpreted the fact when you told me the physician only needs to know the Genus of the bacterium not the species or sero type. I really believed that antisera fell under that restriction," the cynical Leslie replied.

"Really Les, there is no need for sarcasm, you know! I just asked if you had typed the organism for such sero type 3 species tend to be the epidemic strains," replied Dr Gutch, bordering on petulance.

"Yes I do remember telling you that I had spent three months at the Brompton Chest Hospital testing old bronchitic and tuberculoid patients. I believe that was one of the first things I learnt there, when we were studying the number of pneumococcus isolations from the many incarcerated patients. First noted was the colonial appearance followed by the constituents of the surrounding capsule and their extractions using optochin, I believe," replied the over-sensitive Leslie.

"Ah ha! There you go again, it is always about you. My God man! Stop being so sensitive! You were well trained so why do you not do the job properly by sticking to your guns and demanding that your budget is inadequate?" was the heated response from Dr Gutch.

Leslie was becoming overheated as well and angrily responded, "How do I know that the bacteriology budget is inadequate since you keep everything secret? Should I go down to the Sister of Finance and ask for more money?"

The bell had rung as both sparring partners remained silent. It was Leslie who broke the silence. "It is very difficult to emulsify this organism in saline for the large capsule is rough. It appears as a granular suspension, as you know, and is difficult to differentiate from agglutination or clumps on the glass slide." Dr Gutch had lit his pipe as he has done every late afternoon when he gives up the cigarettes. There was a sweet smell of tobacco, the name of which he had told Leslie repeatedly but Leslie had instantly forgotten.

"Try a suspension in 1% glycerol saline to get rid of the rough antigen," Dr Gutch replied.

"Oh! We have done that and it still remains rough," quietly replied Leslie. Then send it to PHL

Leslie retorted, "Really Squire, they will take months to send back their results and invariably it is too late to follow-up for everything goes cold on the investigation. The reason for telling you that the colony was mucoid is that, it is also a factor when an organism is an 'L Form' because their cell wall is partially intact."

Dr Gutch turned and said, "What utter nonsense. 'L Forms cannot grow on our basic media. It is rubbish. L Forms grow only on specific PPLO Medium."

Leslie was becoming exasperated as he quietly repeated, "The organism has only part of the cell wall, so it is able to grow on the routine standardized medium. If it had lost its complete cell wall of course it would not grow on our standardized medium. It is more of a spherocyte."

Dr Gutch looked coldly at his Chief of bacteriology, sternly raised his voice and retorted, "Then it is not an L Form of the organism, is it?"

Leslie tersely replied, "I guess not in the strictest definition of a true L form, technically speaking, but what would you call an organism that only has part of its cell wall?"

"Was a cell wall stain done?" Dr Gutch continued.

"Yes," Leslie replied. "But it could not be differentiated under the microscope as there was a great deal of free polysaccharide floating in the liquid culture, which bound much of the stain masking the parts of the cell wall. The controls were fine, so we know that the stain works."

A stalemate was reached and Leslie stood up to leave saying, "The staff is about to leave and I must go back to the main lab and see what is left for tomorrow and to answer their questions."

"Tell me when the EM results come back from Dr Karl at the University!" responded the red- faced puffing man in the huge chair.

"Well I would like you to give him a call and I am willing to admit that I used your name before getting permission from you to get this work done," a dejected Leslie responded.

"Yes, I think that I will give him a call. If I do not get him tonight I will call him in the morning. Look Leslie, the patient has been treated appropriately and I understand that the mystery of the abnormal shapes that we saw in the smear needs to be investigated. Of course, we must follow up on this puzzle that needs to be solved," said the sedated Dr Gutch. As Leslie turned to leave the office he heard the telephone dial going in Dr Gutch's room and he smiled to himself.

Nostalgia and a Nobel Laureate Maybe??

Les could not recall the name of the German scientist who had a legendary reputation for his microscopic skills and the photos he produced for text books. Indeed, at one time according to the professors at Waterloo, his name was bandied about as a possible candidate for a Nobel Prize. How true that rumour was is unknown but it was said by a Princeton Professor to a very gullible group of fourth-year biology honours students. There was a humorous anecdote which occurred when Leslie first came to town and assisted Dr Gutch in organizing an advanced course for the medical lab scientists at night classes.

One of the lecturers was Dr Karl and to be truthful Leslie was chuffed at the fact that through Dr Gutch's intervention, such prestigious lecturers were able to come in on evenings to give their lectures. It was Leslie's turn to have the lecture room prepared for the students with the slide projector in working order, a clean blackboard, and chalk with a duster and prepared handouts so that many could just listen and not write notes. When it was Dr Karl R's turn to lecture, it was Dr Gutch who went and got the old man out of his lab and brought him to the lecture hall in time for the 7 pm presentation. Leslie was in the front row and was anxiously awaiting the lecture by this very brilliant man. He never heard a drier lecture than what was given on the components of a microscope and the ability of all staff to get Kohler illumination by setting up the light and lenses properly.

Les was about to have a quiet nap when Dr Karl demonstrated this skill on a monocular microscope, so that all twenty-four students had to go down and look at the brilliant field that he had set up. There was no doubt that the field was clear but he used a monocular microscope, similar to *Louis Pasteur*, and *Robert Koch* and all the old microbiologists of the late nineteenth century. The problem is that all the students used binocular microscopes and there was no need for Kohler illumination since the illumination was preset by the manufacturing companies, like the Swiss.

Of course, the lecture had some importance for as microbiologists it was necessary to be intimate with the most important instrument of our profession or trade. As the class settled down, Leslie returned to his seat but the heat was stifling in the room on that winter's evening. Like the rest of the class after a full day's work followed by a full evening of lectures, he too was becoming quite drowsy. Then he heard Dr Karl say to the class that he had set up a practical for all the students to participate in right now. He came over and took Leslie by the arm and led him over to the microscope on the bench desk at the front of the picture theatre. He was told that he was to set up the monocular microscope to show 'Kohler illumination.'

There was laughter for all the students knew that Leslie was the organizer/lecturer and not a student but the dear Professor missed that part of Dr Gutch's notes to him. This was an exercise for the students who had enrolled in the course and who work in primary care facilities. Dr Gutch tried lamely to intervene but he could not be heard or be swayed by this tenacious little bald-headed German scientist. He was on a roll with a set of new adult students and he was determined to teach them in spite of themselves and Les was to be the scapegoat.

Leslie was trained at the WHO laboratory in the West Indies and had worked with the best microscopes that the Swiss had produced back in the late '50s, early '60s. The microscope had to be set up every morning for Kohler illumination before being used for the day's work of screening hundreds of slides for malaria and filaria. Les had a lot of experience in setting up microscopes under the most trying of conditions in the Caribbean. As the class giggled at the possibility of Leslie's impending failure for few wanted to deal with this meticulous Teutonic professor. Leslie's own doubt was, could he handle a monocular microscope, for one needed to look through one eye piece and keep both eyes open. This can be quite difficult without a lot of practice.

He went up and in less than 2 or 3 minutes he had set it up and stood back. The old professor in his open white coat moved from behind the desk and looked up at the students in this massive auditorium. A few filled the first three rows while the others were spread out across the whole lecture theatre.

"You see, no one should spend so short a time in getting the maximum out of a microscope. I can assure you that this man has not got it right for he wanted to sleep a few minutes ago and was not paying attention," stated the serious German professor to the applause of loud laughter of his audience, all at Les' expense. Of course he was quite correct about Les wanting to nod off but he was completely out to lunch on his conclusions.

Dr Karl, like a conductor of an orchestra, moved along his desk which made him even more miniscule in the large auditorium lecture room. He looked up at the audience and waited for them to quiet down. This is the skill and timing of a true 'stand-up comedian' waiting for the laughter to come forth. Leslie saw that this German professor had the timing like all great showmen and it was immaculate. He had obviously honed this skill from years of intellectually belittling undergraduate students too inexperienced to understand the subtlety of irony. After another stab at his dissertation of 'speed over accuracy and efficiency,' he eventually got to the microscope and looked down. The classroom was quiet as he raised his head then looked down again. His fingers twitching to touch the fine adjustments but there was nothing to adjust. He looked at Leslie and said, "You may sit down, young man, Dr Gutch has taught you very well." There was more laughter but not at Leslie's expense but at this old chap and at Dr Gutch, who began to protest but the old German would not listen. Leslie did not know if Dr Gutch ever got to tell Dr Karl about his gaffe on that night's lecture. It does not matter for many of Leslie's staff, who was attending the course, said that they were proud that Les had succeeded that night.

Electron Micrographs Arrive:

It was about two or three days later when an envelope with copies of Dr Karl's Electron Micrographs came to the laboratory. On the micrographs were small drawn circles showing the partially missing cell wall and only bits of capsule on the organism. He had also shown whole cell walls on the organism for comparison. It was absolute brilliant work by this closeted EM Microscopist and his reputation was well justified. There was also justification for the knowledge of the team at the microbiology laboratory. It was indeed a great day for Dr Gutch when he saw the published article with his consulting decision which saved a patient from aggressive and toxic treatment. The information that was collected by the Chief of Pediatrics in preparing the patient case history lacked a great deal. It was poor and incomplete even if he had just instructed his residents in preparing the notes. This revealed the need for more precision in taking a patient's case history in detail by the Chief of Service, the residents and interns. The residents were brought together as Dr Gutch told them the complete story and, in fairness, he was interrupted by the clever resident who explained that Mr. Leslie Paul had told him of this theory three days earlier. This was the opportunity for Dr Gutch to drive home the point to the physicians at Grand Rounds that there was a repository of knowledge in the medical labs and it was up to them to avail themselves of this knowledge.

It would have been quite simple to have sent out the growth of the pneumococcus after 18 hours and allowed the patient to be treated. However, there was a rich amount of information that was derived from this applied research and hopefully, GPs would no longer just give one dose of an antibiotic to their patients and send them out of their offices. This type of treatment is one major reason today for the multi-resistance pandemic developing in isolated organisms from patients. These bacteria have not changed in millennia for they are the same old organisms that cause the same old infections. The publications allowed the health centre to share the results of this very important case with other lab scientists across the country and around the world. The text books, if slavishly followed in their description without regard for the inherent biological differences that can occur in medicine, can be quite misleading.

The Fungus or Candida or Yeast-like Theory in Hodgkin's Lymphoma:

A yeast or Candida species, which is well known by women who occasionally have a yeast infection, is about a million times bigger that a bacterium more or less. The point is that yeast may be round like a coccus bacterium but it is much larger under the microscope.

One very clever lab scientist, who had specialized in fungus work referred to as Mycology, had done a literature search on this interesting case. She brought forward a list of a number of 'small race yeasts' that would have had the same microscopic appearance as that found in the spinal fluid. The cultures were incubated for many weeks and were checked weekly for a possible Candida or yeast growth. After four weeks incubation no yeast type had grown. The reason for following up to such depth is that the text book is still correct in the strictest sense. The most likely infectious agent in such a cancer patient is a fungus, usually a yeast-like organism. However, in this clinical case, it was straight forward bacterial meningitis due to *Streptococcus pneumonia.*

This case history was published and is depicted below with the micrographs.

In the PLATE: (next page that follows) the top two photos show the shape of the bacteria: on the left is the normal shape. On the right top is the appearance of the spinal fluid from the patient. The bottom two photos show the detail that could only come from using an electron microscope, which in those days were only found in universities science departments and very few teaching hospitals.

Darryl Leslie Gopaul

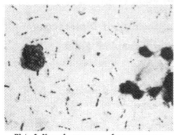

Plate I. Normal appearance of pneumococcus.

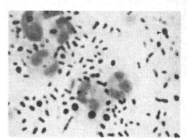

Plate II. Pneumococcus from patient's C.S.F.

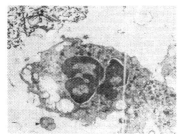

Plate III. Electron micrograph of C.S.F.

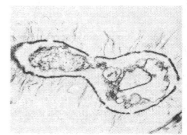

Plate IV. Electron micrograph of pneumococcus from patient's C.S.F. showing effect of ampicillin on cell wall.

NOTE:

PLATE II   Effect of penicillin allows cells to swell up

PLATE III   Bottom left - note the diploid *Streptococcus pneumonia* (small arrow head).

PLATE IV   Bottom right is the individual bacterial form. Note the space gap in the cell wall. The hazy hair-like off shoots is the diffused capsule.

A Discouraged Osteopath

Leslie had met an osteopath surgeon that is, a surgeon that dealt with patients that suffer bone erosion problems and need joint replacement. Leslie was told to stay away from this chap for he was mean spirited and very rude. The doctor had sent some bone for the microbiology laboratory to culture; it was taken from a female patient who had a hip replacement. The new hip had deteriorated prematurely, he thought, due to infection. However, it was necessary to find out what the causative infectious agent was but only from a bacterial or fungal perspective. The request was shown to Dr Gutch who said, "Technically, the lab should not do any research work for the specialists or for anyone else. Due to the limited resources, the lab is only to do diagnostic work on the acute patients and those few geriatric patients for whom we are responsible."

After awhile as the lab technologist waited on Dr Gutch to give a direct instruction, the doctor continued in a subdued voice, "Show this to Les and see what he suggests."

Leslie had no second thoughts as he enquired as to who the physician or surgeon was. He was told that it was the osteopath surgeon. "Dr Philips who does surgery replacement on the patients with bad hips and knees but he has focused on hips," came the reply.

Then another technologist mentioned in passing, "As long as he does not send in his cow's hips or their failed prosthetic hips for culture to us," and laughter erupted. The humour came from one of the older technologists who this surgeon that sent him infected pieces of bone for the lab to culture but they were from his cows that he used for research. Leslie felt that he should go and see this terror of a physician for his direct almost rude manner was quite disquieting to many who had the misfortune to have worked with him. It was late and all the lab staff had left for the day. He called the surgeon and to his surprise he heard the curt, "Dr Phillips here."

Leslie replied quietly, "Dr Philips, I am the new technical Chief of Microbiology and we have a specimen of bone from a hip replacement requesting culture and identification. May I ask what micro-organism you suspect? Is it bacteria or fungal, more along the lines of a yeast-like infection? Secondly, on removing the bone was there any signs of proteolysis such as an anaerobic infection causing an odour or rotting smell?" There was silence before the voice answered, "Look Leslie, can we meet? I really do not wish to meet Dr Gutch for we invariably end up in a quarrel. He is inflexible and never helps us younger guys but preaches the universal line of us young'uns versus old workers. We piss each other off and right now I am very tired."

Leslie answered immediately, "Are you free now? I can come up and see you or you can come down, for I am the only one down here in the lab as the rest of the staff have gone home, your choice."

Dr Philips' response was, "Come up and see me on the sixth floor where I have some research work to complete." Leslie knew where he was for he had seen some of his work on trauma & shock due to blood loss. It was also the sixth floor where the microbiology lab had its own animal house. It was Les duty to check that section of the animal house where guinea pigs were kept. They were still used back in the early 1970s, to detect and confirm the pathological traits of the tubercle bacterium (causing tuberculosis) from patients' specimens or their positive cultures. The lab kept guinea pigs which were inoculated with clinically suspected tuberculoid samples from patients or with tubercle bacterium, which had grown on artificial culture but had to be proven as severely pathogenic. The animals were sacrificed and the samples of their lungs and major organs were stained and examined microscopically for the presence of the tubercle organism (also called acid-alcohol-fast bacilli, which looked like thin red rod-like organisms against a green back ground).

Les ran up the stairs from his second floor lab but then had to walk up the last two flights. He arrived breathing deeply, almost gasping. The door to the research room was opened suddenly and there was an ascetic, unsmiling blond blue-eyed slim tall man, who looked at Leslie with a dispassionate glare and asked loudly, "Are you Leslie?"

Leslie smiled and held out his hand. It was taken and the calm request came from Dr Philips, "Come in and see what I am about to do. There is a mask and a lab coat for you to put on." Leslie masked and gowned himself accordingly. They both entered the room where two beautiful greyhound dogs were lying completely sedated as a drip from a vein went into two large measuring cylinders containing the accumulated volume of blood loss. The dogs were linked to a number of monitoring devices to record their vital signs. There was also a chart that would record the time at which traumatic shock from blood loss would occur. This was explained to Leslie by the intense physician while he attended to the instruments, tweaking the devices into more efficiency or greater sensitivity. Leslie looked at what he had set up with simple pieces of outdated equipment. Dr Philips was engrossed in what he was doing and did not look up at Leslie once during his discourse.

Leslie reached over the monitor and suggested, "If you are looking at the time that blood loss shock occurs then the flow of blood is a bit too fast, maybe it should be slowed to a drip every so many seconds." He was smart enough not to say anything that would upset this very sensitive and focused scientist physician.

Dr Philips looked up, stood and went over to the monitor then adjusted the system to a slower drip writing down the change into his log book which was open on the stretcher on which was a clipboard with numbers in a lined chart. Then again without looking at Leslie he quietly said, "I am also looking at the relative amount or volume of blood loss proportional to body weight. The greyhound has a large heart and because of its fitness, it is close to that of a young human being who has had a traumatic car or tractor accident. He turned and looked directly at Leslie who also looked unsmilingly but more puzzled as he tried to understand the purpose of the research work being done. Dr Philips began to explain, "I still have to assist in the emergency clinic on weekends and I have had to deal with two car accidents involving two young males who went into shock due to blood loss. I was busy dressing their wounds awaiting the lab to do the cross-match of blood to make up for the loss. I patched them up to stop the bleeding but was unable to bring them out of shock quick enough; they were OK, only thing was the possible damage that could have or may have been done due to shock. The starvation of the brain of oxygen due to blood loss for any length of time could conceivable leave the patient with some miniscule damage to their brain function. We never really know how much shock produces how much damage and what that damage is or when it may manifest itself. There is so much we just do not know and we get these patients daily but are we noticing the details recording them trying to postulate outcomes. Les, the frustration in witnessing this major loss of knowledge daily is frustrating beyond all understanding"

Leslie nodded quietly to himself showing a deep respect for this intense surgeon who just wanted to work. The room became silent as they looked without seeing the beautiful dogs and it was Dr Philips who broke the silence by asking quietly, "Where did you train Les?" Leslie was taken aback for he was closely watching the heartbeat monitor and absentmindedly responded, "First in the UK in the med lab sciences for I had to drop out of med school. You know, parents had some difficulty in business. I had completed the second year and so dropped into the pathology program for lab scientists. Came to Canada and after two years went to the University of Waterloo and completed work on a PhD but had a run-in with the Senate Committee who wanted me to stay longer, so I left and came here just to work." He looked up and was surprised to see Dr Philips smiling broadly showing his teeth. Leslie was astonished at this unexpected change and involuntarily smiled back, asking, "What?"

Dr Philips, now smiling broadly, asked rhetorically, "You are a graduate of University of Waterloo, Ontario?"

Leslie answered briskly, "Why yes. I went there for 28 months until they found out that I was really qualified in the UK as a microbiologist, then I received a teaching fellowship and did some research for a great Professor in Microbiology."

Dr Phillips asked, "Was it Dr Kempton?"

"Yes of course it was. How did you know?" asked Leslie.

"Believe it or not there is more to these six degrees of separation." He looked directly at Leslie, still smiling audibly with a gentle giggle. "I too am a graduate of Waterloo and I am a qualified engineer. I had one course in Microbiology and Dr Kempton was the professor. He was a very nice man but I had to book that subject for more detail than he had given at his lectures. He guided me throughout the course and he was very helpful to me." Les smiled back and interrupted saying "I owe more to that man than any other human being in my undergraduate years."

Dr Philips explained, "It was my plan at the time that I could use my engineer's degree qualification and enter medicine. So I completed a fellowship in surgery and specialized as an osteopath. I specialized in hip and joint replacement but industry is too slow in developing the prosthetic devices. I decided to make my own joints and I could charge less than they are doing right now but first I had to get a patent on the design. I also thought that I could make quite a bit of money in this endeavor to keep the family who had suffered much as I was going through university."

The two men looked at each other silently as the darkness grew outside and when they simultaneously looked at their watches, they both said it was about time to go home. Dr Philips said, "I have to go and feed my cattle and take my readings for many have prosthetic hip replacements. I use the farmer's laser instrument which is used to detect the level of the land, to measure the level of their hips as the cows walk."

Leslie replied as he closed the door and headed for the elevators, "Ah! Yes I wanted to ask you about the cows, for the staff have said that you send them bone from cow's hips from time to time for culture. Dr Gutch says you should pay out of your grant for these tests to be done in the routine lab."

"Yes I have a few grants from the NRC as well as from the industry but they are never enough to pay for the technical staff and the feed for the cattle. Every time I turn around everyone wants a bit of the grant. The University wants to slap a research tab of 25% from each NRC grant before any work is done. If that ever happens I will close up shop in London and go to the USA for they are interested in my work."

The elevator stopped and Leslie held out his hand and quietly said, "Can we meet tomorrow morning for coffee in my room?"

Dr Philips replied, "I have surgery in the morning from 6:00 am which means that I have to be in here at 5:00 am. How about say around 3:00 pm? I shall be there all morning and depending on any surprises, it may take longer." Leslie had lots to do but he agreed and went back to his office as Dr Philips went on his way. He blocked off the time in his diary from 3:00 pm and wrote in Dr Philips.

On his way home from the health centre, he thought of the awful ambition of this very lonely man and the stress that is promoting his obvious early paranoia state. How come such a physician, who was working so hard, putting in such long hours and obviously getting little rest, is not allowed to do his work in a rich country such as Canada? It was incongruous that such an ambitious professional would meet with such opposition and obstacles. Of course, he thought to himself, he did not know all the facts but this was not a foolish man. Dr Philips was a highly qualified individual and was capable of applying all these skills to benefit the number of patients who had to have new hips and knee joints. Surely, our country would profit from his development of such necessary primary intrinsic research.

What is wrong with this very affluent society? Why is the message not getting through to the powers that control the research dollars? Why do we have so much competition for dollars for such a worthy cause? We could have a method in place so that these noble researchers can work in peace with all the resources that would encourage and boost their enthusiasm. The professional life of such a man, after all these years of schooling, was worth some support. His number of valuable years, relative to a human lifetime of capabilities, is quite small. He has proved himself by strong academic work over such a long time and by his many publications. There were seven years of training at Waterloo then seven years in medical school, then another five years to get his fellowship in surgery. Add in his years as an intern then years as a resident and the hours of study, the cost of his books and his education. He must have over a hundred thousand dollars invested in his education in this the 1960s era.

He should be given a hundred thousand dollars to start with, to do his research and as many years to achieve what he wished for in this research. Unfortunately, life is not like that and the utopian society where young men and women develop to their full potential so that the rest of humanity can profit from their industry, even in a rich country as Canada, does not exist. As Les' old Volvo wagon turned into his driveway he had made up his mind. He will not 'toe the line' laid down by his chief, Dr Gutch. He will assist as many people in the hospital that need his laboratory expertise, especially the doctors in research. He will not charge for any R & D work unless he was found out by the administration, then he would lower the charge accordingly. He will have to be very careful, he thought sympathetically to himself. He will learn the ways of finance and budgeting for the department and he will work favourably with the administration to learn precisely what they wanted with the sole purpose of increasing resources for 'his department'. This he silently promised to himself and the next day, he began by making telephone calls to all concerned with the budgets of the laboratory. He quickly learned that Dr Gutch controlled all the budgets. He was not likely to give up that power even if he just toed the line with what the administrators asked of him.

But Leslie was not the type of person to give up so easily and he began to plan as to how to arrest this power source from the Director of the department by showing that he could bring more assets to the department. Dr Gutch invariably said that things were not on budget, if Leslie asked for a piece of equipment or some antiserum for a trial. When he explained what he was doing he would invariably get cold water poured on the project. He would be told that if his project did not directly assist the patient on the bed then there was no use doing any research, applied or otherwise. Dr Gutch was quite correct for he was the guardian of the department budget. What Les did not understand was why Dr Gutch did not go and fight for more resources, as the other chiefs were doing, and thereby getting the attention of the administrators and not just wanting to be the nice guy who balanced the budget.

The status quo continued until one day when Dr Gutch was at his cottage, there was a need for invoices to be paid to the commercial companies. Dr Gutch had locked away all the invoices and packing slips, so that no one could find them. Leslie claimed that he was never involved in the basic ordering and checking of the paperwork. The purchasing officer at the time said he will come up and have a word with Dr Gutch when he returns from vacation. This purchasing agent wanted to know why a doctor with his hourly rate was doing clerical work like ordering supplies. We need to know how these people spend their time to justify their large salaries. This was pure treason as far as Leslie was concerned. He warned Dr

Gutch of what was about to happen for he had no intention of replacing the 'devil he knew with one he did not know'.

Besides, he felt a sense of departmental loyalty to Dr Gutch in spite of their differences and for some unknown reason he had bought into the 'anti-administrator' syndrome that all the medical chiefs felt. It was this man who gave him a break to work in this health centre and throughout many years assisted Les, his wife and young family with the pass down of toys from his own children to Les' kids.

The Osteopath Researcher:

Dr Philips came down to Les office at 3:00 pm the next day as promised. Leslie looked at this very tired man and offered him a coffee from his department kitchen. Leslie closed the door of his office and they began to chat on how busy the operating rooms were and how many cases he handled that day and so on. Leslie was pleased to see honesty and calm as this quiet man, who was just about his age more or less, relaxed for this moment. They smiled and chatted and it was Dr Philips who spoke first, "Les, how do you get on with this old Englishman? He speaks continuously about the past and what is being done or was done in England. He left there over twenty years ago and he does not know what is going on."

Leslie again smiled but he felt a loyalty to Dr Gutch even when what this surgeon said was quite true. Les smiled and said, "It is not easy. Yes, at times it is very difficult but he has a great deal of experience so I allow him to go on about the old country. But he left it for a better life and he has forgotten that reason. We do struggle to get along for there are so many problems with the budget, amongst other things. I would like to do more but if I make too many changes, it brings out pangs of insecurity. I have learned that I must take my time and make changes slowly."

Dr Philips nodded in understanding but said abruptly, "I admire your understanding and willingness to give that time but these men must move over for us to have our day. Unfortunately, I do not have that time for I have spent a fortune on my education and now I have a family to support and a career to build. I only have so much time in my profession before my hands begin to tremble and I am unable to hold a steady saw or scalpel or read the notes and plan how to cut a piece of skeleton."

After this rapid dissertation on the inequality of age over youth, it was Leslie who interrupted quietly. "However, if you address all your specimens to my attention, we will process them at no charge and this will be one less obstacle in your path."

These two Waterloo graduates worked together for two more months until one morning, when Les came in to work he was asked by his charge technologist Sandy, "Did you hear the news?"

Les turned to her and asked, "What news?"

She said, "Dr Philips has left the health centre. He could not get any support for his surgical cases. It was said that from his grant he had to pass over money to the university." Leslie was shocked at the unexpected and hurried departure but he was not totally surprised.

He and Dr Philips had become quite close and they shared a lot of information, mainly on his research and his future goals. What drove this man forward was the short time in which he had to achieve these milestones. Les had more informal chats with him than he had with his other surgical colleagues. Many of Dr Philips' colleagues just thought of him as a clever odd ball. Other less industrious physicians took pot shots at him calling him an over-ambitious capitalist wanting to make royalty money on his prosthetic devices. A few more vicious physicians said that they were glad to see him leave the health centre. There were very few who thought that the health centre had lost a real asset.

Leslie had got to know the man well and true to his promise, he had the laboratory do his work which involved the search for the major infectious agents. When prosthetic implants fail, in 90% of the instances it is due to infection by the common bacterial flora of the gut or skin that inhabits the wound but leads to inflammation and disease. On one of the casual interludes as they were both enjoying each other's company chatting about science, Leslie broke the familiar barrier and asked Dr Philips to stay and help build the health centre. He entreated him to stay and help build it into a major world centre for osteopathic surgery. Dr Philips smiled with his head down which was a rarity for this beaten man. He never answered and over the years, Leslie wondered if the decision to leave was already made when he had made that suggestive plea.

Canada lost a brilliant mind and it was tragic for Leslie had seen this occur on many more occasions over the years that he had worked in the health service. It was rumoured that Dr Philips had gone to the USA for more money and had taken a Chief of Surgery position in a major health centre, which promised him full funding for his research. It is again strange to Leslie, who continually puzzled over this indomitable fact, as to why a wealthy country such as Canada allows its major talent to flow south of the border without a fight to retain them. Is it that no one cares that we train these specialists for the USA with our taxpayer's money? Why are there so few resources for ambitious men who are driven to succeed? The power of this country does not lie in the resources buried in the soil but in its educated people. That is probably too novel a thought for our politicians for they are not the brightest stars in the universe even if they think that they are.

Les was flummoxed by the total lack of imagination that the leaders of this great country have demonstrated. It has been shown recently in Alberta, at the beginning of the twenty-first century, a province that had accumulated so much cash and wealth that it could easily pay off the deficit of the whole country. In spite of all this cheap wealth, there are homeless folks on the streets and there are students carrying large loans akin to large anchors to progress, from their schooling but the Premier of the province says, "We did not expect so much wealth in such a short time. We did not know what to do with this cash from the oil revenues" It is the one province where fewer of its youth are enrolled in university or community colleges compared with the rest of Canada. The oil wealth has proven to be a curse not a blessing to that province for it has to import its intelligentsia and manpower from the eastern provinces when there were untrained youths hanging around the province.

There is a political battle of legal proportions when we ship timber, oil, potash and ready-made cars or any other commodity over the border to the USA. There is hardly ever a word of opposition about the human commodity that is lost to our society. The United States have demonstrated repeatedly that it is capable of collecting the best minds from around the world to their country. Their only cost is to give them the freedom and some resources to do what they were trained to do. Its rich neighbour to the north has not learned that lesson in Leslie's forty plus years in the country which he loves and calls home. It is such a small price to pay for so much indigenous wealth.

The Vietnamese War

&

Publish That Case History

It was the year 1974 and the Vietnam War was in full blast metaphorically speaking. For us in Canada, our only exposure was the nightly news broadcasting the bombings as in the war movies of Hollywood back in the early '50s. However, the American public began to take things into their hands and thus began the internal rebellion of the people who wanted out of this losing well-intentioned war. In a lot of ways, this was strictly an American war and the allies were not backing them in any way. The fallout however, from a world humanitarian view, was the plight of the children. It was a situation when several well meaning Canadian couples decided to adopt Vietnamese orphan children. It has always been a wonderful feeling to see the generosity of such people in North America. At the same time, it still takes one by surprise to see the number of really kind people there are in this country of Canada and indeed in the USA. The children are the ones that first come to mind in these conflicts followed by the stressed-out women at least that is from Leslie's perspective.

It should therefore follow that when children are adopted and taken from war zones their first need is love by their adopted parents who see past the physical emaciated appearance of their charges. They then attend immediately to their health by taking them to their family physicians. Invariably, none of these children have the childhood inoculations as our North American newborns do. These children also lack proper nutrition from birth but somehow they survive. However, because of unsanitary conditions, they often become a repository for many illnesses mainly infections such as malaria, diarrhea caused by Shigella, typhoid fever, tuberculosis, other respiratory diseases and a host of other parasitic infections.

When these unfortunate children are first met by their adoptive parents or caretakers, they are often riddled with internal parasites such as hookworms. There are a variety of different types such as the ones that live in their intestines and the ones that can hone into their brain. Needless to say, there may also be fungal infections from the superficial skin forms of tinea, to middle ear infections or chest infections due to *Aspergillus* species. These kids need a thorough clean up from a microbiological perspective both internally and externally for many become repositories of many pathogenic diseases. Unfortunately, Leslie and his team did not usually receive the best of specimens from the local general practitioners.

The main problem, as it is with so many general practitioners (GPs) or family doctors, is the lack of up-to-date information and education. Les was aware that these well-meaning GPs tend to deal with these exotic diseases from a very narrow perspective through lack of tropical medicine experience. These cases turn up as outpatients at his hospital in London, Ontario after the GP has found something unusual, meaning beyond his experience of his otherwise clean practice in SW Ontario. In such instances, even our health centre specialists may also be in the dark as to what follow-up procedures should be initiated, since they also lack the experience of the variety of different tropical infections.

However, in their early days of medical school they may have learned the syndromes from text books or heard from casual discussions with colleagues who may have some experience. Les, because of his own tropical experience, has learned that the term 'bush medicine' can also occur in medical practitioners in the industrial world. In such cases the physicians in the front line act with no better information or skill than that of a witch doctor for his knowledge is based on intuition. The sharper ones do not attempt to handle these cases other than in ordering the standard hematology and microbiology tests and often consult the specialists in tropical medicine. This is not a put-down of the general practitioners but rather a reflection of the poor evolution of the continual medical educational system that does not evolve in a society that flourishes on immigrants. One would imagine that since the work force of this country depends on immigrant workers both now and in the future, that some provision would have been made to check them out health-wise with trained and up-to-date experienced individuals either at their site of embarkation or with properly trained individuals in tropical medicine, in this country. The fact that the North American population has a low fecundity rate ensures that there would be a growing need for an increasing population. The demographics are consistently showing a reduction in numbers of workers who do not work to their sixty-fifth year of retirement. Immigrants are the main source of future workers in our industries, many of which will come from the so called third world countries, where healthcare is nil to nonexistent.

From Desperation the Future is predicted in Infectious Diseases:

This is a case of a young Vietnamese child of about three years old in poor physical development. The child cried incessantly in spite of the food, warmth, and the touch from her new parents. Suddenly, the child developed a high fever and the new parents brought her into the emergency. A sample of blood was taken to the hematology laboratory for a full blood count. The white blood cells were abnormally elevated, which is indicative of a systemic infection. A blood culture was taken and this entailed taking some blood from the patient and placing it into a bottle of a bacterial broth that allows bacteria to grow when incubated at 37 degrees Centigrade for 18 to 24 hours.

If a patient has had some antibiotics before the blood is taken, then the diluting factor of the blood into a large amount of broth would allow the badly damaged bacteria to grow. In those days, there were enzymes against the family of penicillins that would break it down. The labs used this to try and isolate the infecting organism by breaking down any trace amount of penicillin. It is always better to take a sample for microbiological investigation before an antibiotic is administered. When the penicillin is destroyed in the specimen the few bacteria in the patient's sample, even if partially damaged, will survive. This may seem odd to the lay person and the question asked is why does the lab wish to have the bacteria alive and to grow in the lab broth or media? The answer is if the lab isolates the bacterium causing the illness, then tests are done to determine the best drug to administer to the patient to destroy the bacteria and bring about a cure. When the lab scientist can identify and name the bacterium that is causing a set of symptoms, then doctors will know in the future how to treat such patients again.

Invariably the GP will treat the patient empirically with a range of antibiotics that he has heard about from the drug salesperson, who explains how wonderful 'their' antibiotic is compared with their competitors' products. In many instances, the drugs used while it is risky to say, the dosage is usually improper and sometimes inappropriate since the patient may be suffering from a insidious liver or renal problem. Antibiotics work when there is a high enough level circulating in the blood stream or the urine in the kidneys to kill the infecting organism at the site of infection. The concentration of the drug in the blood or urine allows the drug to bathe the site that is infected and kill the bacteria that are infecting that area. This gives the body time to heal itself.

This is the practice in the Northern industrial countries and in some of the Third World countries with an acceptable health system. It is not the same in countries at war. Indeed, it is common practice for antibiotics to be bought over the counter by any patient and used inappropriately to treat the sick in their homes. No one ensures that the drug or antibiotic is at its therapeutic concentration or that it has been stored properly at the right temperature and humidity. Secondly, there is often a misunderstanding about how to dose the patient with the appropriate antibiotic. The dosage given to a patient depends on the health of their liver and kidneys as well as, their weight and overall health. To the lay person in such countries where antibiotics and other drugs are bought over the counter, there is no education to support these parameters. It stands to reason that there are a lot of risks for such poor families who believe that many drugs are the miracle cure and that the more given, the better.

The Vietnamese Adopted Child:

Les was aware of these difficulties and this was typical for the child that had come to St Joseph's Health Centre. The young child went into shock after being examined in the emergency room. The stiffening of the neck is a major sign that there may also be a risk of meningitis. A spinal tap of fluid was taken and sent to the Microbiology Labs. The specimens were cultured onto a variety of media and fluids in an effort to find the causative infectious organism. After twenty-four hours the Petri dishes with the defined media, in this unusual case, were examined and some unusual colonies were seen.

There were two distinct bacteria isolated based on their shape when seen stained under the microscope. One was a black round one called a coccus and they were in pairs. The second one was a tiny red rod- shaped organism when stained. The identification was straightforward - the coccus was identified as a *Streptococcus pneumoniae* or pneumococcus. The second rod-shaped one was identified as a *Haemophilus influenzae*. These organisms were the usual pathogens found causing bacterial pneumonia in chest infections. In patients with acute pneumonia, a septicemia or infection of the bloodstream usually occurs. If the infection becomes systemic or spreads throughout the body then the bacteria may also be found in the blood and in the spinal fluid causing meningitis.

These two bacteria were isolated from the specimens of blood where they were found to cause a septicemia and then from the spinal fluid causing meningitis. The bacteria were also isolated from the urine and the sputum which meant that the child had a systemic infection. The physicians were informed and Dr Gutch was told of the dangerous state of the child's health. He set out to place the child in isolation and to treat her with the appropriate antibiotics. This is how a tertiary hospital works but, as explained before, the work is only just beginning. Thanks go out to a brilliant lab scientist that Leslie would refer to as Caroline since he does not know where she is or even if she is still practicing.

In those early days, it was unusual to have a lab scientist such as Caroline, who had a Masters Degree as well as her technical diploma. She was a great source of knowledge to all the staff even though she had specialized in fungal work. Fungal work or mycology was difficult for many staff practicing bacteriology. She had excellent training in basic applied research and she understood the sciences at a different level than the routine technologists. She was unafraid to do a literature search to trace up the latest information but most important of all to decipher whether the work was done before.

Leslie was just beginning his full-time work as Chief of the department and whenever there was an opportunity to isolate an organism from an unusual source or an unusual antibiotic pattern of resistance in an organism, he would chase it up. When he published these case incidents or patients' histories, his name in the diagnostic field became well established in the province. This professional recognition increased later on across the country, when the national technical journal accepted his publications of patients' case histories. These examples were also sources of novel information in his teaching especially, when he was invited to be a guest lecturer he would stress the need to examine all unusual findings.

In the case of the Vietnamese child and the isolated bacteria, it was Caroline who first called Les' attention to look at the growth of the coccus or pneumococcus on a sheep blood agar Petri plate. The organism grew as a heavily mucoid green colony. When the susceptibility test was done using a paper disk with a concentration of penicillin, there is usually a zone around the disk where the organism is sensitive and showed no growth to the drug. In this unusual instance, there was a small zone but this could be due to the heavy concentration of bacteria used. The size of the inoculum used can also influence the zone of inhibition especially if it was too heavy posing a challenge to the small amount of penicillin used in a small paper strip, from which it diffused across the culture medium. The size of the inoculum can directly affect the reading of the test which determines whether or not to treat with a drug. This can be misinterpreted as resistance to an antibiotic. The test was repeated with a standardized concentration and again there was a heaped-up thick growth at the edge of the very tiny zone of growth.

This observation was seen with the susceptibility testing of *Staphylococcus*, when challenged against a paper disk impregnated with a solution of penicillin. In this test, the bacteria appeared as a heaped edge of heavy growth, at the edge of the zone of stasis. When the test was repeated with organisms from this heap, the staphylococcus was found to be resistant for no zone develops just a confluent growth of the staphylococcus across the antibiotic disk. The explanation is that the staphylococcus produced the enzyme known as penicillinase which breaks down penicillin rendering it useless as a killing agent in a patient's body. However, this enzyme was only produced when the penicillin was present in its immediate environment which means that it had to be induced by the presence of its substrate.

In this case, the test disk placed on the plate held penicillin which killed the organisms closest to the impregnated disk. However, when the staphylococcus was stimulated by its ability to breakdown the penicillin, it grew in abundance some distance from the disk. Hence, the area immediately at the edge of inhibited growth or the zone of stasis is observed as 'heaped-up' growth around a circle of no growth, in appearance.

This phenomenon has been known for many years dating back to the early 1960s. Today, the enzyme produced by staphylococcus that breaks down all forms of penicillins belongs to a huge group known as the beta lactamases. The reason is that the penicillin molecular structure is a beta lactam ring. Hence, the enzyme that breaks down the molecular ring structure is called a beta lactamase. This analogy cannot be used in Leslie's laboratory case for it does not apply to any other organism as a rule. In the lab, Leslie's group had seen this new phenomenon with the new green (known as alpha hemolysis) colony that is common to the pneumococcus and this was a very unusual finding.

It was the same for the other organism which Caroline had seen, *Haemophilus influenzae* that was also isolated from this Vietnamese child patient. The obvious question that all research scientists have to ask is why did this bacterial morphological change take place? The second question is whether this was a different species of the usual organism identified in North America for years? The third question asked is what was causing this morphological change? The fourth question is whether this organism, because of the different appearance, was as sensitive to the penicillins as described in the text books or were we dealing with a different drug pattern? Of course, Leslie could not just leave things alone. He was almost puritanical in this belief and this should never happen in tertiary medicine, at least this was his opinion. His scientific sense would not leave this puzzle alone. Once he was fired up the need for answers became an obsessive task not just a curiosity.

Wandering into Blind Philosophy:

True applied lab scientists are invariably in search of unusual patterns of behaviour in a living forms such as a bacterium, a virus or some other microscopic biological entity. Genetic changes and the ability to adapt to changes in the environment in which living forms survive are the basis for survival and longevity of a species. Les had a puzzle and human beings hate an unsolved mystery; it needed to be solved. So it was not just that the job had to be done in order to bring about the patient's treatment and possibly remove life threatening occurrences. It was important to use these real technical findings to enhance education and fill in the little bits of information missing in standard recognized text books. Only real knowledge comes from the patient and information is often hidden in the case histories that are just filed away without any search for commonality with other similar syndromes.

The more difficult part of this necessary undertaking is challenging the status quo and of any experimental design, especially when it has to be modified. Further, these obstacles are intensively supported by the conservative old guard who quotes the "gold standard" from the out dated text books. This information is placed into the path of the lab scientist who wishes to chase up the puzzle. Leslie did not know at the time, how often he would have to face this ordeal of questioning the tried and true practices of his profession. At a later stage in life, he often wondered why he returned to such a profession after obtaining advanced education. While education broadened his perspective in the biological sciences, it was difficult to convince others of the need to question the "gold standards" made by man in the old days of the practice, which did not have the technology and drugs of today. In one of the after work beer sessions, which he enjoyed, his often callous and caustic Scottish colleague would listen quietly and then mutter into his beer, *"I am no religious being, in fact I do not believe in God. However, Ah cannae help but believe that one is placed into a position for some reason in the cosmos for some people. Nah! It goes against my Scottish socialist realistic pragmatic conscience. You are too religious in your thinking Man. Les you shoulda been a priest"*

Leslie often felt the same way, when he looked at the great achievers throughout history. Destiny interrupts by allowing a slight change in circumstance to be observed, thus allowing such workers to make a positive breakthrough and do great things. The philosopher may ask how much is circumstance and how much is the input of destiny or power of the cosmos in scientific discovery or is there truly something called luck? Whatever the explanation, Les and his group of disbelieving colleagues shared different thoughts as to why people find themselves in different environments in their lives and decide to run with the circumstances. Is that how changes and discovery really occur? Or is it by accident or a pre-ordained divinity for the few who do believe in a religious dogma, or just random chance and selection?

Whatever the reason Leslie and his band of lab scientists had a mystery to solve. There was precedence in an organism showing a phenomenon of stimulated growth in the presence of a poison in this case penicillin, a commonly used antibiotic. The proof of such an observation was simply by selecting the questionable resistant organism and retesting it against dilutions or different strengths of the 'poison' (such as penicillin or any other antibiotics). This methodology has shown that there was growth in the presence of the 'poison' or in this case the antibiotic penicillin, therefore the correct assumption is that this organism was resistant. Observing growth in higher strengths of the antibiotic also defined increased resistance. In order to kill the bacterium an excessively high dose would be required and maybe this would be unachievable in the human body. However, could the human body survive such high does or concentrations of antibiotics? What would be the side effects?

A high dose of an antibiotic could cause major side effects on the human organs. When a poison, such as an antibiotic, is used to kill a microscopic uni-cellular life form, then it also has the potential to kill or damage a multi-cellular life form, such as a human being by killing one cell at a time. This too has been proven in the literature of drug companies and in the medical journals. The skill, with these very precious antibiotics, is to use just the minimum dosage that will kill the infecting organism while doing little or no damage to the patient.

The two organisms isolated by Caroline, Leslie and his co-workers showed a behaviour that was unusual for these 2 species isolated from the baby. This was known to be not unusual for the staphylococcus species to appear as heaped up growth at the end of stasis using paper impregnated disks with the penicillin. Was it safe to make the 'leap in thinking' that maybe the phenomenon was not really unusual for all species of bacteria including these two species? It is just that no one had seen or documented it or, maybe, saw it and just dismissed the observation through lack of knowledge, scientific curiosity or some other cerebral deficiency. It is interesting to hear of Bill Gates saying to the interviewer, *I did not see anything unusual in what I was doing for everyone in this business had also seen the potential of what I had developed. Many chose to ignore the potential but I followed up on this and made my own software.*

The drug of choice in treating patients with infections caused by these organisms was straightforward in those days. Leslie had no choice but to do the test knowing that the patients would be treated empirically. However, the screening test which was to challenge the organism against a paper disk impregnated with penicillin revealed this heaped-up observation. So taking the cue of the acceptable staphylococcus model, the organisms were re-tested from the heap and they were found to be resistant. These results were shown to Dr Gutch and he immediately resisted the testing procedure. His reason was that all the contemporary text books noted that there was *no such thing as a penicillin-resistant pneumococcus or Haemophilus species.*

In Dr Gutch's mind, the in vitro testing was incorrect when compared with the old way and it could not be trusted. Dr Gutch went along with the status quo but he must have been bothered by the results that the lab had produced. He consulted on the case and decided to raise the concentration levels of penicillin in the blood stream of this sick baby. He called Leslie into his room and the discussion began. "You know, that was quite a lot of good work done but you must understand that the baby is getting better."

Leslie said, "Well that is good news. However I need some guidance on how we can find out the true concentration of the drug at which this organism is truly susceptible."

Leslie remained quiet as Dr Gutch lit up his cigarette and blew the thick blue smoke into the air. He huffed. He panted, even wheezed a bit, and then said, "Well, you will have to do the old tube titration test, old boy. That remains the gold standard for susceptibility testing, as you well know. Why not get on with it but do not spend too much time on this work for we are not a research lab." The old tube test is a line of clean tubes in a test tube rack with one mL of saline in each tube. One mL of a diluted concentration of penicillin say around 10 microgram in solution of which one mL is placed into the first tube. This is mixed and one mL is transferred into the second tube until the end. A standardized suspension of the test organism, which in this case are the two organisms isolated from the baby. That means that each organism had to have separate tube tests done along with a known control row of tubes. This is a long and very tedious test. The most difficult part is that this tube test can only be done with fast growing bacteria not those that are fastidious as the ones isolated from the baby.

Leslie impatiently replied, "Come on doctor, you know that these are fastidious organisms and they will not grow in standard lab broth. If we tinker with the broth then there is a risk of incorporating many errors of commission and we will be chasing our tails forever in a circle."

Dr Gutch had a stern retort. "If you know that is the problem then why do you not go ahead and find a broth that works? Do a literature search and work out the details."

Over the years Leslie often wondered if Dr Gutch had not given him such advice just to get rid of him or to get him 'out of his hair'. He surely did not like these technical or academic questions thrown at him so often. In Leslie's case, he could find such a case weekly and he was wicked enough to try and get the old boy into an enquiring frame of mind, throwing him a science puzzle. Dr Gutch was a very practical man and he prided himself on being able to work on the bench better than any of the lab scientists. In fact, he was better at tissue culture work in the old fashioned way, which at one time back in the late 1950s was innovative in virology and he was avant garde in his approach back then.

When he was in the right frame of mind and a puzzle caught his imagination he would ponder it and has been known to seek advice from his colleagues at the university. This was rare but the interplay between these two men was such that one had the authority but not in the discipline that he loved. Dr Gutch had a lab scientist to head Virology, whom he had trained and brought over from the UK. When one simply recreates the same system that one has worked in for the better part of one's working life when creativity and power are at its peak, then it is a recipe for stagnation, if it persists new techniques are not taken advantage of.

Dr Gutch and his senior scientist were two lab scientists who worked comfortably together and the association was not unlike a spousal arrangement, of which Les developed with his senior scientist many years later. The explanation of excellence was thrown at Leslie for many years when these two colleagues, in his opinion, 'ganged up' to overpower his suggestions and ideas. The full array of obstacles ranged from budgetary restrictions to staffing deployment or changes in employees status. Leslie did not let any of these get in the way, for he often refocused his priority in his own discipline. This was simple enough for he could enrich the Bacteriology work with his new skills of applied research, advanced biochemistry and the new sciences of molecular biology.

If there is one thing that one learns when one is building up an idea of what a future project should look like, it is that there is always some new piece of information that comes from an unexpected source. It is usually a gem of information if one listens and keeps the information in the back of one's mind. In the same casual conversation, he was asked by Dr Gutch, "Leslie what is it that these organisms require to grow luxuriantly on lab media?" Leslie invariably always felt when he was questioned on what he was doing just as if he was doing his dissertation again and he had to prove himself repeatedly. In a perverse way, he liked doing his 'orals' so he did not dislike the idea of being questioned but it had to be in the correct tone of voice.

In this instance, it was an enquiring tone so he answered, "What these fastidious organisms need is an enriched concentration of vitamin B, in fact all the B Vitamins."

Dr Gutch pulled on his pipe as if he were the great contemplative scientist. Then looking down on the floor he asked, "Do you know where you can get such a concentration of vitamin B?"

Leslie saw that this was a serious turn in the questioning. "There is no commercial market for such a pure vitamin supplement that is why we use sheep and horse blood. What is needed is a vitamin source that could be added to the broth that does not turn the broth turbid. I need to read the tubes visually for turbidity which indicates growth of the organism. Naturally I could culture every tube but it would be better to use a clear broth and read growth as turbidity."

Dr Gutch then focused on the technique and asked, "How will you approach this resistance to antibiotics especially to penicillin that appears to be present in these organisms?"

Leslie was quick in his reply. "I would use the old minimum inhibitory concentration dilution procedure or the tube test." This technique is in every one of the old text books where tubes of broth were used in which a concentration of an antibiotic was diluted out. A drop of a turbid broth with the test bacteria was added to each tube. When turbidity first shows in one of the tubes, then the clear tube just before is considered to be the smallest concentration of antibiotic that was needed to kill the bacterium. This was called the minimum inhibitory concentration (MIC) of an antibiotic.

Dr Gutch smiled and said, "I am pleased that you agree for that is really the only way to do a proper sensitivity test. I really dislike that paper-disk sensitivity test. It was OK in the old days when there were fewer drugs and we could try a screening procedure which had no bearing on the in vivo dosage necessary to treat the patient."

They both paused and the cigarette was placed in his blackened ashtray on Dr Gutch's desk. Leslie saw the end of the butt just fall into the tray. Dr Gutch scratched his beard, stroked his mustache and yawned. It was around three in the afternoon and he needed his cup of tea which his Virology Chief would soon bring to him. They usually closed the door and lit up their cigarettes while they sipped tea. This was the time for Leslie to get lost. In fact, he usually met with the chief of Haematology and they would go down for their cuppa in the coffee shop on the floor below the lab.

However, the tea did not arrive and he said to Leslie, "You know that the calf serum which we use in virology 'tissue culture work' is rich in all the vitamins and there is a high level of vitamin B, which is necessary for our stock tissue cultures." Yawning broadly, he smiled through the blood shot eyes of an old smoker. Just then there was a knock on the door which meant that tea was to be served. Leslie prepared to leave, smiling at this comfortable duo, when Dr Gutch said to his Virology Chief with the tray carrying the two steaming cups of tea, "Can you let Leslie have some calf serum from your stock?"

His Chief looked up from her tray over which she was bent. "There has been a back order but there might be enough to spare. It depends on how much you would require Leslie?"

Leslie was a bit taken back and said, "Look, why do you not have your tea and when I come back from downstairs, I will do the calculation and tell you how much I need to do the first screening test."

"OK," she replied quietly and as he withdrew, the door closed and Leslie bolted downstairs to join the other chiefs of the departments for the much needed coffee and to have a chat.

How does one break this secret code of antibiotic resistance?

The plot continues to find the smallest amount of drug that will destroy the bacterium isolated from the adopted child. These bacteria are called fastidious because of their difficulty to grow on the common lab media. They required a defined media, with special vitamins and miniscule growth enhancing factors. Defined media could not be used to perform antibiotic susceptibility tests. Les and his technical workers had to use the gold standard but alter it to allow the microbes to grow. The challenge made it a necessity to meet in Les' office with doors closed.

THE WAR ROOM PLAN

Over the years of his practice at the health centre whenever he had a project to undertake, Leslie liked the idea of bringing his enthusiastic and unusually smart lab scientists together in what he privately called 'the war room'. From these brief meetings so many decisions about projects were designed and completed. In many instances, articles were drafted, literature searches analyzed and drafts made, revised, revamped and hence, many a publication was originated. It was from this little 12 x 12 office that his little band of keen lab scientists requested to take on a project of their choosing. It was from this room that he and his supervisors decided where resources should be obtained. It was fun and all staff took part in this open academic conspiracy to promote their department and health centre through applied research and publications. Back in 1972, Les would bring the staff into the old library for his cupboard of a room could only hold two persons not three for it would be too physically intimate. These were his happiest days for the restrictions that he had to undergo for supplies, to do things for the better could dominate his otherwise happy life. These obstacles made him more creative in obtaining resources but were also the cause for much envy and suspicion by his colleagues.

After the serious discussions with his Chief Dr Gutch, Les called Caroline in, for he had decided that she would understand and would be challenged. "Caroline we must develop an enriched broth that would remain clear even if it was tinged a pale yellow."

Caroline quietly enquired, "Is this for the two fastidious organisms from the Vietnamese baby?"

Leslie was smiling and replied, "Yes Caroline, but we also need to do a literature search. I will begin with that part if you will work out the dilutions to do a step-wise range of dilutions so that we can really ascertain the smallest amount of penicillin needed to inhibit these organisms. There is a need to do broth dilutions but we must refine the dilution range. Double dilutions leave too many big steps. After a 1 in 4, the next step is 1 in 8 and this is not good enough. I would like us to get the smallest amount of penicillin that will inhibit these normally sensitive organisms. We shall also work out the bactericidal (the killing dosage) versus the bacteriostatic (preventing the growth from taking place) level at which the reaction occurs. Mathematically we should be able to work out the blood level of the drug needed to kill or inhibit the organism. I will work with the pharmacists to work out the dosage needed to obtain the level to treat this infection."

"Gee Les! That will be very difficult to do, for there is no way of finding a source of vitamin B. I have searched the commercial brochures and asked the university labs for assistance with no success."

"Well Blondie, guess what? The old man just gave me the answer! He said that calf serum has is a rich source of the vitamins, especially of the B types and he is willing to let us have a few milliliters to test out," Leslie enthusiastically replied.

Caroline's blue eyes widened beneath her horn rimmed glasses. "You mean to say that he would let us have some of his priceless precious calf serum! How does he know that there is vitamin B in that serum? I will call the library to get us some reprints on calf serum," she joined in with an equally focused enthusiasm. Les knew that he was correct to ask Caroline to assist in this project.

Leslie interrupted and said, "No Caroline, focus on the series of dilutions first. I will call the company that provides the calf serum and ask them for the literature. That would be the quickest way to get the information."

"However," he continued, "we need to have an electron transfer agent in the broth that would allow the *Haemophilus* to take up its nutrients. It must not be hemoglobin for that will make the broth brown and turbid. This would render the reading of the end point as turbidity or growth difficult to interpret."

Caroline was one of the finest lab scientists that Leslie had known back in the 1970s and she understood a great deal more than many of the other staff in the laboratory. In those early days, it was difficult to get staff that was as well qualified as she was. Actually the reason that she was in town was that her husband was completing his PhD thesis at the local university and she was working to support them both. They did not have any kids, so she was free to do some extra-curricular work. The opportunity to undertake this project with such a supportive scientist was a real bonus for Leslie could return after his supper with his young family then continue their research in peace, away from the routine hustle and bustle of the lab routine during daytime. They agreed to meet around 7:00 pm that evening for she would go to the university and have supper with her husband then go to the library and get the reprints that they needed.

Retrospective:

Leslie had a call at home from the company's scientist that supplied the calf serum, who had left his own telephone number asking that Leslie return his call. Leslie in his excited frame of mind explained everything to his scientifically trained wife, who also had come in from work. She had begun part-time work for they had a newborn baby girl. They had supper together and he told her of the project that they were about to undertake. His wife smiled at his enthusiasm but she remained quiet for she would learn over the years that his curiosity and scientific puzzles meant that he would never be home on many evenings during the week and for the rest of his work career. There was invariably a project, then there were lectures and meetings and that was Leslie's life in the early part of his career. Actually, it continued into his first twenty-eight years but only slowed temporarily when he began doing joint trials with his colleagues around the world.

A Scientist Family Support, Led by a Scientist Spouse:

Leslie thought of his wife, Alice who was a good researcher in her early days. She could have gone down that path and would have been quite successful. She preferred, however, to do the straightforward diagnostic work or as they referred to it 'routine bench work.' She was never really that interested in research and so limited her ambitions to diagnosing disorders by examining her hematological blood smears on patients with abnormal hematological results. She had also specialized in immuno-hematology. She had to maintain her license so she did a number of extra weekend courses and quite a few by correspondence. Fortunately, many sessions were held at the city colleges and health centre campuses after work. They both worked to keep up to date in their respective careers. Over the years when Alice did weekend courses he remained home with the children. They both enjoyed the provincial and national conventions, academy meetings and in house training courses held in the city.

In many instances when their city was the venue of these technical meetings, conventions or educational sessions, they took part in the organization and on the work committees. Their gentle disposition and hard work gained them a reputation as a dependable husband and wife team. They worked for different establishments but they came together especially for the social occasions. This was a time of settling into their work community and into their new city. It was Dr Gutch and his wife who assisted them in settling into their new home environment even to the passing down of their perambulator and many of their children's toys to be used as gifts for their fledgling family.

Money was tight with a mortgage and car expenses. There was just enough for food and some small enjoyment such as the odd fast food meal out. They deprived themselves of a television and movies for many years. The kindness of his Chief Dr Gutch and his very English wife was not lost on this couple. Les and his wife exchanged Christmas cards and a small plant with them at Christmas time for many years even after the old man had retired for well over twenty years. Dr Gutch lost his spouse within the first three years of early retirement. He remained a bit of a hermit but he made time for taking telephone calls from Leslie and his wife. In the early days, he even joined them for supper but by and large he did not leave his home much to meet with his colleagues and it appears that he had few friends. Les missed him a great deal for he shared his knowledge generously at their after work sessions and on the few occasions when Les could get him to present a lecture to the academy or at a convention.

Caroline's Support:

Leslie received the information on the contents of calf serum from the commercial company's scientist. It had a high level of attainable vitamin B which he needed. He went into the lab after supper and Caroline followed a few minutes later. She was hugging an armful of reprints which she had spent the better part of the evening photocopying at the university. She had taken her husband's library card to use the photocopier. She did not have to bear the cost of photocopying so many articles. Les and Caroline sterilized the main work bench in the laboratory and used this clear area to spread out the reprints. Using underliner pens they began bringing the information together.

These were the evenings that not many of their coworkers knew about. He was preparing for the time when he would dominate the technical journal with case histories. Generally, patient case histories come from the routine work that occurred every day in labs across this country and the USA. However many never manage to be published and shared with colleagues;

everyone was too busy making a living. Les and his staff of 30 along with his hematology colleagues successfully began to flood the national technical journals with their publications. Many of his colleagues across the country just wondered how he had the time and resources to keep up this volume of work together with the real daily diagnostic work while managing the staff.

> *"Lives of great men do remind us*
> *We can make our lives sublime*
> *And departing leave behind us*
> *Footsteps on the sands of time"*

Caroline was a great colleague and together they sorted out many technical difficulties such as on the use of immunological and biochemical agents needed for this undertaking. The prime example is a term that they had learned in their notes but never bothered to find out. It was referred to as the co-factor. They never paid attention to the nature of what was 'co-factor'. What was it? How could they find a replacement for this factor and what that replacement would be? These were serious questions that had to be dealt with in the course of their investigations? They tested many different agents until they had a calf serum broth that would allow the growth of these fastidious organisms. They then did the time studies to try and get turbid growth within four hours of incubation at 37 degrees C. This empiric work was never published for they were just two scientists who stumbled into a problem that stimulated their interest. They solved other technical problems along the way, such as an ion or electron carrier that kept the broth clear enough so that turbidity could be seen.

The Testing:
The big task was to calculate the dilutions in small enough steps and to get a reading that all staff could interpret. The

unknown factor was described in text books as *'between 20% - 30% or more of penicillin would be bound to the proteins'* in human blood. This 'bound penicillin' did not help in the killing of the organism in vivo, hence the need for a larger dosage of the drug would have to be administered in order to kill the infectious agent. If the drug is bound to protein it is not available to bathe the site of the infection, where the infecting organism is located. The bound drug will eventually be released from the protein but that is usually over a long period of time up to a year.

There is no simplicity in scientific applied research for as soon as one thinks that a problem is solved, one finds another obstacle. Hindrances that are overlooked or that have just occurred demanded one's full attention before one can progress. In the end, Les and his scientist found a dilution range that they could use which worked. First of all, they had been able to get these very difficult bacteria to grow in their test protocol within four hours, instead of the normal twenty-four to forty-eight hours. This contravenes all the lab protocols in use at that time in labs around the world. Secondly, they had isolated a pneumococcus that was not killed in vitro and was resistant to 16 milligrams of penicillin. Such a result is automatically wrong for all the text books state definitively that all *'alpha streptococci are sensitive to penicillin'* which included their isolate of a pneumococcus from the spinal fluid of their little patient, is always sensitive to penicillin.

The *Haemophilus* species isolated from this child was also found to be resistant to 16 milligrams of penicillin. The test was repeated so many times and the control organisms were consistently killed at 0.2 mgs of penicillin. The identity of the organisms was verified by sending them to the public health reference laboratories in Ottawa. Higher concentrations of antibiotic disks up to 10 mgs of penicillin were tested on the standard media used for these organisms. The results showed the resistance of both organisms even when repeated two more times. In every instance the bacteria showed complete resistance to these elevated concentrations of antibiotics while the standard control organisms remained sensitive. Dr Gutch saw the results of these disk tests and he was truly stymied for an answer. He had run out of possible reasons for these repeated "false results."

The patient was responding to increasingly higher doses of penicillin G which was the soluble drug. The good thing about the penicillins is that they are readily excreted in urine. There were no side effects on the patient at that time, as a result of the extra-ordinarily high drug dosage. Why were these two organisms not responding to the drug *in vitro test*? Caroline found a way to detach the penicillin from the bound proteins, actually not so much as detaching but rather estimating the amount that is removed by serum used in the in vitro test. Penicillin was binding to the globulins in calf serum. Our calculations were done repeatedly and any way we cut it these bugs were showing resistance in vitro to elevated levels of penicillin.

The trouble with their tests regimen, Leslie knew, was that it was a methodology untried by others, and hence would be unacceptable by the few scholarly scientists in the profession. Where could one find support for this new methodology that was very time consuming but terrific in its breakthrough technologically as a method that is comparable with the 'gold standard'? The levels of penicillin in the patient's blood were way over the level needed to kill the normal bacteria.

Eventually, Leslie drew up the experimental design and handed the results to Dr Gutch, whom he knew would fume at their findings. If this did not follow the text book then it was incorrect and he would not wish to know or discuss the details. This was much worse than Les had thought for the idea was definitely unusual. A penicillin resistant pneumococcus was isolated from this Vietnamese girl child who had been given all sorts of drugs since she was a baby. In her short life, being born in a war zone and given medicines over the counter with no regard for her size and weight was in fact now allowing her to live. Dr Gutch remained quiet and kept the document on his desk for over two months but Leslie had made a copy of their findings.

Caroline kept asking why did Dr Gutch not respond and Leslie just said that it was too novel for him and he needed time to process the results. She asked almost every day and Leslie had no more reasons to give her so she became petulant. This normally quiet sensible woman snapped at Leslie, *He doesn't trust the work that we do. We are not British-trained for those are the only people he really trusts.* There was no need for Leslie to respond to her frustration and to point out that he, Les, was indeed British as well as Canadian-trained.

However, in an effort to quash her despondency due to the lack of response to their hard work, Leslie said to her, "You know, Caroline, we should publish the results in the national technical journal. After all, the editor has been quite supportive to our previous case history publications. He had even written to me saying that we must continue to share our knowledge, so we should continue to send more case histories to the journal."

Caroline was ecstatic at the suggestion and smiled broadly saying, "You know Les that is a great idea. At least let us send in the manuscript for review by his consultants." Les knew that this would temporarily redirect her anger and frustration into another direction but he was quite uncomfortable and remained quiet.

There was a feeling of uncertainty in Leslie's gut for he felt what they had done was clever applied research but it was too advanced for even their peers to consider. Leslie said nothing but kept his insecure thoughts to himself. His senior scientist was happy at the prospect of publishing the details of their case history. She had a broader concept than the staid literature, which was the discovery of the first documented resistant strains of two common organisms. This resistance to penicillin had never been recorded before the year 1973-74. This story does not end here and continues into the next chapter.

Fleming Versus Fleming

Microbiology History:

At the end of 1974, a rather obtuse Englishman, who was the head of Microbiology at the Hospital for Sick Children in Toronto, better known colloquially as Sick Kids was doing some strange work. He had been working on a test to detect the by-product of penicillin breakdown or penicillinoic acid, by the enzyme penicillinase. In fact, he had developed a simple test that would have great value to diagnostic microbiology using iodine as a detector. The name of this microbiologist at Sick Kids was Dr Fleming who used his name as a humorous foil as it was the name of the founder of penicillin. In his lectures when asked by his more discerning students whether he was related to the founder of penicillin, the infamous microbiologist Sir Alexander Fleming, he would just say that he had worked in his lab. Les was chuffed in his later years when he met this man who had the British dry sense of humour and loved to have a scotch after his lecture.

There are variations on the anecdotes of how Sir Alexander Fleming actually discovered the fungus known as Penicillium, which was used to produce penicillinoic acid. This basic acid was used to produce the very first penicillin drug that has saved many millions of lives over the past seventy plus years. It was said that a grad student or one of his lab scientists had been doing research using a mixture of fungi isolated from soil. At the end of the research project the individual showed his department Chief, Dr Alexander Fleming, his culture plates. When the lab emptied of the grad students at the end of the day, Dr Alexander Fleming retrieved the disposed plates and on examination, he saw a circle of no growth around the fungal colony. It appeared to him that a by-product was released by the fungus that inhibited the mixture of bacterial colonies in the Petri plate.

He took a pure colony of the fungus Penicillium, sub-cultured it onto a fresh plate of medium after he had plated out a single bacterium colony as a mat across the plate. The next day he saw the same phenomenon of a zone around the fungus where there was no growth. The medium in the zone of no growth was extracted into a sterile broth. Then a drop of the fluid was placed on a fresh plate with a seeded bacterium as he had done with the fungus colony. He found that there was again an area of inhibition where the drop was placed but this time the fungus was not present. He had found the by-product known as penicillinoic acid. The rest is history for Dr Alexander Fleming had found the first antibiotic that had a profound effect against a range of bacterial strains which caused infections in human beings. He was knighted and played a great role in the development of the refined product known simply as penicillin.

However, our hard working Microbiologist at Sick kids did not have his test available when Leslie and Caroline had done their work two years earlier. In fact, it would not be available for another eight months. Meanwhile, the text book continued to advise physicians that all streptococci were sensitive to penicillin. An advanced molecule of penicillin G had been developed and was known as Ampicillin. This was the drug of choice used in the treatment of patients with an infection caused by *Haemophilus species*. Caroline and Leslie carefully described their tube sensitivity test and their new broth enriched with calf serum in their article.

They described their findings of the amount of penicillin bound to the globulins in the test. They showed the controls used which were standard organisms and the dilutions that were used in most diagnostic labs but there were shorter interludes in concentrations and not just two-fold dilutions. They took black and white photos of the colonies and submitted them with their manuscript. They described the background of the baby adopted from Vietnam and from their limited knowledge, revealed that across the counter antibiotics were used on the child during her younger years with her poor family.

They both reviewed the article which was well written and well referenced using the example of the 'phenomenon of heaped up growth in the presence of penicillin' with staphylococcus. In less than two weeks, they received their manuscript back with a very long letter written to Leslie and included the following savage rebuke:

THE ACADEMIC 'PUT-DOWN'

Dear Mr. Paul,

Please find your manuscript returned for this article will not be published. Indeed, I am absolutely appalled that you, a leader, in such a well thought of health centre would submit such a poorly researched and terrible article for publication. Our Consultants were disgusted for you did not even review the basic text books as your reference. I am told and I quote, "There is no such thing as a resistant alpha streptococcus or Haemophilus to the wonderful drug penicillin." This is not the caliber of work we expect from our colleagues in the teaching health centres in Ontario and in Canada.

Please do not submit any such atrocious, poorly literature researched manuscripts to this journal in the future.

Sincerely

M Editor,

Leslie felt hurt and his fragile ego as described by Dr Gutch had been severely bruised by this rebuke from a senior colleague for whom he had great professional respect. When Caroline read the letter she began to cry and ran out his room. She left the lab and entered the ladies room to recover. She returned later and came directly to Leslie. She said that she would destroy all the work that we had done. She said that she would leave the cultures in the refrigerator. They eventually dried out and died. She felt so embarrassed and her professional pride was destroyed. She was a very sensitive person. Two weeks later she resigned her job and left Ontario to work on the west coast as a routine lab technologist in a public health laboratory. Les never heard from her again and their paths crossed only briefly once many years later. She now has two sons and appears to be content.

Leslie persevered on in the same health centre and continued to submit safe case histories for publication in the Canadian, the European, and Alpha Adria and American journals. However, one year later after Caroline had left his lab, he was attending the Canadian Public Health Meeting in Toronto. The erstwhile Dr Peter Fleming (of the erstwhile Sick Kids' Hospital) released his paper test that allowed the fastidious organism *Haemophilus species* to be tested for resistance against penicillin. In a retrospective study at his Hospital for Sick Kids, freeze-dried stored *Haemophilus* organisms which were isolated from cerebrospinal meningitis cases were retested using his screening test for penicillinoic acid. His workers had found that over 7% of the strains were resistant to penicillin. At the end of the twentieth century that figure rose to as high as 30% in some countries. Similarly, the number of *penicillin resistant pneumococcus* had reached as high as 30% – 35 % in some countries.

In his later years, Leslie met the editor of the Canadian Technical Journal, who was about to retire from his job as well as, from the journal. The editor was invited to a private supper thrown by the London group of senior lab scientists. After a wonderful supper with many speeches expressing goodwill and best wishes to this icon of the profession, Les related the above anecdote to this grey-haired old scientist. He asked if Les still had the letter and Leslie lied and said that they had destroyed all the information on that manuscript. In fact, Leslie had kept all the articles and letters sent to him by the editor. He had promised himself, after this generation of lab scientists die off, hopefully before he does, that he would publish these letters. It looks like these days are here. It does not pay to be first in science unless you are running for a Nobel Prize.

Actually, it was Dr Gutch who said to Les when they first met. "You should not try to be the first for you will be hurt." How right he was and he knew Les' temperament better than Les knew himself.

Nothing New in your Tuberculosis Article

Professional Arrogance

(Thanks for the manuscript but I will not use it. Regards, L...
Editor. CJM)

Leslie had insisted that a suitable replacement plan for the retiring Dr Gutch, as Director of the Lab, was to employ an Infectious Diseases Specialist. The Public Health Act stated that the individual had to be a medical practitioner such as a pathologist in order to be in charge of any medical diagnostic laboratory. After all, this was the practice of medicine in diagnostic laboratories. He had heard of a bright newly graduated candidate in another city who might be interested in the job. However, there were tales of him being an autocratic overbearing individual. The important thing to Leslie was that this individual fitted the requirements of the job at that time both politically as well as medically.

This man was quite a clever physician and he should have focused only on his medicine for he was an atrocious leader of people. Alas! Leadership of people, Leslie was beginning to believe, came as a gift with birth; although some principles of leadership in the co-operative world can be taught, true leaders were born with the skill. In the many clinical cases presented on sick patients, Les invariably felt an acute satisfaction at the end of his day, when there was tangible evidence of the patient responding favourably based on the findings of his laboratory. The contentment from this type of work was further rewarding when one shared the experience with others and when education was derived and shared.

As a boy, Leslie remembered the terrible stigma and fears in the general population of people who had 'consumption' or tuberculosis. As he developed in this field of Microbiology, he was convinced (even if his teachers 'pulled the undergraduate legs' about having a disease named after them, thus making them immortal), that there were no new diseases. There were just the same old diseases but the virulence of disease- causing bacteria had evolved into more critical stages of their biology. This fact is tempered by the fact that there has been better scientific investigative procedures and better understanding of pathogenicity of bacteria. This increase in understanding of the pathology of diseases and the way micro-organisms spread, the risk of more complicated damage to the human body if improperly treated made these old fashioned diseases, more sinister.

A simple sore throat is a good example to use for it is caused by a 'streptococcus' which can be treated by gargling with a strong solution of salt water in a normally healthy individual. There was a dye that was used to paint the insides of the mouths of children who had a continual carriage of the streptococcus in the days before antibiotics. The dye is used today in the laboratory on patients' specimens that are dried onto glass slides and examined under the microscope. It is called crystal violet which in the early days was found to kill the beta streptococcus harboring in the crevices of the mouth. In these folds within the mouth acting as a repository, the streptococcus that was not killed caused recurrent infections. This was a time when there was poor nutrition and good healthcare for the populations was still years away. The organisms either killed the individual when their resistance was low or returned again and again causing the same infections. The beta streptococcus or *Streptococcus pyogenes* is the primary cause of a sore throat. However, it also is responsible for such terrible diseases as scarlet fever, rheumatic fever and many other infectious disease syndromes.

History Continues:

As a child growing up during the war days and just after the end of the war, Leslie had seen boys with their blue mouths. Later on, the other aspects of a beta hemolytic streptococcus or a Group A streptococcus infection could be traced to the disease known as scarlet fever. Leslie was involved in culturing and isolating the streptococcus from septic abortion cases when he worked as an intern in the UK. Such abortions were done because of unwanted pregnancies. There were few agencies that would undertake abortions so many were commonly performed even in the late 1950s and early 1960s in dirty surroundings or in 'back rooms' by non-professional personnel. A great proportion of mothers of these risky operations ended up as tertiary cases, close enough to death because of septicemia (bacteria in the blood stream). The culprit in 99% of these cases was streptococcus type A (*Streptococcus pyogenes*). Indeed, it is known that a number of these women died as a result of these 'dirty handlers' and poor sanitary conditions.

This organism is easily treated in the modern late twentieth century medicine with a five-day course of penicillin but was now responsible for more than just a 'sore throat'. It was incriminated in 'septic abortions', scarlet fever, neonatal sepsis leading to death as the fetus passed from mother's birth canal. This was possible when mother was a carrier of the organism either in her throat, axilla, and vagina or from a host such as a healthcare handler. The toxin produced by this organism causes 'tissue hypersensitivity' in chronic urinary infection. The organism is rarely isolated from the urine of such patients for it is the toxin that does the damage. The toxin is detected in high serum levels when the patient's blood is drawn and allowed to clot. The pale straw- coloured serum seen above a blood clot is used by the labs to detect the toxin of the streptococcus.

One of the following damages, or 'sequelae' that a patient may incur from a case of whooping cough, is a hernia. This is caused by the physical stress of trying to expel the thick mucus formed in the upper respiratory tract. These examples show the power of increased scientific knowledge shared through publications by professional scientific and medical staff. In the medical diagnostic laboratories, there is a greater need than in any other disciplines to publish the shades of new knowledge uncovered daily by the lab scientists. It is the diagnostic labs that first pick up the causative infectious organisms and are the first to identify the causative agents.

Ever Heard of SARS?

One of the biggest medical managerial fiascos in this discipline was an outbreak of the disease called by the acronym 'SARS' or 'sudden acute respiratory syndrome'. There were about forty plus deaths in Toronto, Canada as a result of this 'new disease'. In some ways, it was the suddenness of the onset of the disease and the rapid mortality associated with this 'new 'disease that caused the furor. It was thought at first, to have come from the Far East countries such as China and Hong Kong which were incriminated as the source of this outbreak. A few Infectious Diseases specialists were called for an opinion by the provincial government but it was doubtful whether any medical microbiologists had been consulted.

The provincial government decided to make this a public health issue and the press made a 'meal of this outbreak' causing panic to all the citizens in the big city. The poorly informed and until then respected body known as the World Health Organization or WHO, placed Canada on a quarantine alert to the rest of the world. There were just a few cases and there were a few deaths but this occurs daily with ordinary diseases. There are more planes from these Far East countries landing in LA and other California airports than in Toronto. It is strange that no cases of SARS were reported in those states that take in more oriental travelers than any other countries of the world.

From then, public health directors, who had always lain low from public scrutiny making this government job, a very secure place to work, found themselves in the public light. They were found to be less than informed and made public gaffes. This changed when a very clever assistant, who had remained in the shadow of the bureaucracy, became Director of Public Health Services. She was given the task to keep both the public and government informed through the daily press and television interviews. She gave details of the spread of the disease and the control mechanisms that were in place to limit spread. This professional woman, who was of an East Indian race, was absolutely brilliant and was a role model to many young women in Canada. She died at a very young age and the city of Toronto lost a very valuable human asset.

However, there was not one microbiologist that was given the task to control the spread in the surrounding hospitals; in fact, the task was given to the administrators of hospitals. It was not given to the professional 'Infection Control Practitioners' who worked closely with the medical microbiologists and who were trained in the process of 'cohorting infected patients'. Rather it was given to the medically untrained administrators of hospitals, who had the power to close their doors to patients in need. Like the 'idiot savant', they arduously restricted access to hospitals and what a "meal" they made of this episode! This meant that they could increase their global budget from the provincial government for all inconveniences incurred. Their financial losses from these increased measures of safety due to the crisis would be taken care of by the provincial government. There was a need for more barrier nursing units and for a host of other reasons. The government had their proverbial 'balls in the grip' of some very cagey administrators whose major task was to get as much funding from the government. One would not say that this was done deliberately by all administrators but if ever there was a case of putting the cat among the pigeons, this was it.

Television Medical Doctors:

There are several television physicians and one of these individuals contracted the disease. This caused even more panic in the public, as well as among the governing administrators who were given the task of informing and handling the public.

The first thing that they did was to institute a ban on all visitors to hospitals. This is not necessarily a bad thing for Leslie believed that generally there is too much visiting by family and other non-related personnel in hospitals.

Leslie, now retired, was furious at the lack of professional microbiologists being involved throughout the country and enquired from the practicing microbiologists why they were not involved. He was told by their representative that they were never consulted by the government, their colleges, medical associations or the administrators of the hospitals. It is interesting to note that this 'television physician' was photographed by the television cameras regularly in the Microbiology laboratory but *'her lab coat is never buttoned up in front of her'* but open like those of the actors depicting shows in emergency medicine. She is never seen wearing gloves or a surgical mask and the lab staff pointed this out to Leslie commenting that *No wonder she caught the disease, she should show herself as a better example to the public. She took poor precaution to protect herself.*

This physician went on lecturing to many sympathetic emotionally charged audiences loaded with female activists groups. Canada has one of the finest medical services in the world which is available to every citizen from Toronto, Vancouver or Montreal to the outer northern regions of Nunavut and Tuktuyuktak. All its citizens get the same cost-effective medical services which is paid for by the taxes from its citizens. Canada has the largest land mass of any country with a small population of just over thirty million citizens but it has universal health coverage. Are there problems with the health services? You bet there are and Leslie just wanted the world to know that the WHO did a lousy job not taking into consideration that they were dealing with one of the finest health services in the world.

There is the wonderful agency in the USA known as the CDC – Center for Disease Control, who offered their services and assistance to Canada. They gave a clean bill of health showing that all that should have been done was done during the SARS crisis. They did not give an opinion on the follow-up throughout the health service. The hotels in Toronto instituted a tax to keep their premises clean and free of this epidemic. This tax was kept for almost a year after the outbreak of SARS, causing the expenses for many individuals and small businesses to be increased. This press-induced scenario also assisted in destroying the tourist industry with poorly publicized information. From his home office, Leslie thought that so many facts should have been considered and explained to the public but the press went for the cheap shots as usual, under their puritanical umbrella of the public's right to know.

For example, thousands of older and geriatric patients die yearly from respiratory distress and infections but no one bothered to mention this in the light of 42 dead patients with SARS. The use of special journals in medicine should be the source of information on the spread of disease not the poorly informed lay reporter whose motivation is to sell newspapers. This group of 'press reporters' borders on the unethical as far as Leslie was concerned for they cause panic with their limited knowledge and great skill for sensationalism. This criticism also applies to the television reporters as well, for they now use their position to bring the economies of the world to a standstill with their continuous reporting, really harping on the world's economies, in this recessionary period of time in 2009. The reason is invariably the same which is lack of in depth knowledge of the subject covered and sugar coated with their need for sensationalism, under the veneer of a camera induced sincerity. Duh!

Ethics and Public Need to Know:
When the (mis)/uninformed reporters take valuable scientific facts and mangle them to produce sensational stories, there should be laws or policies by the print media to prevent

this from happening. Leslie was terrified of the way the press convey details that are of medical and scientific value to the lay public. In fact, these organizations, if they must report should hire or use professionals to do this work along with a ghost writer. The public's right to know is often over played. There is a lot of information that tired depressed workers who come home from a hard days' work, do not wish to know. Highly sensational and depressing panic-driven stories of what has happened in the world or is happening in a neighborhood far away are the least interesting to them. Yes, there should be a free press but that freedom comes with a great responsibility. It must be ethical for much of what is reported as news today borders on the unethical, in Leslie's opinion. The public can indeed turn off the channel but when all the channels combine to have commercials and sensational stories all broadcast at exactly at the same time, then choice is taken away from the consumer.

The Case History:

It was well past 7:00 pm as Leslie was closing up his office and all the lab staff had long left to go home for the day. He turned off the lights in his cluttered office and went through the dark lab to do a last check, when he saw the light on in the Infectious Diseases physician's office. He went in to check and saw a very worried ID Physician, who looked up as he entered the office. "Hello I did not know that anyone was still in the department," he greeted ID.

"Oh Hi Les, I am working on a case that has just come in and it looks like this man will not live through the night," ID replied.

Leslie then asked, "Is there anything that I can do to assist?"

"No Les, I understand that you already looked at the ZN Smear this afternoon and verified the organism from the lymph gland as likely to be infected with tuberculosis."

Leslie remembered the Charge technologist, Sandy bringing the smear for him to review under the microscope to verify the staff findings and to sign off on the report. He thought that happened over five days ago. The staff had seen the red rod-like forms indicative of the tubercle bacillus known biologically as *'Mycobacterium tuberculosis'*.

"Oh! Yes I did have a look at it and I am convinced that it is *M. tuberculosis var hominis."*

The ID looked up at him and said, "Look Les, I know that you have a lot of experience but how are you so certain that it is the 'hominis strain" from the microscopy?"

The hominis strain meant that it was indicative of a virulent form that caused the scourge which killed many around the world in the year's pre-1940 and throughout history. Les was quick off the mark in saying, "I have seen the 'cording' phenomenon typical of this organism. I can get the slide out of my office, if you would like to have a gander under the microscope."

ID just quietly sat down and quickly told Les the following, "Would you like to see this patient with me, I am going upstairs? I have placed him in an isolation room."

Leslie declined but followed up with, "The Bactec instrument tagged it culture positive two days ago and at your request we sent it to PHL who did some preliminary susceptibility testing. They found it to be highly resistant to four of the major anti-tubercular drugs. But surely these drugs can all be administered together to get an additive effect and there is a good chance of synergy."

Change in Therapy:

ID looked up from the computer, where he could get the Medline to find the latest publication in any medical discipline and on any subject, and replied, "Yes that is why I came back tonight. As you know the regimen for treatment of patients with tuberculosis is to place them on one drug and look for a response. Well, I had him first on streptomycin and the lymphatic gland under his axilla (arm pit) has remained like small pods hanging down. I added INH and still no response, then a third and fourth for these drugs have an additive effect. There is no cross-inhibition between them. The patient did not improve and he is getting worse. I am afraid that we will lose him if there is no let up in the disease."

The Value of a Medical Seminar at International Conventions/Congress:

After a pause this pensive ID colleague, who stared at the ground unseeingly, replied, "I came to check on him and his glands are even worse. I was about to do a Medline search to see what the latest therapy is or whether I had missed something in the treatment strategy."

Leslie asked, "Why do you not use that new drug that the Greek medical scientists used to treat their TB patients? Do you recall the meeting we went to last month in New York, at the World Trade Center? It was chaired by Dr Neu. It was a symposium on ciprofloxacin." ID stood up suddenly and stared at Les.

"Gosh, I had completely forgotten about that symposium. Thanks Les; I think I have the article in my filing cabinet. I completely forgot about that meeting. I wonder if the pharmacy has this drug in stock."

Les volunteered, "You trace up the details of that drug and I will call Chris, director of pharmacy at his home and you can have a chat with him."

Les contacted Chris and passed him over to ID, who wished to know if the drug was available. He wanted to have the approval to use this new but very expensive drug. Leslie left for home as the two men discussed the need to have this drug available immediately.

ID, still on the telephone, waved and said a happy, "Thanks." The next morning Leslie called his colleague at the local Public Health Lab and asked if any more anti-tubercular drugs for our strain of TB were tested and if he had any results. His colleague said that he had to send it off to Toronto for he has never seen such resistance to such high levels of drug as he had with this isolate that Les had sent to him. He said that he will trace up the results and try and get back to him some time that day. Les asked, before putting down the telephone, if he would add ciprofloxacin to the testing regimen. His colleague said that he will get onto it immediately.

It was well past 5 pm when Les had a call from his colleague at the public health lab and it was terrific news. Les paged ID to come down to the lab. They met and Leslie showed him the results that he had written down. This tubercle was resistant to the highest levels of the 7 drugs used to treat tuberculosis patients. The good news was that this strain was highly sensitive to ciprofloxacin on which ID had placed the patient the night before having had the approval of Clinical pharmacist. The next day ID came to the lab to fetch Leslie and they went up to see the patient, who was a new arrival to Canada from Cambodia. He looked emaciated and small as he was standing looking through his window at the sunshine outside.

ID and Leslie masked, gowned and put on gloves before they went in to see the man. He raised his arms and Les could see the shrinkage of the brown-skinned glands in his armpits where they appeared as slightly raised bumps. ID looked at his glands in the groin, turned around to Les and described what it had looked like just 24 hours earlier. After 5 days on a regimen of combined drug therapy, he withdrew all of them and just used the single drug known as ciprofloxacin.

Five days later ID released the patient with a course of the new drug but there was a precaution from the Greek scientists on the use of this drug. They had reported that the drug should only be used once for the TB developed resistance rapidly. The hospital infection control nurses and the barrier head nurse were pleased at this patient's response. The barrier room was cleaned according to the protocol and left to aerate for two days. This would have been a normal happy ending for what followed was that the public health inspector would go to the patient's home to inspect and examine the other family members. He would take the case history of the other members of the family and medically check out the rest of the family for tuberculosis. ID received the letters associated with the public health follow-up and to all intents and purposes this was a closed case from the health centre's perspective.

Grandfather Missed:

Four months later the same patient returned with just as severe an infection as when he had originally been admitted. Infectious diseases practice is similar to the work done by a detective for there was a need to know why he had been re-infected after he had returned back to his job in a bakery. Leslie and ID combined their contacts and called in the Public Health personnel. They were asked by ID to return back to the home that had a mother/wife of the ill patient and two children but this time they found out that there was a grandfather upstairs who was bed-ridden. They did not know of this individual on their initial visit and so missed the carrier of this resistant tubercle organism. The whole family was treated including the re-infected father. The grandfather died soon afterwards of an overwhelming tuberculosis infection, the isolate did not respond to the anti-tubercle drugs tested in the laboratory. The house was apparently well cleaned under the supervision of a public health nurse with some input by the hospital infection control officer.

Publication of the Case History:

Leslie's colleague at the Public Health Lab was Dr Abdul who had a great deal of experience with tuberculosis when he worked in the Middle East as well as in Pakistan. They met and decided to write up the case history of this first truly multiple resistant *Mycobacterium tuberculosis*. The literature research was done but Dr Abdul said that he knew resistance was developing in the poorer countries but no one had documented these facts and this was back in 1987. The Canadian Society of Microbiologists was publishing their new journal and Les sent the manuscript to the editor, who returned the article saying that *there was nothing new in the treatment of tuberculosis and while it was an interesting case, this will not be a problem in Canada and she would not publish the article.*

Les and Dr Abdul sent the article untouched to the national technology journal which published the case history without changing a word. The response from the numerous workers in the smaller community hospitals was unbelievable for they said that this article had put them on alert. In the five years following this first recorded isolate from our Cambodian patient, due to the increasing number of AIDS patients and immigration from the poorer countries, the cases of multi-resistant tuberculosis have increased nationally and internationally to frightening levels. Leslie's colleague from the UK who worked with WHO in Africa, warned that multi-resistance in tuberculosis was on the increase (1992) and it would soon reach the northern countries including Canada and the USA. Before he left to go on sabbatical leave, Leslie learned that the number of resistant cases of tuberculosis had increased twenty-fold in the American continent and it continues to rise.

The workers in the field were not alerted to the possibility of such an old disease coming back into their healthy population with such a vengeance. It is also the arrogance and naivety of the specialists in the field who did not take a living biological entity such as the TB organism as a serious contender in their practice. Another important factor is their deceptive overwhelming belief in antibiotics to kill all organisms, not keeping in mind that one day an organism may be very sensitive to an antibiotic but on the next round be resistant. It has been known for years by epidemiologists that in every population of 10 million organisms there will be over 100 – 1000 that will be resistant. Antibiotics may kill the majority but then they will select out the resistant strains, such is the dynamics of bacterial populations. Their generation time varies from minutes to a few hours, so their ability to mutate genetically and resist a poison such as an antibiotic, can occur rapidly, relative to the human life span.

Wealth is what is keeping Canada, Europe and the USA from being overrun by these common diseases. Wealth allows these countries to obtain drugs fairly easily and to have stocks in hand that are available at the physician's whim. This scenario is changing for the big drug companies who spend millions of dollars to produce the new drugs are no longer making the profit for their shareholders. They also lose their rights to the patent of antibiotics or other drugs after a shorter period of time thereby allowing the generic companies to reproduce the drugs cheaper and to take over the market. These market changes along with a complete lack of applied knowledge and respect for the microbes spell danger. If a single staphylococcus has the genetic capability of producing over a million inducible enzymes then it must follow that all drugs will eventually succumb to these powerful microscopic life forms. Approximately one billion cells make up a human body but that body has over ten billion bacteria in and on it, which should make everyone in the pharmaceutical industry think on their future.

Strategy:

The armamentarium of antimicrobial drugs against the common infectious agents is being greatly reduced as multi-resistance develops. The best example is the organism that causes upper respiratory infections such as a *Streptococcus* in the throat or in pneumonia, a deep chest infection, which is due to the pneumococcus. These illnesses are quietly becoming resistant to standard antibiotic treatment. Young mothers are getting more biased information from their women's magazines, the newspaper health sections and the internet. They go to their physicians demanding immediate treatment for their children and the tired GP dishes out antibiotics because of the parental demands. Usually, these tots get their first viral and bacterial infections from their schoolmates and antibiotics do not treat viral infections.

All that normally healthy children need when they contract a sore throat is to be kept warm, nourished, lots of fluid and an opportunity to rest and allow their bodies to build up antibodies to their silent microbial companions. The scientific and medical reasoning is that a sore throat is caused by a virus. This is first observed as lethargy, quieting of behaviour, lack of purposeful interest and physical restlessness. There might be a runny nose of clear fluid but warmth, lots of fluids including warm soups and bed rest is the first line of treatment. At this stage antibiotics are useless and dangerous for it can begin the process of bacterial resistance in the normal organisms' resident in our gut and mouths.

If the sore throat persists, there is an elevated temperature followed by swollen glands in the neck, then it is time to see the GP. The GP should first take a swab for bacterial culture before initiating an analgesic to control the fever and an antibiotic treatment to kill the causative organism. Parents should avoid panic and should refrain from demanding that antibiotics be given immediately. There is concern by many GPs in such instances of mothers' rights that they tend to treat the mothers keeping them quiet by administering antibiotics for the sick children.

Monologue:

There is one more bit of information that the health services along with the public health authorities need to follow up on and that is our food source. Just before the venerable Dr

Gutch died, Les and his Chief were having a telephone chat. Dr Gutch advised Les, *"Look Les, you are still in touch with the lab folks, tell them that the resistance in bacteria is coming from their foods especially their meat"* He is quite correct for the farmers use antibiotics with impunity, thanks to savvy sales personnel of the major pharmaceutical companies. There is a need to measure the drug levels in our animals which would eventually find its way onto our tables as our food. Antibiotics given to our animals remain circulating in their tissues long after the company's direction of being safe to sacrifice or butcher. This phenomenon is known as the 'residual drug effect' in humans for a percentage of the drug binds to the proteins of the animal. It is only removed after months free of any drug. If such a treated animal is sacrificed before the drug is excreted or detached from its binding site then it may be destroyed during cooking.

However, many folks enjoy a medium to rare steak, indeed many of the meats such as lamb or steak tartare of any kind is usually totally uncooked. Antibiotics are transferred either directly from our meat, other foods or through the antibiotic resistant bacteria. They enter the human body daily and that does not include directly from kitchen cutting boards, dirty hands and utensils. The normal gut bacteria of the animals ought to be checked for antibiotic resistance just to trace the resistance that is developing in human patients and hospitals. Bacteria do pass along their genetic traits sexually as well as through their normal means of replication.

Les has repeatedly said to colleagues and to groups of people that they should learn to live with their bugs for they are ubiquitously present in our environment and in food products. The multi-resistance seen in the common bacterial flora on and in the human body will continue for it has come from the over-usage of antibiotics in our food sources and are the same used to cure animals or to help them gain weight.

The Sobriquet of Arrogance

The Trial:

Les, in one of his more thoughtful and contemplative periods, has wondered about destiny, luck, 'right place at the right time' and the old Shakespearean poetic line in *Julius Caesar,* his great stage play that states, *"There is a tide in the affairs of Man, which taken at the flood leads onto fortune,"* and the reality of ordinary men such as he. Is there indeed a 'destiny that shapes human lives' until the end? While not being a practicing Christian, Les began to wonder in his more mature years whether he has missed it all. In spite of himself, has God looked after him throughout his life? This was not a result of being scared or of facing old age and his final destiny. No, this thought came to him repeatedly, for as a scientist he has always been prepared to die.

His dilemma is why for some at an early age and for others a sustained sentence? Of course, all animals and people die is an indisputable fact as do all plants and all bacteria eventually die, so all living things have a designated shelf life. Dying held no fear in his mind. His reason for this luxurious contemplation at his retirement age, is his wonder as to why certain events happened to him at the right time throughout his limited life span and more so throughout his career? Many will say that this idle speculation is blatant arrogance and aligns itself in the belief in 'luck' and spiritualism influencing the destiny of humans.

As a medical lab scientist intern in the UK, Leslie had the unique opportunity to take over the running of a small hospital lab at St Nicks Hospital in Woolwich for a month. First of all, he was fully qualified although he still had his final examination to do that summer. He was a senior intern for he had his intermediate examination which he completed in two years rather than three which was the standard time. A number of circumstances occurred at the same time leading to a shortage of senior staff in this small hospital that was one of a group of over 10 or 12 in the Woolwich Group of Hospitals. He would be under the direct tutelage of the Microbiologist Pathologist, Dr Ken Sumner, the second in command of this South Eastern London Hospital Group. *"Now look here, young man you will be left on your own for most of the day, do you understand!"* said the smiling buck-toothed, red-faced Englishman. He had white hair and all his jackets had dandruff on the shoulders. It was no different on that day. His dark blue jacket showed the white glistening speckles, which looked like fairy dust as if Tinkerbelle had blessed him. Under his suit jacket which he wore every day, was invariably a white shirt, with a crumpled tie and ashes, from the ever present cigarette which hung from his lips most of the day, matching the dandruff over the rest of the jacket.

Smiling broadly, Leslie raised his right hand to his forehead in mock salute, "Yes Sir! I shall be here every minute of the day, Sir!" Removing his hand, he stood in mock attention. Les was secretly enjoying this opportunity to do all the bench-work in the absence of Alan, who was the Chief of the small combined Biochemistry and Microbiology Departments. He had gone off on a much needed trip with his family to Somerset on the West Coast of England, for three weeks vacation. Before he left, Les and Alan had gone over the routine and Alan cautioned, "Do not let the docs walk in and demand that you drop everything you are doing to look at a specimen they had urgently collected."

"Yes Alan, I will do as I have seen you do, which is to look them in the eye and say sorry I cannot do that. I shall then suggest that they call Dr Sumner for a consultation or to get his approval to leave what you are doing. Right?" Leslie responded again with a bright smile and a wink. He was enjoying this occasion immensely for he had grown up under the guidance of some of the finest human beings who were in practice in this profession and he was very fortunate to have met them in his lifetime. They were his tutors, his colleagues and that gave him a confidence based on their trust.

Alan's bright blue eyes lit up. "Saucy little bugger! How did you notice this escape? I have taken years to come up with this plan to keep unavoidable interruptions from delaying my work," he responded equally delighted.

Les retorted, "I can also mutter under my breath - *Piss off you silly bastard and leave me alone.* Hello how can I assist you?" Les continued, "You see Al, I have been practicing in the event that such an occasion should ever have arisen."

Alan burst out in loud laughter just as Mr. Bowden entered into the room staring at his next in command, his face also cracking into a smile. "Alan, what the heck is going on here?" Alan could hardly contain himself but through his red face and spittle he told the Chief, Mr. Bowden, what had just conspired between us. Les had turned his back in mock comedian timing for he had them both laughing early that morning. The Chief also bellowed in laughter and they both turned around to see Les with a slight smile about to address them.

"Well Alan, I will do exactly as I have seen you do with the exception of the flirting deep look that you give to Valerie, when she comes into the lab to ask you to do a sperm count on a patient. What do you whisper to her to bring out that red flush on her cheeks?"

Amid a roar of laughter, the door opened and in came the old Mrs. Kelly, who looked after the wash-up room and the autoclaving of all the old smelly micro-cultures, but she also made tea and coffee for us chaps in the labs.

"What are you gentlemen laughing about so early in the morning?" she quietly asked as she laid down the tray with our much needed coffee. She came promptly every day at 10 am with coffee and every afternoon at 3 pm with tea.

"Mrs. Kelly, you must look after this young man when I am away for he will get into trouble," Alan replied to her awakening smirk. Mrs. Kelly usually remained quiet most of the day until one went into her work area then she was very accommodating with whatever the task one had to do in her room.

"Well if you ask me he should be in more trouble for he is young and very handsome. If I were a young lassie today, he would never get away. Actually he could put his shoes under my bed any day." She winked and turned red in her protruding cheeks that closed her wicked eyes when she laughed as she moved quickly through the swing doors of the lab.

Again loud laughter as Alan gleefully admonished, "I do not know if I should leave you both alone for you will just encourage him. Anyway keep him away from Valerie!"

She looked seriously at him and then said, "Why should I? You are married with kids and Valerie is unattached except for a lousy boyfriend and young Leslie is also single. They should get together and have some fun." With that she left the batwing doors swinging. Alan, Mr. Bowden and Leslie could not stop laughing as they washed their hands and moved over to the tray of coffees. Alan sat on the high chair and began the ritual of folding his own cigarette by licking a strip of paper, filling it with a bit of shredded tobacco, slipping the folded open cigarette onto a wheel edge of his tobacco tin and out came a whole sealed cigarette. He lit and drew heavily while his right hand felt the tray for his cup. Leslie had witnessed this ritual so many times as he sat opposite this very clever lab scientist with a happy and casual approach to life as he sipped his coffee.

Alan broke the silence saying, "You are a great fellow Les. This is the first time I have heard Mrs. Kelly say anything saucy in all the years that I have worked here. I really think that she likes you." Leslie always took his time sipping his hot coffee and dared not move to handle anything he had started to attend to. This was sacrilege to the British tea-break rules. There were jokes to tell, or discussions on what was on television the night before or an anecdote to relate. Little did he know that the new world order would never be as wonderful as this? He had tried over his years to bring about an atmosphere of happiness in his labs in Canada and maybe in a majority of the time, he might have been partially successful. It was never as humorous or as clever as when he was a student in England. Those days of intense learning, of little food and few luxuries, combined to make his internship the only focus and he loved every minute of his training. He could hardly wait to go to the labs on a morning. In some ways, he almost disliked the weekends but it was the time for him to 'swot' and retain new jokes for the Monday coffee break.

Alan never told Les what he had said to Valerie when she brought in a semen specimen for analysis. This test had to be done immediately when the specimen was still warm and fresh. This was the only time that he had to leave whatever he was doing to attend to this test request from the obstetrics and gynecology specialists. When this beautiful blond with curly hair large blue eyes came into the lab as they were sipping their coffee, Alan stopped her, to mention that from next week Les would be in charge. She looked at Les, with flushed cheeks smiled and said, "Congratulations, Les! Will you be doing the sperm counts as well?"

Leslie was also smiling and replied, "Yes, thanks Val but I need to know what Alan says to you to bring those red cheeks up every time." She stared at him and blushed even more, if that was possible.

"I thought that you would be better than 'im but you're going to be worse, 'ent you?"

Both Alan and Les again laughed and saw the batwing doors flap for a second time that morning. Les had his notes from Alan, who had dictated the routine of which he was very much aware but he felt that he should have them for reference. Essentially, if he got into difficulty he was to call Dr Sumner. He was told that he should leave the good doctor to do the contacting with the wards, the nurses and physicians. However, Dr Sumner who had met with Les earlier that week had looked at Les with a serious grin and said, "Do not call me for any technical problems unless you have read all these books on the shelf," pointing to the floor-to-ceiling library of books present in the main lab.

"Yes Sir, I will not dream of disturbing you during the daytime," Les again saucily replied.

"What is that you said?" shouted the smiling red-faced Dr Sumner and continued, "Look here Laddie! I shall be covering the other 10 hospitals in this group, for both Dr Williams and Dr Gorman will be away. It is I, alone and you alone here to keep the South East Group of Hospitals afloat in the absence of the other lucky bastards who have taken all this time off. So be as smart as you like but do not call me unless there is a catastrophe."

They both laughed good naturedly as Leslie put on his clean white coat that Mrs. Kelly had brought in that Monday morning.

Solo Performance:

Les smiled to himself as he unloaded his Petri dishes, placed the urines for analysis into the refrigerator and filled up the Gram stain bottles. He sat down with a sheaf of requisitions from physicians both within the hospital, as well as a number from outside physicians or general practitioners. He carefully placed the Petri dishes on top of each requisition with the same lab number to ensure that all the specimens were there and that each specimen had been cultured the night before according to their specimen type and clinical diagnosis. He quietly removed the plates into a complete stack as he read the cultures. There were no unusual organisms other than the common *E.coli, Proteus sp, Staph aureus* and enterococci. He carefully picked off the bacterial colonies on which he would perform antibiotic susceptibility testing, added them to a labeled broth and placed them into the incubator for four hours. Just in time for Mrs. Kelly had brought in his coffee.

He thanked her and went over to wash his hands. He set up the microscope and placed his coffee on the bench and so in the absence of everyone, he began to sip the hot coffee intermittently. He examined the Gram stains on the specimens, which he had just read the cultures. This gave him an opportunity to relate and compare his microscopic findings with what grew on the Petri dishes. He could see the benefit of this type of process especially when he did both the microscopy and reading of the cultures. This did not happen when other staff was present, for some read the microscopy while others read the cultures. His training was being enhanced with the routine challenges of every different difficulty he had to solve on his own every day.

At around 6 pm on his third day in charge (he liked to remain late to read the microscopy first before reading the cultures the next day), he was visited by the boss. Dr Sumner barged through the batwing doors and looked at Les with the usual red face, protruding teeth and a grin. "Aha! Cannot complete the day's work in time, eh?" he blurted out.

Leslie stood up and smiled. "No Sir! I have completed the day's work, would you like to check it out?"

"Ha! Always an answer, smarty pants. Yes I would. Have you kept the Petri dishes from today?" Dr Sumner asked as he put on his white lab coat. He sat on the chair next to the main reading bench and Les drew up a chair next to him. He passed the cultures over to him, which he had kept from the mornings reading. He held a well organized clipboard of requisitions and placed the numbered Petri dish cultures with the requisitions. Dr Sumner looked at the plates rapidly and after about five minutes he pushed everything aside, next to the stack of Petri dishes that were in chronological order, and smiled as he lit a cigarette. He looked at the smiling Les who had begun to put away the plates and requisitions when Dr Sumner said, "I am satisfied with your work, Les. We knew that you could do it.

Alan said that we should leave you alone to get on with the running of the lab here. Well done, Lad!"

Leslie did not smile or try to pass one of his smart-assed comments for it was not often that he received any praise for the work that he did. In fact, when he thought more about verbal support, this was the first time that a father-like figure such as Dr Sumner had ever passed a comment that was positive and encouraging during his limited working life. "Thank you Dr Sumner, I would never want to disappoint you in any way with my work. I really love what I do and it is never a hardship for me to stay and get my work organized for the next day. In fact, I almost hate leaving this old place at evenings," he honestly replied. Then, as is the British way, to give with one hand and to take away suddenly with the other, Dr Sumner replied: "Look Les, you need to leave on time. You need to get yourself a girlfriend go out and have some fun."

"That's OK boss, when I find a rich millionairess then I will go out," he wickedly responded. His never wanted to disappoint his boss but he did when he failed for he did fail his final exam at his first attempt because of a practical glitch and he had to swallow his pride and face this gentle person who had given him such great training.

"Look after yourself old son!" Dr Sumner turned around and left for home. It was then that Les realized that this gentleman worked the five area hospitals in the group by himself and must have been quite tired at the end of the day. He made time to check up on his young grad who was doing the senior scientist job all by himself. This was a time that Les would never want to fail in his duties and he wanted to be squeaky clean in everything that he did for the mere joy of it. This type of practical training still has merit and the world would get better workers in all fields of endeavor. If the practical was taught with the theory rather than the separation of the two that has evolved, which keeps the students out of the job market, then there would be a better trained individual.

How Long Can Joy Last?

In the third week of his enjoyable control of the whole laboratory with no support from anyone, he still thought of work as fun. It was fun to produce the many reports when he entered every morning identifying a *Salmonella* or a case of gonorrhoeae along with the many 'sparrows or me too' organisms. He had taken a page out of Alan's book and had the beautiful Valerie in stitches with his early morning jokes. As he laid out his plates and patients' requisitions, he noticed a number of swabs from throat, nose, rectal areas, ears and the skin areas around the genitalia - all from one ward.

He counted the number of different children's names that numbered ten, all from the pediatric ward generating over 50 samples. These specimens had arrived the day before but as he worked on batches of samples during the day, he did not see the connection until he was about to read the Petri dishes of all the work the next day. It was customary to place similar specimens together then to read them as a group. He had no idea how this unwritten protocol had evolved but it made a great deal of sense to him now that he was reading all specimens.

Problem Uncovered:

He thought he would begin with this big batch of swabs and without a word he saw that all the cultures had heavy growths of *Staphylococcus aureus*. This organism is the commonest cause of patient infections and acquired hospital infections. His slide testing revealed the pathogenic strain was present in all and he had isolated it from the whole batch. This allowed him to make a list of the patients noting their names, their sex, the ward, the specimen type and the amount of growth. He called the ward and asked to speak to the head nurse.

"Hello, this is Sister Mary-Anne, what are the lab results that you have for me?" came the heavy Irish accent.

Les began carefully, "Good Morning Sister, this is Les in charge of the Laboratory. I have found that there are a number of your patients' specimens all carrying Staphylococcus aureus and felt that I should notify you as soon as possible."

Sister replied, "Are you a new pierson (person)? Where is Mr. Alan Holbrook, he normally calls with the results?"

"Mr. Holbrook is away Sister, on vacation and I am his understudy intern here," Les responded.

He had heard, over many coffee breaks that no one crosses the Sisters in charge of the hospital wards. That included their charges the nurses, the doctors on staff not even the consultants who came from the Harley Street Private Clinics weekly or monthly depending on the need.

"Ah! Mr. Les, then you are a student here, are you not?" she asked in a firm voice.

Les quickly replied, "Yes Sister I am a resident here and have been placed in charge by Dr Sumner."

"Where is Dr Sumner?" she asked abruptly. Leslie was getting a bit testy at this time for all he was trying to do was to pass on the information on the suspicious number of patients with this dangerous pathogen on her ward.

He replied tersely, "Dr Sumner is covering the Woolwich Group of Hospitals because the three other pathologists are all off for seminars and vacation. He is terribly busy but I can call around if you would prefer speaking to him directly."

"You do that Mr. Les and have him call me directly with the lab results," she answered in her firm but very Irish twang. Les had hoped that he would never have to call Dr Sumner for the next week until the staff came back from their vacations. However, he went in to the office to see the blond secretary, Valerie, who looked at him and immediately stopped smiling and asked, "What is wrong Les?"

He looked at her with a sheepish grin and said, "I think that I just blew it with a Sister on the pediatric ward."

She stood up suddenly. Her blue eyes showed shock and asked, "Not sister Mary-Anne?"

"Yes! Is she the terror of the ward?" enquired the now worried Les.

Valerie smiled, "She is not as bad as the others. What did you say to her?" Valerie asked.

Les spelled out what he had done, justifying himself for what he felt was the correct thing to do. The lovely Valerie smiled and quietly said, "Leave this with me. I will call around to find Dr Sumner. It will be difficult to know which hospital he will be at but I have a good idea where he normally begins his rounds. I need some time. I will ask him to call me and I will tell him what you have done. I will also tell him that Sister would like to speak to him directly." Les felt a great weight taken off his shoulders. He smiled awkwardly and thanked Valerie profusely. "Do not worry Les you owe me and I will collect," she teased. Les was tempted to say he was not into loose sex with strange women but he held his tongue until she did what she had promised.

Professional Support:

It was about mid-morning just as he was about to sit down for a break, when Mrs. Kelly came in with the coffee but she had two cups on the tray. She said the usual, "Good morning and I brought one cup for Dr Sumner. I saw him driving in just now. I thought that he would like a cup on this early morning. He never comes in when he is on hospital rounds unless there is an emergency."

Les felt some more relief as he had written out the list of patients' names to which he had added more information. He quickly pulled out the relevant plates into a stack for reading just so that the boss can have a quick review. There was nothing difficult about isolating the staphylococcus and to do the first screening test. By this time he also had the antibiotic sensitivity tests available so he began looking at a comparison of their patterns of resistance.

Every first year technology student knew how to do this test. He began to have second thoughts as to why this group of patients from one ward had crossed his mind and why he had brewed up a 'storm in a tea cup'. He geared himself for a quiet but firm rebuke even a reprimand by the normally tolerant Dr Sumner, for taking on such a Sister and inferring that 'her ward' had a problem. His self confidence plunged and he felt terrible for the next hour. What made it worse was that he could not understand why Dr Sumner had not come into the lab immediately, for a long time had elapsed and he had made no contact and no appearance. He had waited anxiously and sipped his coffee which had begun to cool off. He continuously looked through the window at Dr Sumner's old white Ford parked in the slot reserved for the Pathologists.

He completed reading all the Petri plates, finished putting all the antibiotic susceptibility tests up for the morning. He made copy slant cultures of the staphylococcus and placed them into the incubator, as these will act as a stock if further tests needed to be done. The benches were clear except for the 'questionable pile' waiting to be examined when suddenly his quietude was shattered by a great number of voices outside the laboratory coming along the corridor. The din was increasing in volume when the batwing doors flew open and Dr Sumner, two male residents and a Sister in a dark blue uniform and bright blue eyes came into his small laboratory room. Dr Sumner was explaining something or replying to a question from one of the senior residents when they stopped in the middle of the room. Les stood quietly in the background facing their little circle, his back against the work bench.

After his explanation to his entourage, Dr Sumner drew on his cigarette in the middle of the group who had all eyes on him. He whirled around suddenly and said, "Good Morning Les, have you got the requisitions on these patients for me?" Les said that he had and he had a summary on a sheet of paper on his clipboard, which he handed to Dr Sumner. The doctor turned directly and winked in his direction. "Thanks son, get me the requisitions as well, will you old man?" he briskly asked. Les withdrew the fifty requisitions, which he had placed in chronological order onto the clipboard.

He did not have them typed as yet. He wanted to send out a preliminary report but Valerie was too busy with assisting him, he explained quietly to Dr Sumner. "Thanks Les, you can give these to Valerie and ask her to drop everything that she is doing and make a preliminary report on each patient. Tell her to bring them in for me to sign," Dr Sumner asked politely. Turning to his group he said, "Come into my office next door" and lead the group through the batwing doors.

Consultant as Tutor:

As this little group moved into the office next to the main lab, Les hurried to tell Valerie what Dr Sumner wanted and to thank her again for her assistance. He began to feel that there was some order taking place and his carrying of all the information which caused this situation was now being shared by his mentor and boss. This is a time when one feels the need for supportive surroundings and to have the team of professional colleagues assisting when the occasion arises.

She smiled and said, "I will get on with it right away and bring them into his office when I am finished." Les hurried back to the lab feeling a bit better but nervous for he still thought he had put the old man into a difficult position to explain why this 'upstart' of an intern would have the audacity to call a Sister about a possible problem on her protective territory.

As he entered the protection of his lab, now free of all personnel, there was a loud bark from the pathologist's office as Dr Sumner called loudly, "Les are you there? Please come in. Can you bring that cold cup of coffee for me?"

He was taken by surprise and replied as loudly, "Yes I am Sir. I am coming right away." Les hurried with the cup of coffee with the two spoons of sugar but it was cold. He entered to see two residents standing backs against the wall near the window, Sister sitting in front of Dr Sumner's desk and Dr Sumner who had his back to the door as Les entered. He placed the coffee in front of Dr Sumner, who stood up abruptly and said, putting an arm around Les' shoulder, "Let me introduce you Mr. Les Paul, one of our brightest interns that we have seen around here in many years of training lab scientist students. He is not that inexperienced for he is a WHO-trained Malaria Scientific Officer from Trinidad in the Caribbean and he has been with us for the past four years."

To say that Les was uncomfortable was to say the least for he could feel the hair rise on the back of his neck and head and itchiness on his back, indicating a rash of nervousness. The two residents came forward briskly and actively with hands out saying, "Hello Les, good to meet you." Les shook their hands. Sister did not rise but met his eyes.

"Aye! Sorry for the mix-up of your name but it is customary to use the surname, Mr. Paul, when you call with lab reports." She smiled and Les mumbled an apology to her.

He moved closer to the sitting Dr Sumner for protection, who was sipping his cold coffee. "Yes Sister, Les was quite shrewd to make the observation among so many specimens. This situation should really be handled by the large centralized lab on Shooters Hill Road."

She was astonished and said, "Dr Sumner, I would not wish the larger laboratory to come over here and tell us poor community hospitals what to do!" Her sarcasm and dislike of the larger hospital's intrusion into the workings of St Nicks was like a personal blow to her pride.

The Plan:
Les stood back against the wall for support behind Dr Sumner's chair facing the group. Dr Sumner suddenly spun his chair and asked Les directly, "What is the next move in this possible epidemiologic problem, Les?" This was dissertation

of the best order and this is what attracted Les to his colleagues for they asked him questions daily and he had to cough up the answers. It was why he had improved so much at classes and held the first place in the weekly exams for many months. His material was always reviewed.

Les looked at Dr Sumner then at the others and answered, "I have made copies of the cultures to send to the main lab for verification. Tomorrow I will have the antibiotic patterns and will document the antibiogram to see if there is commonality of a pattern. I would suggest Sir, that maybe 'phage typing' be done by a reference lab if the antibiogram is the same. This will verify that it is the same strain of staphylococcus biologically and maybe see if it is one of the epidemic strains phage types 80 or 81 that are infecting patients on the floors. It would also follow that all staff on that floor should be screened for carriage of the staphylococcus and to find out whom the carriers are or if it is one individual." He was stopped short by Sister.

Sisters Pride:

"Are you suggesting that all my staff succumb to being screened, Mr. Paul?" The Irish terror stood up when she asked the question. Les' retort came back very quickly, "If all the steps I outlined are followed, then you will have little choice if you want to prevent future spread of the infection to other wards and you want to have it stopped, do we not Sister?"

"How dare you Sir, suggest taking my choice away!" came the outburst from the Irish terror.

Dr Sumner stood up and said, "Really Sister, I know that you do not have the staffing to swab all your workers but these two residents would be only too glad to do this task, would you not gentlemen?" The two residents, caught by surprise nodded in a mumbled affirmative then said that they would have no problems taking the swabs. He continued, "Les is quite correct but let us take one step at a time and not start a panic. My first concern is the status of the patients, our babies, how are they Sister? If there is any sign of sepsis I would like to have blood cultures taken so watch their temperatures carefully gentlemen." With that last suggestion he stood up and as if by some unspoken signal, they all left the room pleasantly shaking hands and nodding with smiles, except Sister. They left for the ward led by this indomitable Irish commander.

As they left the room and Les went into the lab, he was followed by a smiling Dr Sumner. As they went through the batwing doors Dr Sumner began to laugh loudly, "So you took on the dragon of a Sister, eh Les?"

Les bowed his head for he had been exonerated by his chief. He looked up to see the encouraging smile of his boss and mentor and sheepishly said, "I am truly sorry Sir. I really thought I was doing the correct thing by alerting the floor of so many patients with the same bacterium."

He was cut off by the tolerant voice, "I know, I know, Les. You did what you knew was the right thing to do and I support your initiative. Secondly, you have really put me in the loop for I have no idea who will do the phage typing. Do you know if the central public health lab still does this work?"

Execution:

Les nodded negatively and suggested, "Maybe I can ask Valerie to contact the Public Health Lab and enquire without giving details, but I will have to use your name."

Dr Sumner said, "Do not worry at this stage, your idea of checking for the similar antibiogram is a good one. Follow through with it and by the way, I like the summarized sheet and if you have time maybe you could do the same again with the new specimens that will come down."

"I can certainly do so Sir, but I have also kept the original plates for you to see and read," he answered.

"Ah! Yes Les, I must see the plates and the requisitions but I also need to know who labeled the specimens. Was it Valerie?" he asked as he put on his lab coat and began looking through the requisitions. "Find out for me Les and have Valerie bring the roll of numbers that she used on the matching requisitions and patients' swabs."

Les went in again to see Valerie and delivered the message to her. She promptly got up and took the roll of duplicate numbers with her. Les hurried back to sit with Dr Sumner and watched as this aging doctor patiently, like a detective, went through the forms, names and the numbering system with Valerie quietly looking on. Dr Sumner then began examining the plates and he saw where Les had taken part of the colony to either subculture or to do the coagulase test to identify the staphylococcus.

The process was done very quietly until just before the end, Dr Sumner got up and looked at Les. "You have done a very thorough job, old boy. Continue to keep the original plates in cold storage. I know that they will smell like hell but make the subcultures. I have to go to Eltham and will not be back until tomorrow. If a great number of swabs come down use half plates for this survey. Do you think that you can handle the volume or would you like to have some assistance from the central lab?"

Silly question for Les never felt better than now and wanted to show that he could do more than any of the other interns. He did not ask for or wished any assistance from the central laboratory. Pride has its price and so Les worked through late evenings but he never complained. He had to explain to the family that he was living with that he was working on an outbreak but he never knew if they believed what he had said. He was so tired and really did not care much at that time of day.

On the Friday of his last week, the swabs came down in large numbers as well as blood cultures, which he sub-cultured onto two half plates and incubated for 18 hours to be read on the Saturday morning. He arrived early and to his astonishment he found a number of the blood cultures growing the same staphylococcus. When he consulted his summary list he could see overt sepsis in seven of his patients. He had the approval of Dr Sumner, to call the results to the ward, to give a rapid verbal report and later to have the office make preliminary reports, which he signed and made sure that they got to the ward on time. He left that Saturday near enough 3 pm, having been in at 7:30 am that morning, but he was pleased at the work that he had accomplished.

His mind was in turmoil, for positive blood cultures on patients invariably meant death from septicemia. He had done all that was asked of him and more than the lab protocol demanded. He was told to return to the main lab on the Monday for Alan and the big Chief would be back. He had left copious notes explaining everything that had happened for the returning senior staff, without being asked.

End and the Beginning:

After a lazy Sunday at home Les read the Sunday Times and the Telegraph. He usually read over his notes from college on Sunday evening, as he lay in bed to keep warm. He had polished his only pair of black leather shoes and had a clean white shirt, clean underpants and socks all ready for work on the Monday. He used the same old tie that belonged to the Institute of Medical Laboratory Technicians. It was wrinkled and had seen a lot of wear.

On Monday, he did not have to rush to work down into Plumstead; instead he just had a short walk along the walkway next to the Greenman Pub and caught the bus to the top of the Hill. He entered the main driveway of the Brook General Hospital that was opposite the army training grounds. He waved to Reg, his landlord, in the gateway porter's lodge. Les went directly to the large Bacteriology Laboratory. He met the Charge Technologist, Maureen and said he was ready for duty after being away for a full month.

"How was it Les?" his charge asked politely.

"Great Mo, I really liked to be in charge and to organize the work my way. I set a time to have everything completed before my coffee break then looked at my smears from the evening before. Yep, I feel that I have learned a great deal." He was very positive.

Maureen replied smiling, "Great to hear that you enjoyed the experience."

Les had the urine bench to read which had the greatest number of specimens to handle but was fewer than the total he read routinely at St Nicks. He tackled the number of plates with relish. When he looked up he had very few cultures to pick for the antibiotic susceptibility. He saw Gwen opposite him, the next in charge; inundated with many respiratory specimens to read and asked if he could read a few. She looked up at him surprised and quickly said; "Sure I could do with some assistance for many of these cultures are quite dirty." Les took over the reading of sputa from the respiratory patients, which came from the old people's homes. There were a few hospitals in the group that were known as 'old people homes' as well as, a tuberculosis sanatorium or TB hospital. He completed these plates with a few isolates of pneumococci, Haemophilus and coliforms in pure growth. He began the picking off to do the susceptibility testing and identification by sugar fermentation.

The benches were cleared off by 10 am and Maureen said, "Wow, you chaps must have had a great weekend to have finished off all the reading so quickly. Well done troops." She laughed as she left for the back room to call through a hatch in the wall that opened into the kitchen and autoclave room, where the ladies made our coffees. Maureen also went to complete some paperwork. Les was the last to go in for coffee as he had done the staining on all the slides made by the four readers that morning. He then began the staining of the smears for TB screening. He completed all the subcultures when Maureen came to the entry door and said, "Hi Mister Man, come in here now for your coffee. That is an order."

Les smiled and in mock saluted. "Aye, Aye Skipper, just washing hands."

The staff members were all relaxed and they had begun the Telegraph Cross Word as a group activity while they all sipped their coffee. There was the usual banter of what films were worthwhile to see or the latest on television but mostly there was input into the crossword. As the room quieted concentrating on the crossword, the front door flew open and the loud voices of Dr Sumner and Dr Gorman echoed into the back room stirring Maureen to get up and to meet them in the main lab. "Hello Mo, have you already read all your plates? Wasn't there a lot of work on the weekend?" as the pathologists laughed loudly.

"Well, gentlemen, we are very efficient so if there is need for assistance anywhere in the group you know where to come," she remarked with her blue eyes smiling at them.

"Ah! Glad to hear that! It is for that reason that we came to see you." Dr Sumner could be heard from the back room. Les did not move for he heard his name mentioned a few times then the voices dropped off. He finished the coffee and moved nearer the crossword writer and pretended to pay more attention for he could hear the voices coming into the room.

"Still trying to get the cross word done for today," loudly remarked the tall Irish doctor in charge of biochemistry. "I did it before breakfast this morning" he boomed as his eyes closed with laughter at his own joke. The staff stood up and began moving back into the main work area and Les was following them when a large golden hairy arm stopped him from going further. He looked into the smiling face of the intrepid Dr Gorman. Dr Sumner was speaking sotto voce to Maureen.

"Yes this clever intern has put us all in trouble and we need him to sort out the mess," was the reply from the red-faced, smiling buck-toothed grin of Dr Sumner. "Are you ready Squire?" he said looking at Les.

Les stared with a grin and calmly replied, "Who me Sir? I thought that I had to report to the main lab Sir."

There was laughter which included Maureen who broke in saying, "Yes you Sir. You have done quite a job over at St Nicks. The department cannot run without you, it seems. You are needed elsewhere."

"I shall go back there tomorrow then shall I?" Les replied.

"Oh! No Sir you will go there right away,' echoed the booming voice of Dr Gorman.

"When shall I go Sir? I have some smears to read here," asked the now more serious Les.

Maureen interrupted, "Do not worry Les; we can take over from here." She winked taming her irony. "We will try to work without you but I think that we can take over now."

"Look Les," said Dr Sumner who had lowered his voice. "We have a lot to do over at St Nicks. Your notes were great and Alan went through all that you have left but we lost seven children over the weekend." There was a stunned silence as the smiles became frozen on everyone's face. Les could feel his heart pounding in his neck and his ears. He began to feel hot and his back itched. For some unknown reason he knew that patients will die from septicemia but to be in the middle of this disaster he did not know how to take this news. He felt tears coming but he held them back.

Post Mortems:

His eyes moved from one physician's face to the other and again Maureen's voice broke the silence. "Would you like to have Martin or Gwen come along as well?" she asked.

"No! Absolutely not," said Dr Gorman who continued, "Sorry Mo, but there are to be post mortems done on all the dead patients, as well as, detailed notes to be taken and Les has been in the middle of it. He will spend the next month working with Alan, Stan and the others at St Nicks, so you must run the lab with one short for that time. Can you?"

"Of course, we can," she replied with no hesitation. "But will Les be able to get in his applied practicals in time for his finals this summer?" she concluded.

"Yes I know that I can Mo, for I am already more advanced for this time period. This will only give me the confidence and the focus to do more work on my own," Les replied more convincingly than he had intended.

"OK, get your coat, old man and come with me," said Dr Sumner, who turned around to march out of the room and to the car park outside the lab. Les hurried out after him, discarding his lab coat. He went over to Gwen to show her what he had done and what he had intended to do.

She looked up at him and smiled, "You have done more than I could have in that time. Thanks Les and have fun over there," she said.

He was almost half way out of the door when Dr Gorman followed and in the driveway met up with Dr Sumner and Les.

Dr Gorman put his heavy arm on Les' shoulder. "You have done stellar work, Les. We are all very proud of what you have done. Dr Sumner feels as do the other pathologists that you should complete this very difficult project in finding the carrier of the organism and either have them placed elsewhere or try to isolate the individual. The important thing is to prevent this catastrophe from ever happening again," he reiterated.

With that reaffirmation, Les sat in the front seat of Dr Sumner's old white Ford car that smelt of cigarette smoke. It was filled with old journals and newspapers; in short, it was a mess inside this car. Les did not smoke and could tolerate the smell but it was the excitement that he felt of being with the old group at St Nicks that brought about his happiness. He knew that he would have to go over all that he had done and hopefully Alan would not find any mistakes that he may have inadvertently made. Dr Sumner smiled and then went quiet as Les tried to make small talk but his boss turned to the subject that was on both their minds. "You know Les; we do not have the antibiotics against these resistant organisms. I noticed that you had put these strains up against the disk of mercuric chloride. You know that this is just a quick screen for phage type 80 and 81 but there is no scientific explanation for this test."

"To be honest Sir, I just tried all that I had at my fingertips at the time so that at least these simple tests would not have to be repeated again. We will also have to await the results of the phage typing and the MIC tests to see if there is true resistance," Les replied.

"Good thinking old man," Dr Sumner replied then remained quiet as the car crossed over to Eltham Road towards the Memorial Hospital for we had to pick up some antisera for St Nicks Hematology section.

After which they headed into Woolwich and entered the grounds of St Nicks Hospital. Les picked up the box to take to Hematology as Dr Sumner closed and locked his car.

Les heard him say, "Wait a minute, Les. Look, I will do the post mortems but I want you with me. We will culture the heart blood, the spleen and the spinal fluid and I will take blood cultures. Get the supplies ready as well as a sterilization oil lamp for we do not have gas for a Bunsen burner in the PM Room or Morgue. Make some new Pasteur pipettes for this project. I will be ready this afternoon."

With that Les went into the main lab to be met by the smiling Alan and the serious Mr. Stan Bowden both with cigarettes in their hands. Shaking hands around he noticed that Alan had a bit of a tan which he remarked on. This made his friend blush enhancing his tanned face and Stan just looked rested. It was Alan, who burst out laughing and said, "In all the years that I have worked here, we have never had an outbreak and in one month you had to identify one from the lab specimens. Great work old boy."

Les cannot remember a happier time in his career even after over forty years in the lab science business. Stan who was quieter but an equally brilliant man said that he felt that it was one of the finest moments in the lab's history. Now the wards should pay more attention to what is being sent to them daily by thousands of labs across the country. Little did Les know that he would be working on an allied research project with Stan on phage typing for the group of hospitals in about one year's time.

Les enquired from Alan if the notes that he left were OK and was there anything he could explain to him. Alan said, "All was well done mate!" and continued, "Get the stuff ready for the PMs this afternoon. Pay attention for you will get a good handle on anatomy and listen to the old man for he will tell you more on the physiology of the body than any text book could ever do. It is a great learning experience."

Alan would leave in a year's time for a position in Somerset in a town called Yeovil. In a letter to Les after his departure, he made the offer for Les to join his new team when he had passed his final exams. Les never took up the offer and instead, with his girlfriend in tow they left for Canada in 1967.

PMs on Babies:

Les found himself in the damp dark cold room of the morgue with Dr Sumner, masked and gowned, motioning Les to do the same which he quickly did. The mortician was known as Ed and he was a quiet introverted man who kept out of everyone's way. He was rarely seen outside of the morgue and was one of life's loners. He brought in the corpses of the babies and placed them one at a time as Les watched. Dr Saunders handed a pad to Les to write down what he described in the Post Mortem pathology reports. Dr Sumner stated the length of the body, the size of the brain and the weight. After opening the body cavity he dictated the appearance of the heart, liver (normal) and kidneys. He then asked Les to pierce the heart tissue with the newly-drawn glass Pasteur pipette. He withdrew a sample of blood which he placed aseptically into a blood culture bottle. Dr Sumner then opened the back of the skull and showed Les the 'meninges' and again asked him to pierce them and withdraw a sample of the spinal fluid for culture.

"When there is meningitis, these become inflamed and show up as yellow glands," Dr Sumner explained. The process continued until all seven children were completed but unknown to them, there were two more deaths and Les had to return into the main labs for more supplies. He had begun the incubation of the first seven post mortem blood culture bottles that contained heart blood and spinal fluid as well as plates.

It was well past 6 pm before they got out of the mortuary. There were oodles of notes that Les had taken for Valerie to type the following morning.

Dr Sumner said to Les, "I will give you a lift home Les. Sleep in tomorrow and do not get in before noon. That is an order!" To which Les just smiled.

He had no intention of doing so. Alan had the task of reading these post mortem specimens and Les was ferried back into the routine reading of specimens but he was not to interfere with the epidemiology that was being done in house. It must have been because there was legislation that stated only a qualified individual could do this work. This did not bother Les in the least.

Of Harley Street and Arrogance:

Specialists in medicine are used by all the teaching and tertiary hospitals in the greater London area. Many of the staff are full time and are paid a salary but those brought in from outside the system are paid more for their services. In those days, if there was a hospital that needed a specialist, one of the specialists in Harley Street was hired through the old boy connection. Back in the early 1960s, these specialists were treated by the nurses and lesser staff like the 'Gods of Medicine.' However, to their hospital peers, there was a bit of jealousy, a conniving respect but an acknowledged fact that Harley Street Specialists were an invaluable source of clinical expertise. These gentlemen were no longer called by the title of 'Doctor' or 'Dr'. No, these men became 'Mister' or 'Mr.' and they were well connected to the very wealthy population of the world.

The stories that come out into the world of medicine from this branch of elite medical practitioners to the poorer National Health Service workers are legion.

Example Overheard of such a Conversation:

"Well Old Chap, I was called by the Sheik, who said that one of his wives had a recurrent urinary infection. He had his jet ready at Heathrow Airport and a limousine picked me up at around 6 pm. I was treated very well on the flights with the usual Cubans and you know the 125 year-old Napoleon after a supper of Canadian salmon. I had the documents from the wife's GP with me to study and it seemed to be quite straightforward. We arrived four hours later and I was rushed to the Palace but it was still dark and I did not have to do much. I met the Sheik, quite a nice fellow. I met the wife and after examination, saw that she had a recurrent UTI because of being a bit heavy and slightly arthritic. I gave her a wide spectrum antibiotic, an amino glycoside, mm... maybe streptomycin with penicillin and gave strict instructions that she should not wipe her tail from in front but backwards. There were no problems with her kidneys or her bladder but only with her arthritis. I changed her prescription. I rested well for the remainder of the night. I again met the Sheik and explained what I had done but he was not too interested in the details. He just wanted to know if I would be available should this event was to recur."

"Of course your Majesty, I am at your service at any time. I was flown home after 18 hours and got home in time for supper."

To the crass question as to how much he had been paid, the reply was simple.

"You know Old Chap. I really do not know, the cheque is paid directly into my Swiss account. Oh! Yes there is a regular retainer but you would not be interested in that, would you?"

While many of these practicing specialists are remarkable as they have acclaimed knowledge and skills as well as the best bedside manners and interpersonal skills to deal with any aspect of society, there are a few extremely arrogant practitioners. It is those few specialists that go by the Harley Street sobriquet associated with snobbery and arrogance. A pediatrician specialist was needed down in the Woolwich area to cover the difficult patients. Through some 'medical mafia' contact a Harley Street specialist was found. Unfortunately, he was the one who drove a blue Rolls Royce and had his own parking lot close to the hospital emergency entranceway. He also had an arrogance to go along with his expensive tastes. He was revered by Sister Mary-Anne but he showed great disdain for the other nurses, sometimes including the patients in this poor part of the outskirts of London.

Summary:

After over several hundred swabs had been taken on all the staff which included nurses on all three shifts, residents, interns, nursing aides, porters and lab personnel associated with the pediatric ward, there was no staphylococcus that matched either the antibiogram or the screening test for phage type 80 and 81. The phage typing results came back and the strain that gave the epidemiology phage type 80 was common to all those strains isolated from the deceased patients. There were a number of staphylococci isolated from the nose swabs of many staff but none was found that matched those from the dead patients. The swabs were repeated and it was months afterwards when the three head Pathologists met to analyze the data and to give their final report.

Les was enjoying his morning coffee looking idly through the lab window, when he saw the blue Rolls Royce drive into the courtyard and asked Alan who it was that had come down to the slums. Alan came and looked through the open lab window, and said to Les, "Why that is Dr Winslow-Smith. It must be his visiting day."

Les smiled to himself as Alan went back to his own coffee at the microscope. Les did not have a car and wondered how one actually got a car but more important how does anyone get a car like a Rolls Royce. He asked Alan, "I wonder where he consults in the hospital." He turned around to see Alan with eyes focused on the microscope, his glasses resting on the bench. Alan moved his eyes away from the eyepieces, put on his glasses and wrote his findings down on the requisition, then turned around to look at Les.

"I believe that he is a pediatrician," Alan thoughtfully stated. Just then the batwing doors opened and the ever blushing Valerie entered and saw them both being pensive.

"What is wrong with you chaps today?"

Alan smiled and asked, "Do you know where the Harley Consultant works in here?"

She still with the red cheeks asked, "Do you mean Dr Winslow-Smith?"

Alan stood up and went nearer to her, "Yes, you know he drives the Rolls outside."

Valerie looked at him then at Les. "Why, he is a pediatrician and works on Sister Mary-Anne's ward. Did you not know that?" she teased and walked away.

The two men in the lab laughed and Les asked Alan, "Hey Mate, would you like me to write while you read the microscopy? That way we can get this bundle of slides done faster."

"Sure if you wouldn't mind Les, there is a bit of a back-up here!" Alan replied.

They sat side by side and as Alan went about reading the slides through the microscope, Les wrote down the results. After he had about two inches thick of requisitions he took them to the office for typing. He repeated this trip twice more until the back log was cleared. They got up and decided to put up the sensitivities on all the organisms that they had picked off and Les completed his summary sheet of the last set of cultures related to the catastrophe on the pediatric ward.

"Hey Alan, I do not have any swabs from Dr Winslow-Smith," Les called out to his colleague.

"I am not surprised," said Alan. "He is not the type of person who would allow himself to be part of this survey." This exchange was followed by a silence and mumble coming from Les.

Then he felt the hand on his shoulder. "Look mate, you are right, he should be swabbed as well but I bet you a dime to a dollar he did not have one done."

"Then you are to call Sister for she likes you and see if he has had or will give his permission to have his hands swabbed," Les shouted across the room.

"Oh! Yes, you would have Sister come and tear me off a strip with such an insane idea, eh!" answered Alan. Just then a nurse came down into the lab to deliver a specimen from the pediatric wing.

Alan called her back and nicely asked if she had been swabbed in the survey, "Oh! Yes we all were," she answered. Then he asked quietly again allowing her to come back into the main lab, "Do you know if Dr Winslow-Smith had his hands, nose and throat swabbed as well?"

"Are you crazy? He terrifies all the nurses!" she responded with her eyes wide as saucers. "We have asked and offered him a coat and a mask to wear for everyone has to, but he just ignores us and goes in with his suit on," she continued.

Alan persisted, "Will Sister ask him, do you think?"

"Not 'alf mate she thinks the sun rises out of his arse," this Cockney nurse earnestly replied.

She left cautioning us not to repeat what we have heard. However, Les went off to lunch and in the afternoon he focused on his TB cultures, making smears under the hood. He had been reading his text books on skin pigmentation and laughed to himself about how some Caucasians actually get a deposit of pigment making them look quite tanned in certain diseases.

It was around 2:30 pm when Dr Sumner arrived loudly through the batwing doors and shouted, "Stand by your benches Gentlemen! It is inspection time." This was his standard joke which invariably caused laughter for there was a repartee that broke him and everyone else up. The atmosphere at work was so enjoyable in those heady days of Les' youth and his training.

"Sir," Les called for Dr Sumner's attention.

"What is it now young man?" asked the ageing Dr Sumner.

Les continued, "I believe that I am quite sick Sir."

"You look as healthy as a horse. What makes you feel that you are ill?" asked Sumner knowing that some joke was at hand. Les continued still working under the TB hood.

"Well Sir, is it true that with Addison's disease, there is a liver dysfunction that allows a deposit of melanin to increase making their skin brown and tanned?" Les was born in the West Indies and was of East Indian parentage. The roar that went up in the room stopped everyone other than Les who was masked and gowned and could not move until he had completed his TB work. He was nearing the end of this aseptic work on live tuberculosis cultures. He looked up from his work bench and saw Dr Sumner red-faced as was Alan roaring away, doubled over with laughter.

In comes Stan, who was in the next room bleeding patients for the Hematology department. "What the heck is going on in here?" he asked unbelieving that Dr Sumner was doubled over with laughter.

Dr Sumner recovered sufficiently as Les began undressing from his coat and gloves, relating to Stan, "This Laddie wants to have a month off work to get a cure for his Addison's illness for his skin is brown."

Stan lost it as the three of them broke down with red faces and laughter flared up again. Les remained with only a shy grin on his face.

"You silly, sod! Where did you get that crack from?" asked Stan as Dr Sumner left the room to go into his next door office.

"From my text book on pathology," Les replied straight-faced with the innocence of a straight man to a comedian. A few minutes later Dr Sumner came into the main lab room to have tea with Alan, Stan and Les. This was the time that they all questioned Les on his recent notes and on the syllabus. Les loved the quizzing and could never get enough for his marks at night school were all in the nineties with a few hundred sprinkled in between. He was always asked what his marks were after a night class and he would show them to Alan who would pass them on to Stan and their medical boss. These were serious men and were genuinely interested in Les' welfare and scholarly advancement.

It was Alan who brought up the observation that one Harley Street Consultant was not swabbed. It was Dr Sumner who became quite serious and asked, "Are you sure that he was not swabbed, Alan?"

Alan brought out the lists of names of all the staff and showed them to him still smiling but one look at his face showed he was not being funny but very serious indeed. Dr Sumner said that he will be off to see the other pathologists and will not be back for the rest of the day. Unknown to the workers in the lab at St Nicks this is what was rumoured to have happened:

Dr Sumner met with Drs Gorman and Williams and explained that there was a loophole in their tying up the case of a hidden carrier of the infamous epidemiologic staphylococcus phage type 80. He had the summary sheets and they poured over the results and the different results from the Reference Labs. Then Dr Sumner dropped the aside that Dr Winslow-Smith, the visiting consultant from Harley Street, was not part of the results. Dr Williams asked, "Was he asked to participate?"

Gorman interrupted, "Well Dr Williams, he is not one to agree with this type of random searching. His time is too valuable, you know."

Dr Williams was the Regional Chief of Pathology and he understood the reason, but none-the-less called Sister Mary-Anne and explained that they were about to prepare a final report. He just wanted to know if all the staff had co-operated with their search. She said as far as she knew the staff had no choice but to cooperate. Then he asked if the medical staff also co-operated. She was adamant that they also had no choice but to take part or they will not enter her ward. Dr Williams was persistent in his own quiet way but like the iron fist in a velvet glove, he went in for the kill and asked, "Does that include Dr Winslow-Smith?"

"Really! Dr Williams," she remarked, in surprise. "How could you ask such a question?"

Dr Williams asked again still very politely. "I noticed his name is not on the list." Sister then sheepishly replied, "That is because he was not asked to take part in it."

"Thank you Sister. You have been very helpful," said the charitable Dr Williams.

He turned to his colleagues and asked, "Dr Sumner, will you get the necessary swabs for me?" Then he continued, "Gentlemen, it looks like I shall have to invite Dr Winslow-Smith to the club for lunch and 'drinkee-poos'" and the two other pathologists gave their best wishes to him. The three pathologists left for their individual labs with Dr Williams setting off to do the impossible.

Final Report and a Cure?

It was two weeks later when Les had come back from his final exams that he was quizzed on how well he had done. He was quite happy but he did not especially like 'pre or post mortems of exams'. He knew that he had prepared well and was not unhappy with his write up for he completed the whole paper with time to re-read the questions. His hand had caught a cramp several times for the volume of writing. He had to ask for more paper twice to complete the exams.

He went to the bench where Alan and Stan were working and asked if he could assist them and they looked at each other and winked. Les saw them closeted and asked, "What is going on here gentlemen?" There was silence as Stan sat down near the microscope and Alan drew up a seat and motioned for Les to sit down. They explained that Dr Williams had waited for Dr Winslow-Smith to respond to his invitation to join him at the 'club'. They met and became quite inebriated and so they had wondered back to Dr Williams' office late at night. As a result, they had swabs from his nose, throat, his wrists, his groin and his ears for culture. He also wanted to have the results. A staphylococcus was recovered from his nose but that is expected since 99% of the population carries this organism in the nose. However, it was also recovered in all the other swabs and they all had a similar antibiogram to the causative organism.

They had sent the organism for phage typing and QED – *quad erat demonstranum*. This was the same organism that caused the deaths of the other seven plus two children. Dr Winslow-Smith has never again returned back to St Nicks and he had asked for some treatment from Dr Sumner, who had to explain that once a 'carrier always a carrier.' Les listened intently to his tutors and colleagues and there was no answer.

They looked at him and it was Stan who said, "We still cannot say that he was the cause of the infection, you know."

"Why not?" asked the inflamed naive Les.

"Because one of the patients could have brought the organism in with them and could have infected the good doctor. It could just be co-incidence, is there no room for reasonable doubt?" responded Stan.

Les was out of his depth and he gave up this line of argument and remained quiet.

It was the sensitive Alan who responded, "That poor man, what else can he do, apart from pediatrics?" and Les had not thought about this part of the argument.

Les was working away on the benches doing some agglutination for possible Salmonella isolate, when he came to the technological task of making an antigen for the 'flagella'. It struck him immediately. He got up, as Dr Sumner came over to the desk to see his slide agglutinations and asked if he thought it would be *Salmonella*. Les said that he was 90% sure but will perform antigen suspensions of the flagella and the body and do a tube agglutination test in an effort to prove the identity.

"Dr Sumner, is it possible to make an antigen extract of Staphylococcus aureus?" Les asked.

"Why sure Les! It should be possible to make a vaccine of any organism but the best success has been with virus and the Gram negative rods, except for TB. Why do you ask?" inquired the doctor.

"Well I wonder if one can make an autogenous vaccine for carriers of this strain of Staphylococcus aureus and if it works just for a bit, that surely would be useful. Such carriers can get rid of the organism temporarily and have booster vaccinations as needed. I would like to try to make one," Les offered.

There was silence as Alan and Stan joined in this now silent thoughtful group session. "You know what Les, go ahead and make a vaccine but do not suspend it in formaldehyde. Make sure that the organism is dead after boiling by sub-culturing. When we have a sterile suspension, let me know. I believe that there is one person who would like to try this vaccine," Dr Sumner replied.

Les took about a week to have a heavy enough suspension of the staphylococcus vaccine and handed it to Dr Sumner, who had the pharmacy re-suspend it so that he could use it on the Harley Street Specialist. The vaccine was used and it worked for about three months before the staphylococcus returned. No one had ever followed up on this test case as a treatment 45 years later, as far as Les is aware.

NOTE: This vaccine was made in the rough old days and the product, by today's standard, was crude in every sense of the word. It was before the time of the electron microscope (which is in common usage and a routine today), density gradient centrifugation, the measurement of the molecular weights of haptens and the in vitro challenges of cytokines.

With all the new technology today, in the twenty-first century, surely it is possible to develop a vaccine to the *Staphylococcus aureus*.

The most Interesting

Lecture to Medical Students-

"Sexual transmitted diseases"

Sexual Gymnastics:

By far the best lecture that Dr Gutch ever gave to his fourth year medical students was the segment on venereal diseases. The students' one complaint was that they could never understand his Churchillian verbiage and phrases through his 'gargled' old English accent. However, it is interesting to note when he gave this lecture on 'Sexually Transmitted Diseases' the auditorium room was filled. Many students could not control their laughter, as he took this difficult subject and presented it as a humorous discourse, where everyone appeared to understand. Les' task was to prepare cultures of real gonorrhoeae-causing bacteria (better known as 'the clap'), where all the kids had to do was to place a drop of an oxidase reagent onto the Petri plate cultures and a purple colour was seen. This was an identification test to screen out suspect colonies growing on a chocolate agar Petri dish.

However, it was interesting to note that with every 'giggle' or outburst of laughter, like a true comedian, he would pause for effect then continue to explain in even more graphic terms the methods of contracting syphilis in its many stages, the description of a soft Chancre, 'the clap' or gonorrhoeae, ectoparasites such as crab lice or scabies, Trichomonads, genital Herpes, Chlamydia, genital Candidiasis, Papilloma warts, pox virus, and all infections of the genitalia associated with sexual intercourse. He moved his audience with ironic wit, with bordering coarse jokes and euphemisms which he created. Les enjoyed this lecture every year when he was asked to assist Dr Gutch.

When it was Les' turn to give similar lectures across the country to nurses, medical scientists and public health staff, he was not ashamed to use similar colourful metaphors to get the point across. The microbes that are the cause of venereal infections are not new; indeed, they have been recorded from biblical times to present day. The difference is that in today's world, there is more openness by society to saying clearly what they are infected with. They know how these infections are spread, what their clinical appearance and symptoms are and more importantly, how to treat and prevent their spread.

The young university students who are still exploring the excitement of sexual adventure and embracing this novel activity are also curious about protecting themselves from these infections. It is said that imitation is the best form of flattery and so Les confessed to copying some of the phrases used by the venerable Dr Gutch. He used this man's humour and was convinced that his overriding success as a lecturer and his popularity in being invited to speak around the world in his later years was as a result of this material but also of a practiced ease of delivery. This was invariably the cause of much mirth with his daughters now in their late twenties, when they heard his peers at functions say, "You do these presentations so easily, it must be a gift". They knew that their dad put in at least six hours of work on every lecture.

When he lectured on sexually transmitted diseases, Les would quote the exact words of his mentor, imitating the accent. Timing was crucial and when it was right he would say, "If you young men intend to dip your wick indiscriminately be prepared to get indiscriminate infections."

On the other hand in addressing the female cohort of students he would state, "When you young ladies embrace the privilege of sex with unknown donors of these microbial gifts, rest assured that you will have the gift of giving indefinitely if you are not treated immediately. Remember Herpes is forever"

Needless to say in sexually active (conscious, curious) 'twenty-somethings', this was as close to a legitimate porno lecture they would legally receive from university. The laughter reverberated for days and the quoting of his phrases could be heard being repeated, usually by young men enjoying their university stay and their courses.

Of Physiology and Principle:

The principle of venereal infections is that they are primarily infections of the genitals and are obtained through sexual intercourse. Secondly, they are highly contagious and if not dealt with quickly the sequelae (progression to other disease states) can have a lethal effect on the overall health of an individual. Examples of the effect of the '*clap or gonorrhoeae*' infection in females, is the development of a viscid discharge, usually yellowish in appearance. There is destruction of the superficial layers of the endocervix, cervix and if untreated can spread into the uterus, the ovaries and fallopian tubes leading to potential infertility. The vagina becomes contaminated with the pustular discharge. Secondly, in the early stages of the disease there are no symptoms and many females have a mild non-infectious discharge or genital wetness that can be easily ignored. It is normal for sexually active females to have a non-infectious clear discharge. In the event of a 'pus-like' or yellow sticky discharge after contact with an infected individual, that indicates infection. If untreated and intercourse is continued then the infection spreads rapidly to other partners.

In males the disease causes great pain for there can be blockage in the shaft of the penis making it difficult to pee. Then again there might be a little watery, sticky discharge to begin with, followed by a thick mucus yellow discharge. A male knows when he has the 'clap' because of the pain when trying to pass the mucus through the shaft of the penis. It is not unlike a masturbation and ejaculation of semen but definitely not as pleasurable as the pain is excruciating. If not dealt with in a timely manner the pus builds up, making the passage through the shaft of the penis difficult and extremely painful. From the urethra through the orifice in the shaft of the penis that is blocked, pain is the indicator. The surrounding parts of the male genitals become inflamed, the testicles become swollen, tender and painful, as the organism stimulates the production of large amounts of trapped pus.

This is the commonest communicable disease after the common cold and the incidence increases yearly. It was thought that the use of the pill by females allowed for more freedom to enjoy lots of sex while preventing pregnancy but instead it just allowed more infections to spread and to persist. From a professional standpoint this was great news to Les and the lab scientists for they were in a 'growth industry' and had little chance of losing clients. After all one may go without food but there is always a lot of sex among the young, the middle-aged and sometimes among a mixture of both age groups. These were the caustic comments discussed by lab workers of both sexes over coffee breaks unlike any other industry; no names are ever used just the isolation from the type of individuals.

Les was asked to deliver a lecture on the 'clap' to a batch of non-scientific students in one of the West Indian communities. These were not the intelligent students of North American universities but young people living and working in tight family circles. The cultural and community restrictions and the economic realities of the third world countries are unknown to European and North American workers in healthcare. There is a need for understanding how a family combines resources to exist under a patriarchic arrangement to use and accumulate wealth. These families and communities live in a deprived state, relatively speaking. Les rarely did these open public health related presentations but he was asked by a GP while on tour of a Caribbean Island where he had just visited the closest community. The GP described this incident of tale graphically, especially stressing what 'quickies' can do, 'venereal speaking.' Les knew that his 'humorous cracks' normally made to a North American audience would not translate very well to this more 'primitive' society. This was obvious to him judging by the fact that everyone was very serious so he amended his talk accordingly to this suspicious society. They looked up to him for he was from Canada and he was a university-educated man

– all crap as far as Les was concerned but he toed the line to get the message across.

After his presentation, the attending GP invited Les over to his home for a drink, local food and a chat. In the third world societies, where these physicians practice either because they originally came from the country or some wish to do some missionary work, they find after awhile that they lack peer company, discussion and understanding. "You know Les, thanks for telling the story of VD to these folks. They are not stupid and they know what they are up to most of the time. There is a family with two daughters and the parents could not stop the big daughter from going out to all-night parties. The big daughter had a job and she paid her way in the home thus was important to the home economy. At carnival time the parents suspected that the girl was promiscuous but the parents could only advise. They suggested that she should use a condom and their daughter would saucily remark, 'I always do'. However, the younger daughter was typically the one not allowed to be like her big sister. She was forever griping to her parents and wanting to join the big sister at her parties but she was just a teenager."

This GP continued, "The younger daughter was brought to him for she had a vaginal discharge. As soon as I examined her, I knew it was gonorrhoeae and I had to ask the questions before passing the report to the Public Health nurse to follow up for contacts etc., you know, the usual. The young girl insisted that she did not have sex with anyone but she must have caught the infection after 'using the underwear' of her big sister. I was adamant that it was not possible to contract such severe 'clap' this way. The big sister was clean after my examination. The family, when told the whole story in confidence by myself, did not believe me but believed the daughter's story. It was only after three other teenagers contracted the 'clap' did we find the culprit who was an older male with no job and lots of time on his hands to seduce these young girls. He was a carrier and was riddled with all sort of pustules, never mind the details."

It was only to be expected that Les in his retirement years knew that he had to write for there were so many stories to tell from his experiences during his travel and work life. The first anecdote of many examples was of a traveling laboratory sales person who visited him at least once a year but one time when Les saw him he had a patch over one eye. On enquiry, he asked Les' confidence and he shuffled through his briefcase to find a coloured photo showing a patient (himself) with overt pus draining out of a closed eye. Les' surprised explicative, "Holy shit Man! How the hell did you get that infection?" The story was that he was in Winnipeg and was a bit spunky one evening and had lots to drink. He picked up a hooker on his way to the motel. The next morning he had a sticky eye which he tried to wash off as he prepared to go to the next client at a hospital. By midday, there was pus oozing out of his eye and the manager of the lab had noticed his red eye that was oozing and took him down to the emergency. A photo was taken for there was so much running pus and the lab identified *Neisseria gonorrhoeae*. He was treated systemically after telling the ID physician what he was up to but unfortunately his eye was severely damaged and he lost the sight in it. Les asked for a copy of the photo and he changed the face so he could use it as an example of cross contamination. This occurs when one wipes one's eyes after a pleasurable evening, with a digit used to 'explore the nether regions' of the female host. Of course the excuse was this all occurred when drunk and the moralist would say the results can have a disastrous effect.

Again the young university students loved these anecdotes when peppered into an otherwise dull lecture. I believe that it was Dr Gutch who created the phrase when a lab scientist went to him for advice with a sample of a louse taken from a 'hippy person' in the emergency. This 'hippy person' had come in with his female companion who was about to deliver their baby but she was riddled with 'crab lice'. The problem for the lab scientist is that a louse taken from the genital area was invariably a crab louse especially from such a patient with poor hygiene. The other body lice would cover the whole torso but the crab louse is easily identified for it has a great big claw. This is the unique feature that scientists use to identify, under the microscope, the body and head louse as different from the crab louse. It uses this huge claw to cling to the pubic hair unlike the body or head louse. In this instance, the louse was taken from the eyebrow of the male patient to which there was a guffaw and, "Well Gin, there is no end to the **sexual gymnastics** that some youths get up to these days, eh!"

Les was within hearing distance when the comment was passed. He had to see Dr Gutch in his office and as the door was open, he said to the still smug smiling medical director, "Pray tell Sir, how many sexual gymnastic positions are there and art thou speaking from personal experience, Sir?" The laughter and the bawdy tone meant that the door had to be slammed shut. This discussion went on for another two hours well past 5 pm. These were the fun days of Les' early years in lab medicine. Dr Gutch had a great deal of experience for he worked with the returning military men, many of whom had different types of illnesses but the most spectacular ones were those associated with venereal diseases.

The final anecdote deals with the classical sexually transmitted disease - the dreaded syphilis. The organism is contracted by sexual intercourse and becomes invasive in the primary stage. It passes through intact or damaged mucosa of the genital tract. This is a bacterium that appears, under a special dark field microscope, as a coiled, 'like a bed spring' shape. It is very delicate and is dies quickly at room temperature. When introduced into a warm wet place like the urethra of a male or the cervix of a female, it thrives. The course of the disease after contact occurs about three months later when a sore or 'chancre' is formed on the genitalia. From this sore or chancre, spiral organisms known as spirochetes spread rapidly throughout the body. The secondary stage occurs several weeks later and appears as skin rashes with other lesions in the throat and mouth as ulcers, also lesions of the anus and vulva. By this time, the primary sore disappears leaving only a scar. Many years later (up to 30 years), the tertiary stage occurs and it takes the form of granulomatous lesions in the brain, bone skin and other internal organisms.

A Vignette:

The case Les was involved in was found by accident in the health centre for it did not deal with chronic infections of the venereal kind. Indeed the Public Health Laboratories deal with syphilis testing in their centralized laboratories in Toronto. Hospitals in Ontario send all their specimens for syphilis testing to this facility, which do several tests. The first is a quick screen test or VDRL; if this is positive or indicates some positive agglutination then it is followed by a more sensitive test for verification. Today, there are better tests based on Nucleic acid or DNA testing. Reports are sent back to the laboratories in the referring hospital. In Les' lab, the staff usually brought the results to Les' desk.

It was just a formality for in all his years of looking at these results neither he nor his staff have ever had a true positive result in Canada. But here was a result of a serology test (antibody against the syphilis) that was positive. Les called the physician in charge and reported this abnormal result after checking with the centralized public health labs in Toronto. The physician just broke up laughing and asked that Les come up immediately to the ward to meet him. This situation occurred back in 1990 and when he went up to the ward the doctor was waiting with two nurses standing next to him. They had smug smiles on their faces.

The physician was a friend of Les' and he put his arm around Les and led him to the ward with two beds, but one was empty. On the other bed was an old woman who was asleep and she was surrounded by her personal things for she was a long term patient.

The physician looked at Les and asked, "Well old boy, what do you think?" pointing to a very old 80 plus years sleeping woman. "Do you think that this old gal had a good old fling recently?" His sarcasm was bold and loud and he bordered on the caustic remarking, "I believe that your lab has buggered up Les. We do not know how many other such wrong reports you have sent to us."

His glee was overwhelming and he was moving in for the puritan's kill. Needless to say, Les was stunned to see an eighty year- old patient who began to stir. She quietly opened her eyes saying, "Ah! Doctor you are waiting for me to get up?"

"Do not worry dear, rest yourself for we were discussing your problems with the man from the lab downstairs," the amiable doctor said enchantingly to the dear old girl. Just then Les looked up at her comfortable surroundings and saw an old black and white photo of a soldier in uniform. He looked at the old woman after picking up the framed photo and he stooped to hold her hand, "Tell me dear who this handsome soldier is?"

She brought it close to her face and smiled. "That is me husband, doctor. Aye and he is a handsome man isn't he?" she replied softly.

Les agreed smiling and asked, "Which war was he in?"

The old woman replied, "Why in the first big one, WWI.

Les asked, "Did you have any children?"

She replied that they could not have any because he was damaged during the war. She continued that, "He died when he was just about fifty years old."

Les thanked her and walked out with the physician following him curiously asking, "Les what was that all about? Why all the questions?"

Les turned around and within the hearing distance of the two smirking nurses remarked loudly enough for them to hear, "You should read up on syphilis especially the tertiary stage and the first world war veterans." This was Les' turn to be smug for the old girl had given the typical description of a treated old soldier with syphilis. She further reported that they had no children. There are many cases of the wife contracting the disease but the symptoms only showed up as tertiary syphilis. However, the blood serology would remain positive for life.

Climax of a Career

Les Paul is retired from a career spanning 40 years; this book has covered his 28 years at the health centre where he had been in charge for most of that period. About 1993, Leslie looked at how the laboratories were delivering the service to the wards, physicians and nurses. He found that the old problems hindering immediate interference on a patient when laboratory results were completed remained unchanged. This included his computer interface to his automated equipment that identified a bacterium and tested a range of antibiotic susceptibilities in less than 15 hours, with over 80% within 6 hours. This change allowed his lab to send direct results 24 hours a day. However, results were sometimes left on the printer or if a nurse had picked up the printed report it remained on the nurse's desk until she got around to placing it on the patient's chart. Several variations were tried to show haste and need for this shortcoming to be corrected. Les decided that his own staff who knew the need for such a change should be involved.

This is when he introduced the concept of a bedside lab scientist or a Clinical Technologist. Today such bedside laboratory workers are called Clinical Laboratory Scientists and their duties include having the latest lab reports available when they attend bedside rounds with the physician, specialist, interns, residents, nurses, infection control practitioners and clinical pharmacists. Their contributions to daily bedside consulting include making sense of the lab reports not only if they were normal or abnormal but the story behind the results, especially in microbiology. An example would the presence of a hemolytic streptococcus type B also known as *Streptococcus agalactiae* in the female vagina for it lives and thrives in an acid pH. However, in the pregnant individual this organism is capable of invading the fetus at delivery or when there is premature ruptured membrane and has been known to invade the uterus causing a neo natorium sepsis. If undetected it has been known to be the cause of death in a full term child. Another important duty of these new bedside professionals is their ability to combine the results reported by the hematology and/or biochemistry labs. The combination of an elevated white cell count and the isolation of a bacterium imply an infection, probably by the isolate made in microbiology. It should be noted that the mere isolation of a bacterium from a patient does not necessarily mean that there is an infection since many pathogenic bacteria live as commensals on and in the human body.

The use of the laboratory staff trained as bedside support professionals has taken on an even more important role with the change in instrumentation used to test small samples of body fluids including blood. The miniaturization of the new technology allows bedside results to be available within minutes, even seconds. These results are either printed onto self-adhesive mini-reports which can be affixed onto the older paper patients' charts or they can be electronically downloaded onto electronic charts.

Les was very fortunate for the educational qualifications of his scientific staff continued to increase because of the competitive job market demands at that time. In his last few years, many of his staff was highly qualified, more capable of taking on advanced technical tasks and this in turn motivated him to keep them achieving more than the average bench worker. He deliberately moved ahead with challenging them at every front (including their inter-relationship behaviour with each other) scientifically by continually evaluating diagnostic products, new technologies and in producing defining results that were publishable. Almost every one of his scientific staff had their name on one of these publications. Over his career, nine of his staff achieved their advanced scientific diplomas and well over twelve of his colleagues across the country, whom he mentored, also received their advanced degrees. Les was pleased at the quality of the staff in his last five years for they adapted to advanced training including new clinical challenges. He knew and felt that with any major change in hospital amalgamation, they would survive for they had the education, advanced skills and many could take on clinical roles and become successful.

Les left when he was called to serve the amalgamation of three health centres and make the weaker specialty testing laboratory profitable and sustaining. He was also asked to make the transfer slow down so that the staff with different institutional cultures would eventually get used to the idea of change. As soon as this was done, he was asked to remain and work in a senior administrative position. Les declined and began his new consulting and writing career. His work was complete for one is placed on the bicycle of life and so one must pedal fast and hard. When the propulsion takes a life of its own then it is time to get off the bicycle and let someone else take over the pedaling. He was tired of this ride and it was time to seek new challenges. This is Les' story and this is where he ends his journey on this leg of his life's path.

Afterword

On this book

This book is non-fiction and is entitled, *"Diagnosis"* in which I use a number of case histories to demonstrate the great detective work done by medical laboratory scientists across the hospital laboratories around the world. Their work allows patients to be treated by providing scientific analysis information to assist general practitioners as well as, clinical specialists in making or confirming an accurate clinical diagnosis. These scientific folks are never mentioned in television shows but rather their roles are usurped by so-called "heroic physicians and more recently heroic cops in street clothes" who do very little to none whatsoever of the technical work.

Laboratory scientists may intercede when the lab results are generated to suggest to their non-lab peers further tests that should be done. For example, the laboratory scientist may suggest other antimicrobial drugs that should be tested that would be equally beneficial and may be cheaper. This advisory process has the added benefit of a cost effective benefit for it is based on the formulary of the pharmacy department. During my tenure as Chief Scientific Officer of a Microbiology Laboratory, there have been very skilled colleagues with whom I have worked. I owe a great deal of any success that I may have garnered to many of them who were part of the team. To name a few, there were Kenneth Saunders, Sandra Brown, Paul Hostetler, Leslie Hatch, Enal Ram and a host of many others too numerous to mention, mainly because I cannot remember their names. A few have died and others have moved across this great North American country never to be heard of again.

At times my wife, who is unaware of how the writer's mind works, contributes to my work by allowing me to keep out of her way during the day. She takes the easy way out and just allows me the time to write and to go to book shows. That is what happens after 43 years of living together as a couple; there is a profound understanding through benign neglect. We both enjoy the lifestyle as a writer and lecturer for it provides us the opportunity to travel, to meet wonderful human beings and to enjoy their fellowship around a meal or a glass of wine.

My constant colleague who has been my supporter and the producer of many of my book covers and marketing materials, as well as, advisor on all matters associated with audio-visual and artwork is Tom Pridding. Tom has his own company www.*Priddingdesignsolutions*. Tom is my constant companion in the production of these books and his advice is immeasurable on artwork and on the book format; he is an invaluable ally. I also owe a great deal to Dorothy McKeown for suggesting more case histories during the first cut and to my daughter TG who does not want her name used for her computer assistance, without which I would be very frustrated and lost. However, special thanks to my conscience probing, willing associate and friend Lynda Murch, who never misses an opportunity to improve or suggest a correction or a better word to implant.

Lynda and I were at the University of Waterloo together but she is younger than I was. She found me after 36 years as she was cruising the web and found out that I was now writing books. She immediately ordered the full five books which we gathered from our bookshelf. She has become my e-mail colleague and our friendship was renewed. When I asked if she would read for me she did not hesitate. Lynda as you discard one manuscript for another one to correct, know that you have been a wonderful support to me – I owe you supper and a bottle of the best Chablis or Shiraz, but I wonder if your erstwhile husband would allow you one evening with a very old friend – I stress 'old'. To Sandy Causyn Brown who took time, from her work and building a new house, to *mine out* a case history which appeared to have vanished from my records. Thanks for all you have done and for being the great colleague that you are over our twenty eight years and still continue today. I could not have wished for anyone better to associate with over those years and counting. Of course, there is that Zeta-Jones bit and that Nigella woman but they could never tell an Eikenella from a Pseudomonas.

FOR THE BACK COVER AND TO BE USED AS NEEDED INFORMATION.

OTHER BOOKS:

The publication of this book marks the seventh year in my career as a full-time novelist and writer of non-fiction and fiction, says Darryl Gopaul. My first book was a non-fiction spoof of my profession as a Medical Microbiologist entitled, *"Bacteria, The Good, The Bad, The Ugly"*. This was followed up by a book of fictitious short stories based on my upbringing on the island of Trinidad. This was a very cosmopolitan island in the Caribbean and I was brought up under the British Colonial System of Government. I am of East Indian origin born to three generations of the same race on this island. I had a wonderful education in the grand system of a British subject and had the best of a college education based along the lines of a highbrow boarding school. At least that was how it was perceived in those early days of the late 1940s, 1950s and even into the 1960s.

The interweaving of tales brought over by African slaves and indentured workers from the Indian continent, similarly for the Portuguese, Spaniards and French, was combined to form a rich encyclopedia of imaginary tales. Many of which, I heard from my grandparents and my mother, as bedtime stories. There was no television and films were a treat and far too expensive for us to go regularly. This book is fiction and is entitled *"Tales of Myths and Fantasy"*. Our family has given all the rights from the sale of this book to an Ottawa group called 'Project Tembo'. The organizers of this charitable endeavour raise funds to support female students up to the high school level in Tanzania. They have also begun a micro-business project supporting African women, who are the mainstay of the family. Neither the author nor any of his colleagues who assist him or his family get any benefit from the sales of these books or from the possibility of TV film development.

The next book is non-fiction and is based on our travels, that is, my wife and myself, as we ventured around the world and is entitled, *"Around The World on Three Underwear"*. This is a humorous look at travel for it is not a very easy thing to do when one has only his spouse as his companion for five months. My wife and I looked at the different cultures and their foibles, the difficulties we experienced, the foods we ate and the wonderful wines consumed from many countries. We laughed a lot, met folks from different parts of this small planet who were also in transit. We exchanged experiences and goodwill to many who have since become our friends.

The next book took me back to my roots and followed my path from childhood to adulthood. Essentially, this was my journey through life in the countries that gave me an education and an experience that has made me the man I am today. In England, I got my advanced education all paid for by the government. I had a permanent career which spanned the better part of over thirty years most of which was in Canada. But the story began in the country where I was born, Trinidad in the West Indies. This is a book of non-fiction entitled, *"Six Decades To Wisdom (maybe)"*.

I then brought together fifteen years of written poetry in a book entitled, *"Sonnets Of a Human Soul"*. This was followed by *"A Collection of Fables & Tales; A compendium of Short Stories"*. See www.iuniverse.com for hard cover, paperback, and e-books as well as Amazon.com, Barnes&Noble@bn.com, alibris.com and many other electronic web sites.

All these books belong to my wife and to her small company, which was formed to assist me in publishing this collection. She has ownership to the rights of these books for her to dispose of as she deems necessary.

Author's Bio

Darryl Leslie Gopaul has written and published over 130 medical case histories, scientific research and administrative articles in his thirty-seven plus years of practice. He received his Medical Technologist training in Trinidad, through a WHO/ UNICEF scholarship grant. He went to the UK where he spent 5 years in a *co opt like program* to get his Diploma in Medical Microbiology. Over the many years and through different universities, Darryl has earned a Doctorate in Microbiology an MBA, specializing in Healthcare Administration. His total years in the profession were spent lecturing to many professionals across Canada, USA and Europe. He has been a member of the Ambassador Program to the former USSR and the old Czechoslovakia before the fall of communism. On his other Ambassador Trip he was the Scientific Leader to the middle east countries which include Egypt both Alexandria and Cairo, then to Israel visiting colleagues at the Hadassah Medical Centre, visiting Tel Aviv, Jerusalem. The Central Public Health Laboratory other scientific as well as many of the holy sites. From there he took his small group of sixteen professionals from the US, Canada and the West Indies to Turkey visiting the professionals in Constantinople.

Darryl continues practicing as a Consultant to small hospitals, commercial companies where he supports them with both his technical and Microbiology expertise. His training in business also allows him to contribute to the HR functions of his major client in Toronto, Canada. His income supports his travels and time off for writing. He is unafraid to give his opinion at any press interview after his books are published. See the following newspaper article after his first book was published.

Too much paranoia about microbes and bacteria, microbiologist says

By Peter Epp
Chatham This Week

The news media is fostering a climate of fear that encourages an unhealthy paranoia about bacteria and micro-organisms, says a London microbiologist.

Speaking in Chatham on Aug. 13, Dr. Darryl Gopaul said micro-organisms have a purpose in nature and most of the time are very necessary in the continued maintenance of human health.

But events like the SARS epidemic and the discovery of BSE in a single cow in Alberta have allowed the media to promote fear and paranoia, rather than provide a thoughtful analysis of what has happened or, in some instances, what has not happened.

In most cases, he said, the general public has been left with a lingering fear about "bugs".

Gopaul, who spoke to the Rotary Club of Chatham, used the SARS epidemic as an example. As a scientist, he said he wonders why Toronto experienced an outbreak of the respiratory disease when centres like Los Angeles didn't.

"There are far more flights between L.A. and China than there are between Toronto and China, and yet Toronto had a SARS outbreak and Los Angeles didn't," said Gopaul. "It doesn't make sense."

He hinted that people in Los Angeles possibly did die from

Darryl Gopaul

the same respiratory illness, but their conditions were never publicly identified as SARS.

"Thousands and thousands of Canadians over the age of 75 die every year because of respiratory illness, and yet 45 died because of SARS and look what happened," he said of the Toronto quarantines.

While not suggesting that the SARS epidemic should have been covered up or ignored by officials, Gopaul said the news media had a responsibility to provide a balance and accurate account the epidemic and its relationship to other respiratory illnesses.

"SARS was terrible, but the epidemic was only half of the truth," he said. "Instead, we had the news media feeding paranoia."

Gopaul, who for 29 years

worked as a microbiologist with the St. Joseph's Health Centre in London, has recently published a book, entitled Bacteria... The Good, The Bad and The Ugly. The book, he said, attempts to provide some balanced analysis of "good bugs" and "bad bugs" and provide some basic information for people without a scientific background.

He said humans are "loaded with microbes" and in almost all cases these microbes provide a beneficial service in maintaining health.

As an example, Gopaul said there are microbes in a person's stomach, part of the e.coli family, that provide a useful service in extracting Vitamin K from digested food. The Vitamin K component is necessary in the process of blood thickening.

"If you didn't have this form of e.coli in your stomach, you could potentially bleed to death if you cut yourself when you shaved in the morning," he said. "Yet if this bug is ever transferred to your bladder, you're in for big problems."

Because of the public's general fear about microbes, even those that are beneficial, Gopaul said some health products may do more harm than good.

He said antibiotics must be used carefully during an illness. There is a danger that the overuse of antibiotics will kill weaker bugs, and allow

stronger bugs to develop a resistance. He suggested that it's better in some cases for healthy individuals to allow their own bodies to marshal the resources to fight back on some illnesses.

"There's a lot of marketing that's done based on fear," Gopaul allowed.

At the same time, the microbiologist said people should maintain a healthy respect for some of the "bad bugs", and should wash their hands on a regular basis.

"Teach your children to properly and thoroughly wash their hands before they eat a meal, and to properly wash their hands after they use the toilet," he said.

He added that research has shown that 70 per cent of the men who use public washrooms never wash their hands after using the toilet.

Gopaul said people who use public restrooms should be wary. He doesn't use his hand to flush a toilet; he uses his foot. And after he washes his hands in the sink, he holds a paper towel in his hand while shutting off the tap.

"I always have a paper towel in my pocket, and if I'm leaving a public washroom, I'll use the towel to push open the door," he said.

Gopaul said he once rented a car and wiped down the steering wheel before using it.

"I didn't know who had used it before," he said.